GERALD B

❦

THE DAUGHTERS OF
MRS PEACOCK

LONDON
J. M. DENT & SONS LTD

THE CHAPTERS

CHAPTER ONE

Five in Family

§ 1

TAKING their seats at the breakfast-table this April morning, the three Peacock daughters—Julia, Sarah, and Catherine Ann—could have no thought to spare for the character of the epoch in which an obliging Providence had placed them. Living in the green middle of England, untroubled by politics, untouched by news from abroad, they accepted without question the world they shared with each other and with their parents. Each in her dreams and daydreams, her bright hopes and shadowy fears, was a person apart, a solitary spirit; but so soon as they came together, as just now in the mere act of entering the breakfast-room, their individual isolation was dissolved in a warm if unthinking family relationship. They had a mother to rule them, a father to provide for them, servants to minister to their comfort; and it was beyond their imagining that things could have been or ever would be different. God was in his heaven, Victoria on her throne, and all was right with the world. True, there were wicked people here and there, atheists and law-breakers and the like; there were poor people, who did not get enough to eat; and somewhere in distant parts of the earth there were the unfortunate heathen, of various colours, for whom it was one's duty to pray; but these three categories did not constitute a serious problem.

The poor were conveniently divided into two classes: the deserving poor, who could be visited and helped a little, and the undeserving, who were best forgotten. There were also, of course, the rich: people with titles and large estates, all busily engaged in propping up the divinely-established order. They too were taken unenviously for granted. The Peacocks did not consider themselves rich, but they were comfortable, and well content to be so. They occupied, both geographically and socially, the best position of all, the middle position; and having no taste for extremes they were proud of it, or would have been had they given it a thought.

'Good morning, my dears,' said Mrs Peacock, sailing into the room in the wake of a large silver teapot, which was carried, like an emblem of state, by Jenny the parlour-maid, prim and respectful in cap and apron. The girl had been christened Euphemia, but Mrs Peacock considered the name unsuitable for one in her station, and being precluded by good sense and natural kindliness from aping the manners of the upper classes and calling her Briggs, she had decided on Jenny, to everyone's satisfaction.

'Good morning, Mama,' said the girls in chorus.

'We shall not wait,' their mother announced. 'Your father is out of sorts. I'm keeping him in bed. Catherine!'

To Catherine, as the youngest, fell the duty and privilege of saying grace.

'For what we are about to receive, may the Lord make us truly thankful. For Christ's sake, Amen.'

The bowed heads lifted. Napkins, extracted from

their rings, were unfolded. Breakfast began. Sunlight
from the broad sash-windows overlooking the street made
the silver and crockery on table and sideboard gleam,
enhanced the whiteness of the napery, set the glass
lustres on the chimneypiece brilliantly glittering, and
gilded the contours of a pair of equestrian bronzes that
stood, high rearing, on either side of the great marble
clock, in front of the overmantel looking-glass. From
the opposite, pink-beflowered wall, Grandfather and
Grandmother Bartlow, in maple frames, gazed selfconsciously at distance, seeming to set the seal of their
approval on the cheerful domestic scene: even in heaven,
Mrs Peacock believed, it was a satisfaction to them that
their daughter held them in pious and dutiful remem-
brance. The space above the sideboard was occupied
by an engraving of Landseer's *Shoeing the Bay Mare*. Its
fellow, *The Old Shepherd's Chief Mourner*, was elsewhere, in
the servants' parlour. Both were from the Bartlow home.

A curious observer might, though with some difficulty,
have discerned a likeness between the venerable Bartlows
on the wall and the ripe fruit of their marriage who was
now, and had been for a quarter of a century, Edmund
Peacock's wife. Tall, and with a certain stateliness of
carriage, she in her middle years was still both comely
and vigorous: dark eyes, dark hair, decided features, a
gipsy-brown complexion, and a slim but womanly figure
which child-bearing had surprisingly not impaired. The
only one of her daughters who resembled her, and that
to an almost comical degree, was the firstborn, Julia,
who had just completed her twenty-third year. Julia,
earnestly co-operating with nature, by force of filial

admiration had made herself into an echo of her mother, copying her manner, adopting her opinions, and blushing with pleasure, prettily enough, when strangers remarked on the physical likeness between them. She was in fact Mother's Blessing, zealous to establish her law in the minds of Sarah and Catherine, and shocked when, as sometimes happened, they showed signs of indifference or even of rebelliousness. For these younger girls, especially Catherine who was but lately emerged from her teens, were highspirited and inclined to be independent, so far as that was possible in a rigidly ordered world: it was sometimes difficult to believe that they were their mother's daughters. They had nothing of her darkness, Sarah being medium-fair in colouring, brown hair and blue eyes, and Catherine fairer still, with a sanguine complexion and eyes whose fugitive bronze gleam, like fire in a sky-reflecting pool, matched the warm tone of her hair. Sarah was round-faced and comely; Catherine was slighter, with smaller and more delicately modelled features; both were by an inch or so less tall than their sister. Julia loved them dearly, as in duty bound. So far as they would let her she watched over them with anxious affection. But Mama was the centre of her universe. She was happy in having one of Mama's names, Emily, for her own second, and was a little jealous of Catherine Ann for having the other. Sarah, the middle one, had received only one name at her christening, perhaps because she was not the boy her parents had petitioned for in their prayers. She suffered the penalty without complaint, and now, at twenty-two, she enjoyed being Sarah Peacock, contemplating her image in the glass with a mixture of irony and resignation. The world had been at no pains to conceal from her that she was less pretty than her sisters, but nature had compensated by giving her a keen eye for human absurdity and a rich capacity for enjoying it.

'And what are my girls going to do with themselves this morning?' inquired Mrs Peacock with a commanding smile, as breakfast neared its end.

Recognizing the question for what it was, the prelude to instruction, Julia waited meekly for the sequel, turning dark eyes on her mother. Catherine, absorbed in thoughts of her own, paid no attention.

'We don't know yet, Mama,' said Sarah. 'But we shall in a minute.'

'You, Sarah, shall help me with the butter-making,' said Mrs Peacock. 'And my Julia, I think, must go and see poor Dolly Bateson, with a basket of eggs. She wasn't at church on Sunday: that means she's had another of her attacks.'

'Very well, Mama,' said Julia. 'That will be nice.'

'Then one of you must get Harry Dawkins to drive you into Newtonbury with a message for Mr Crabbe from your father.'

'Would that be Catherine, I wonder?' said Sarah. 'I knew we should learn our destinies in time, if we were patient.'

'May I, Mama?' said Catherine eagerly. The prospect of Newtonbury allured her. 'And may I go and speak to Papa first?'

'If you do, you must be careful not to disturb him. He may be asleep.'

'I do hope Papa is not ill?' said Julia, on a note of anxious inquiry.

'No, not ill, my dear. I wouldn't say ill. But his cough's troubling him. I'm afraid he's caught a new chill.'

'Shall you send for the doctor, Mama?'

'Time enough,' said her mother. 'We'll see how he is after a day in bed.'

'Poor Papa!' said Catherine, who hated being kept in bed. 'It's such a lovely day too. The sunshine would do him good.'

Julia's admonishing look said as plainly as speech that Mama knew best. It was the first article of her religion.

Mrs Peacock said, in gentle rebuke: 'Your father, Catherine, is not a young girl.'

'Else we should not be here, Kitty,' explained Sarah gravely. 'Remember that, child.'

'What are you giggling at, Catherine?'

'Nothing, Mama.'

'There is no need for *you* to be silly, just because Sarah is.'

'But we like being silly sometimes,' said Catherine, with simple veracity. 'Don't we, Sarah?'

'Innocent laughter,' said Sarah, 'is said to be one of the privileges of the young, Mama.'

'I like to see happy young faces about me,' said Mrs Peacock, 'but there are times when laughter is out of place. With your father lying ill in bed——'

'But, Mama,' cried Sarah, 'you said he was *not* ill!'

'That will do, Sarah. I do not *argue* with my children.'

'How true,' murmured Sarah pianissimo. Only Catherine heard her.

Julia said earnestly: 'We are all very sorry for Papa. Aren't we, girls?'

'Indeed yes,' said Catherine. 'Mama knows that, don't you, Mama?'

'But how will Mr Crabbe manage without him?' asked Sarah, joining in the peacemaking endeavour. 'Is he a clever man, Mama?'

'With your father to guide him, I fancy he does well enough,' said Mrs Peacock loftily.

'But *without* Papa?' Sarah insisted. 'Will he ruin us? Shall we all starve? That will be a new experience.' Her placid smile made it seem an attractive one.

The greater part of Edmund Peacock's income was derived from the firm of Peacock and Crabbe, solicitors, of which, inheriting from his father, he was the senior partner. He had rural interests as well, in the shape of some sixty-five acres of grass and ploughland, with a bailiff and three men to do the work, and enjoyed nothing so much as riding round his estate on summer evenings, counting his sheep, admiring his cattle, and discussing crops and weather with John Sampson. Farming, he believed, was in his blood, transmitted to him from his father's father, who had devoted his whole life to it, with much profit to himself and his heirs. It gratified Edmund that though only a tenth part of the original farm remained to him he was living in the same farmhouse, with its barns and granary, stables and byres; and he sometimes regretted that his father had broken with family tradition by taking to the law. It was a long stone house, decently proportioned; and that its front door opened straight on to the road was no hardship in these days of horsedrawn traffic, of which, moreover, there was not much. Here was rural seclusion, enlivened by the serene leisurely bustle of seedtime and harvest, milking and sheep-shearing: yet the thriving town of Newtonbury, where in black coat and white collar he practised his major profession, was only three stations away, on a branch line. Mrs Peacock, therefore, enjoyed the best of two worlds. She had the status of a professional man's lady and the homelier pleasure of being a farmer's wife. She played both parts with an equal and effortless facility. Her butter was without peer. Her cheeses were the pride of the county. And her handmaidens held her in high respect.

'I am sorry not only for Papa,' remarked Sarah with mock-solemnity. 'I am sorry too for poor Mrs Bateson. She missed a treat by not going to church on Sunday. But don't tell her, Julia. It wouldn't be kind.'

'What *do* you mean, Sarah?' said Julia unguardedly.

'Have you forgotten? You can't have. It was dear Mr Pardew's turn to preach. He was *so* amusing.'

'I didn't know he was amusing,' said Julia.

'Nor did he. That was the best part of it.'

'Mr Pardew,' said their mother, 'is a very good young man. And a *great* help to the Vicar. I don't know what's come over you girls,' she continued, with a glance that excluded Julia.

'Us, Mama?' said Catherine, making big eyes.

'You and Sarah are a pair. She'll cut herself one day, Sarah will, with that sharp tongue of hers. And gentlemen, let me tell you, Sarah, don't like cleverness in young women.'

'How funny of them,' said Sarah. 'Do they prefer stupid girls?'

Ignoring the pert question Mrs Peacock said, addressing Catherine: 'Yes, child, you can get down, when you've thanked God for your good breakfast.'

The four heads bowed. 'For what we have received . . .' murmured Catherine.

Heaven placated, the napkins were replaced in their rings, the chairs pushed back from the table, and the family dispersed.

§ 2

THEY dispersed to their appointed duties. Later in the day, after luncheon, the girls would be allowed a little judicious freedom, freedom within the limits of decorum to follow their own devices and cultivate their several talents. Julia would bend over her embroidery frame by the hour together; Sarah was accounted clever with her pencil; Catherine, when she had spent some of her young energy on outdoor pursuits, liked nothing better than to lose herself in a book, with Bundle the golden tabby purring sonorously in her lap. Evenings were another matter: they were sociable occasions. Lutterfield was a scattered and not populous parish, but there were three or four congenial families within visiting distance, and seldom a week passed without some getting-together for whist or cribbage, well spiced with gossip and good fellowship, at one or another of their houses. And often, whether guests were present or not, there would be music round the piano, if Mama were in the mood. She was a tolerably good accompanist, and the girls' voices went

B

pleasantly together in catches and part-songs. It was no part of Mrs Peacock's plan to make fine ladies of her daughters, but the elegances of life were not to be neglected and they had all three been suitably educated: first at home, under the governance of Miss Smith, and afterwards at a young ladies' seminary at Cragford, which was one station distant from Newtonbury. Nor was their education yet ended: it would never end so long as they were in their mother's care, for it was her constant endeavour to make good housewives of them and see that they employed their time usefully.

Mornings, therefore, were dedicated to industry. For Julia, on this particular morning, this was no hardship. Quite the contrary. To visit Mrs Bateson in the character of Lady Bountiful was by a long way more agreeable than mending linen, making preserves, helping Alice the housemaid with the dusting and bedmaking, or seeing that Jenny remembered to clean the silver. On her return there would be a number of small household duties to perform; but meanwhile she could enjoy the walk into the village, the respectful welcome of Dolly Bateson, and half an hour's genial Christian gossip about her aches and pains, in which, though she deplored them, the old woman took great pride, having nothing else but her many years to be proud of.

'How are you today, Mrs Bateson?'

'All the better for seeing *your* bright face, Miss Julia. But I've had a bad turn, there's no denying.'

She proceeded to describe the bad turn and her present sad condition in avid detail: yet cheerfully, even boastfully, as if conscious that they were much to her credit and must be to Julia, as they were to her, of consuming interest. Julia, who had a sympathetic nature and did nothing by halves, in a measure shared this view, exclaiming, condoling, asking questions, and saying everything that was kind and proper to the occasion. Her basket, covered with a cloth, stood at her feet on the much-worn brick floor, mute token of an impending charity and carefully ignored by both. A moment of unwonted disquiet visited her, a half-heard whisper like the beat of a dark wing, as with smiling solicitude she watched the aged animated features of this little old woman, who with sunken cheeks and knotted misshapen hands sat so carefully still in her straight-backed chair, like a ship in dry dock waiting to be broken up: though indeed the small bright eyes, from which the imprisoned spirit looked out, betrayed no consciousness of that coming event. Where and what shall I be, thought Julia, when I am as old as she is? Still at home, still helping Mama, came the comforting yet not quite satisfying answer. She did not pursue the thought, did not pause to calculate that Mama would then be within sight of her hundredth year, still less that she might be no longer alive. A world that did not contain Mama was beyond her imagining.

Uncovering the basket, she said: 'I've brought you a few eggs, Mrs Bateson.'

'There now!' exclaimed Dolly Bateson, with well-simulated astonishment. 'Isn't that kind! I'm sure I'm ever so obliged, Miss Julia, if it won't be robbing you. And aint they beauties too! Such big ones as I never seen. So kind. So kind. Precious as diamonds they are, for I had to give up my few chicken, you know, what with my rheumatics and all. But my son Willie,' she continued, going off at a tangent, 'he's very good. Writes to me regular, and always sends me a little something when he can, him being at sea, you know, which was a great surprise, running away from his poor father, the bad boy, though forty-nine next birthday.'

'What a pity,' said Julia lamely, 'you can't see more of him. And your grandchildren too.'

'Fine big boys now, they tell me,' said their grandmother proudly. 'But Liverpool's a long way, and a body can't have everything. We shall all meet in heaven, I daresay.'

'Before I go,' said Julia, rising, 'is there anything I can do to help?' Her discreetly roving glance took in the dinginess, the near-squalor, of the little room, with its almost dangerously low ceiling, its flaking walls, its patch of threadbare carpet in the middle of the damp brick floor, and the dirty remains of breakfast on the table. The only adornments were a framed text, *God bless Our Home*, and a crudely coloured sketch of a ship at sea, Willie's ship no doubt. 'Yes, let me tidy you up a bit.' Ignoring Dolly's protest—'Dear me, no! Tis no work for a lady!'—she gathered up the crocks, carried them to the sink, and at once set about washing them, in water from a big iron kettle that was simmering on the hob. 'There! That's done. Now where shall I find a broom?'

'Ah, Miss Julia,' said Mrs Bateson at parting, 'it'll be a lucky gentleman as gets you, my dear.'

As she made her way home the words echoed for a moment in her mind, but she dismissed them with a smile that was only half a sigh. No gentleman, so far, had manifested more than a friendly interest in her; and it did not enter into her scheme of things, or into Mama's, that anyone should. Her destiny seemed to be already fixed and foreseeable. Not so Sarah's. Not so Catherine's. Being neither of them Mama's favourite daughter and right-hand man, anything dangerous and exciting might in time happen to them. Catherine indeed was too young to be the subject of prediction, but already it was tacitly assumed, though perhaps not by Sarah herself, that Sarah, the comparatively plain one, would some day marry a gentleman-farmer, of whom there were several likely specimens in the county. She was being diligently trained to that end. Nor, whatever her secret intentions, did she resist the process. The life of the fields, the energy of growth, the sowing and reaping, the changing moods of the sky, all were congenial to something deep and inarticulate in her nature. She was genuinely interested, too, in the work of the dairy, this morning her allotted sphere, taking pleasure not only in the process of buttermaking or cheesemaking but in the very tools she must handle, their shapes and functions: the milk-sieve, the skimmer, the butter-scoop, the butter-worker, and not least the churn itself, agent of that sublime moment when to a quick ear, or some other more mysterious sense, it becomes apparent that the butter has 'come'.

Mrs Peacock, too, was alive to the homely drama of that moment, and she enjoyed Sarah's enjoyment of it: in this work together they achieved an unspoken harmony of companionship that was sometimes lacking between them. It was perhaps as much for that, as for the training in a marriage-marketable skill, that she continued week after week to command Sarah's attendance in the dairy, where Julia, having served her apprenticeship in past years, was no longer needed, and to which Catherine was not yet promoted. She would never admit to herself that she did not quite understand this unpredictable and some-times disconcerting daughter, with her odd smile, as at some secret joke, and her habit of urbane impudence: such a suggestion would have seemed to her preposterous. To understand and control, to mould and guide, was as inevitably the prerogative of a mother as was implicit obedience the duty of children. All she could allow, even in the privacy of her mind, was that Sarah had certain faults from which Julia, dear girl, was blessedly free, and which Catherine, she rather feared, was in process of acquiring by force of imitation: an unseemly degree of independence, a cool yet stubborn adherence to her own opinions, a disposition to pertness. It could all be summed up in one sad word, conceit. Where did she get it? Not from her parents, that was certain. Dear Edmund was a clever man but no one could call him conceited or self-willed: he was always ready, in matters outside his own sphere, to defer to his wife's better judg-ment. As for herself, conceit had no part in her. She was always willing to learn from anyone capable of teaching her, and took no credit to herself for the inescap-able fact that in her maternal capacity she was always and necessarily right.

'I think it's come, Mama,' said Sarah, at the churn. She wrinkled up her nose in a pleased, triumphant smile. 'Shall you look and see?' It was a diplomatic question:

she had no doubts.   But Mama liked to be consulted and liked to instruct.

'Yes,' said Mrs Peacock, having looked.   'There's a clever girl.   Now a pint or two of cold water, to harden the grains, and a few gentle turns.   Then we'll draw off the butter-milk and wash the butter in the churn till the water comes clear.'

'Yes, Mama,' said Sarah, betraying no consciousness of having heard it all a dozen times before.   Though amused she was an affectionate girl, not unduly impatient, and found the ritual repetition endearing.   Old people were like that.

'I'm pleased with you, my dear.   You're picking it up very nicely.   Not that you won't have maids to do it for you, if you marry well.   But it's good to know how.'

'Yes, indeed,' assented Sarah.   'Besides it's rather fun.' She poured water into the churn and set it gently in motion.   'And since I can't be ornamental I must learn to be useful, mustn't I?' she said with deceptive meekness. 'Do you think Mr Pardew would have me, Mama, if I asked him?   I could write his sermons for him as well as make his butter.   It would be a splendid match.'

'Now you're being silly again,' sighed Mrs Peacock. 'Why must you spoil yourself, my dear child?   I know it's a joke,' she added quickly, lest lack of humour should be imputed to her, 'but not a very sensible one.   Marriage is a serious business.'

'Is it Mama?   Then perhaps I'm not cut out for it. But it wouldn't be serious with Mr Pardew.   It would be comical.   He's so exactly like a curate.'

'What *can* you mean, child?   He *is* a curate.'

'Yes, Mama. So he is. Look, the water's coming pretty clear already. But I'll give it two or three more rinsings, shall I, to make sure?'

While the butter-making was in progress, and Julia on her way to visit Mrs Bateson, Catherine, well wrapped up against the north-east wind, was engaged in conversation with Harry Dawkins in the stable-yard, a slow-speaking, weatherbeaten, rubicund old man of sixteen, whose duty it was to look after the horses, clean out the pigsties, water the bull, fetch the cows in from grass, limewash the fruit-trees, kill the rats in the granary, chivvy the hens to bed as dusk fell, lend a hand with the milking, and when not otherwise occupied be at the beck and call of Old Piggott, the gardener. It was a perennial joke among the girls, and a mystery, that though all these multifarious jobs somehow got done, and by Harry, he was rarely, if ever, detected in the act. To hurry was alien to his nature: neither urgency nor threat could persuade him to it. He was nearly always elsewhere when wanted, and when at last run to earth he gave the impression—maddening or soothing, according to one's mood—of having an infinity of leisure and of being mildly astonished that anyone should require action of him. The world is a pleasant place, he seemed to say: why not sit quiet and enjoy it?

It was therefore no surprise to Catherine to find him doing just that: sitting on an upturned bucket, his eyes half-shut, his back against the stable half-door.

'Good morning, Harry,' she said. His eyes opened wider. 'Had a nice sleep?'

'Morning, miss.' He shambled slowly to his feet,

touched his forelock in mechanical salute, and stood, a looselimbed overgrown lad, awaiting her pleasure. 'It's a good un, too,' he drawled, 'though a sharp little wind.'

'Now listen,' said Catherine. 'Are you sure you're awake?'

He grinned vaguely, puzzled but unresentful. 'Yes, miss.'

'My mother says you're to drive me into Newtonbury.'

'Ah,' said Harry. The idea sank slowly in. 'When, miss? Smorning?'

'This very morning. This very minute. Now.'

'That'll be old Judy and the trap, I reckon?'

'Of course,' said Catherine. 'Come along. Let's go and say good morning to her.'

'She's a good little pony for her age,' said Harry, as they entered the shadowy warm-smelling stable together. 'Spanks along like one o'clock, yet quiet as a mouse. Kimmup, Judy. Kimmup, old girl.'

With her arm round Judy's neck, and her cheek resting lightly, caressingly, on the smooth mane, Catherine fed her with lumps of sugar stolen from the breakfast-table. 'We're going for a drive, Judy. Won't that be nice?'

Unhurrying, yet without losing time, Harry did his part. The pony was harnessed, gently backed between the shafts of the trap, and all made secure, Catherine herself, with a murmur of reassurance to this old friend of her childhood, buckling the last straps. While she was so engaged a new and audacious idea blossomed into decision.

'I shan't need you, Harry, after all,' she said. 'I shall drive myself.' Harry hesitating, bewildered by the change of plan, she took the reins from him and sprang into the trap: whereupon Judy at once plunged forward, to be restrained by Harry's hand on her bridle. 'Let her go,' Catherine commanded. Her tone was impatient, imperious. With a shrug he obeyed her, spreading his hands in a gesture of humorous resignation. 'Don't tell anybody,' she called over her shoulder, 'unless you have to.'

The yard gate, luckily, stood open; and unless Alice or Jenny should chance to be staring out of an upper window her exodus would not be seen from the house. Away they went, she and Judy, at a smart trot, along chalky white lanes, between hedgerows full of young green, under a sky so vast and bright, so all-embracing, no hills intervening, that the roundness of the green globe, magically suspended in space, was no theory but a sensible fact. To Catherine's exalted sense the trotting hooves and turning wheels seemed scarcely to touch the ground: she had the sensation of flying or floating through the intoxicating golden air. To be driving was no novelty, she handled the reins with all the ease and assurance of second nature; but to be alone, and free, made the outing a delirious adventure.

Some forty or fifty minutes later, arriving in East Street, Newtonbury, she was confronted by a question to which she had given no thought: what to do with Judy and the trap while she went to see Mr Crabbe in his office; for that Judy would wait patiently for her return was more than she could be quite sure of. As she sat considering the matter, five yards from the elegant Georgian building whose door bore the legend *Peacock and Crabbe*,

a small tow-headed child, who was gazing in rapt contemplation at a glass marble cupped in his hands, got up
from his seat on the pavement and transferred his open-
mouthed philosophical stare to Catherine.

'Hullo, Tommy,' said Catherine.

The stare did not waver, nor the lips utter speech.

'Would you like to earn sixpence?' An immense sum,
but her mood was reckless.

'Yessum.'

'Can you hold the pony's head for five minutes? See
that she doesn't run away?'

'Yessum.'

'You're not very big, are you? Are you sure you know
how?'

A faint smile, scornfully confident, added ten years to
the child's apparent age. Without troubling to answer
he stepped to the pony's head and attached himself to
her bridle. Catherine, alighting, said: 'That's right. I
shan't be long.' To make sure of his loyalty she showed
him the sixpence. 'Only five minutes, Tommy. There's
a good boy.'

Mr Crabbe, in his dark little room that smelt of leather
and mahogany and black-japanned deed-boxes, greeted
her quietly, concealing his surprise.

'Good morning, Catherine. This is an unexpected
pleasure.'

'I've brought you a note from Papa, Mr Crabbe.
He's rather poorly this morning. My mother is keeping
him in bed.'

'Dear me! Nothing serious, I hope?'

'I don't think so. Just a little chill.'

'Ah, yes. This treacherous weather. Never cast a
clout, you know, till May is out. Though I must say it
seems to agree with *you*, Catherine. You're the picture
of health.' And of beauty, his glance added. Over the
years he had seen her mysteriously change from a leggy
and romping schoolgirl into a demure and dazzling young
woman.

Robert Crabbe was a tall clean-shaven man, very neat
in his dress and very precise in his movements, with a long
straight nose, alert grey eyes, a rather severe mouth
except when he smiled, and brown hair that was already
beginning to go grey at the temples, above the two inches
of side-whisker. He looked, in fact, far more the solicitor
than her father did. Though it was Mrs Peacock's habit
to refer to him as 'young Robert Crabbe', perhaps by
way of emphasizing his junior status in the firm, he was
not young in Catherine's estimation, for he would never
see thirty-five again. She did not however hold his age
against him; if anything it enhanced her interest in him,
by stimulating her curiosity. Here was a man who had
lived and suffered, who had known marriage and bereave-
ment. His allusion to the weather and its treachery gave
her a moment's wonder; for it was in just such an April
as this, three years ago, that pneumonia had carried off,
as they said, his beautiful young wife. She remembered
vividly the doleful faces and shocked voices of that tragic
week, when to be specially kind to poor Mr Crabbe had
been everyone's ruling thought.

'Yes, yes,' said Mr Crabbe, having read his letter. 'I
see. Give your father my warm regards and my hopes
for a speedy recovery. Everything is in hand, tell him.

No need to hurry or worry. And thank you, my dear Catherine, for coming.'

She offered her hand in farewell. He took it, bent over it, and ceremoniously kissed the finger-tips.

'Good-bye, Mr Crabbe.' Surprised into blushing slightly, she turned quickly away; but he accompanied her to the street door and bowed her out. 'I think it will rain before nightfall,' she said, for the sake of saying something. There was not a cloud in the sky.

'Perhaps, when the wind drops,' he conceded politely. 'Good-bye.'

Judy and the trap were waiting for her. The child she called Tommy was still at his post. She remembered, just in time, to give him the sixpence, still puzzling over Mr Crabbe's odd behaviour.

§ 3

As she drove into the yard she was met by Harry Dawkins, fully awake for once, and out of the corner of her eye she saw Mrs Peacock disappearing into the house.

'You'm got me into trouble, miss,' said Harry, ruefully grinning. 'She's in a rare taking, the missus.'

'Why?' asked Catherine. It was an idle question, and she did not wait for an answer. 'Don't worry,' she said loftily. 'I'll put it right for you. It was none of your business.'

'No, miss. I didn't tell on you, miss,' he explained eagerly, 'not till she caught me unexpected. "What are you a-doing of here," she says, "and where's Miss Catherine?" And then, don't you see, the fat was in the fire, as the saying is.'

'What nonsense!' said Catherine. 'Judy behaved splendidly.'

Though inwardly trembling, she held herself proudly, a disdainful smile on her young lips. The long habit of subservience could not be shaken off in a moment: hidden within her was a small scared child, detected in a misdemeanour. But it would never do to let Harry Dawkins see that, or Mama either. There was a battle ahead, and she braced herself for it. If she was in disgrace she was resolved not to seem aware of the fact, a resolution reinforced by a sense of the indignity of having been discussed, in terms of disapproval and apology, by an irate woman and a stable-boy.

Leaving pony and trap to be disposed of by Harry, she sauntered into the house, where, though she did not encounter Mrs Peacock, signs of an impending storm were not wanting. Julia, with a sad reproachful look, murmured: 'Oh Catherine, you've made Mama angry.' Catherine answered, with a toss of the head: 'Dear me! What a pity!'—and exchanged a bold wink with Sarah.

'These children!' said Sarah, in her mother's manner. 'What a trial they are, to be sure! . . . Did you have fun, Kitty?'

As the girls foresaw, it was not until they were all assembled at the luncheon table, Papa alone being absent, that Mrs Peacock opened the attack.

'Catherine, I am displeased with you.'

'Are you, Mama?' Her heart beat furiously. Her mouth was dry. 'May I ask why?'

'Don't ask me. Ask your conscience.'

'Very well, Mama.'

'Well?' said Mrs Peacock sharply. Catherine did not reply. 'Answer me, child.'

'Perhaps,' Sarah suggested, 'Kitty's conscience has nothing to say.'

'Be quiet, Sarah. Let your sister speak for herself.'

'Gladly, Mama, if she wishes to.'

'What did I tell you this morning, Catherine? What were my instructions?'

'To go to Newtonbury, Mama, with a message for Mr Crabbe from my father.'

'Don't equivocate. I don't want a sly daughter. I told you to get Harry Dawkins to drive you in. My words were quite plain. And you deliberately disobeyed me.'

'Oh no, Mama!'

'Don't contradict. Never before have you gone so far, and into a busy town, by yourself. You know that perfectly well.'

'There must always be a first time, mustn't there? And, as you see, I came to no harm.'

'That is beside the point. The point is that your behaviour was improper.'

Improper? This was strong language indeed. Unladylike would have been bad enough, but improper was by many degrees worse. Even Julia was startled by the word, which to her suggested unimaginable depths of infamy. Catherine continued to face her mother with a look of stubborn, faintly smiling incomprehension; but suddenly remembering Mr Crabbe's impetuous gesture she felt herself beginning to blush. There was no logic in her sense of guilt: Mama could not have intended that Harry Dawkins should chaperon her at that interview, nor could even she, whom so little escaped, possibly know what had happened. It was less than nothing anyhow, the girl told herself: the merest, meaningless civility. Yet its memory momentarily confused her and tied her tongue.

'But why, Mama?' pleaded Sarah, coming to the rescue. 'We know it must be so if you say so. But do please explain. It's so important that we should know what is and what isn't proper. Do you mean that a strange man might have spoken to her? But he couldn't have without stopping the trap. And if he'd tried to do that she'd have run over him. Wouldn't you, Kitty? Or beaten him off with the whip,' she added irrepressibly. 'Young girl defends her honour.'

'Have you finished, Sarah? Thank you. Then perhaps you will allow your mother to speak. The impropriety, as you ought to know, was in the disobedience. That is the long and the short of the matter. You and Julia have reached years of discretion, or so I like to think. What is right for you to do is not necessarily right for your little sister. If Catherine had asked my permission I should very likely have said Yes, young though she is. But no, she preferred to deceive me. She preferred to go behind my back. And I forbid you, Sarah, to try and make a joke of it.'

'But aren't you forgetting, Mama,' said Catherine, 'that I am turned twenty?'

'I do not propose to argue, Catherine,' said Mrs Peacock, resorting to her favourite formula. 'You have grieved me very much.'

It was clearly her last word. The meal proceeded in silence. Julia shot an anxious glance at Catherine, waiting for the words of contrition that did not come. Catherine, feeling like a whipped child and angry with herself for so feeling, swallowed the food with difficulty. She wanted nothing so much as to leave the table and hide herself away but was determined to resist the impulse. Sarah, shocked at last into gravity, kept her eyes on her plate.

Yet the sequel, as they all knew, was not in doubt. If dear Mama was grieved, or claimed to be so, there was only one thing to be done. Sooner or later, and the sooner the better, the ritual of apology must be performed, that the cloud might be lifted and all breathe freely again. Sarah knew, and Julia knew, that it was only a question of waiting until Catherine, her resentment subsiding, her lifelong affection reasserting itself, could for all their sakes bring herself to the point of surrender. This she did, later in the afternoon, choosing a moment when her mother was alone. She said she was sorry, shed a few tears, and received a kiss of forgiveness. Peace and happiness were restored: the family was united again.

A sweet child though wilful, thought Mrs Peacock, with a backward glance at her own spirited girlhood. As for Catherine, though in her heart she did not repent, and thought her mother unreasonable, she bore no grudge. If Mama was like that, knowing herself to be always in the right, that was how she was made, and the harmless fancy must be humoured. It did not prevent her being Mama —the best in the world.

C

CHAPTER TWO

A Proposal

§ 1

BEFORE the week was out Mr Peacock, Edmund, Papa, was in circulation again. He was a restive patient and could suffer his wife's coddling no longer. Dr Witherby, whose appearance suggested an amiable eagle in spectacles, solemnly pronounced him to be out of danger, but taking his cue from Mrs Peacock he advised him to have a few days more rest at home, to get his legs back and build up his strength before braving the east wind again, which, it appeared, was for some unexplained reason more to be feared in the neighbourhood of Newtonbury than here at Lutterfield.

'Nonsense, Witherby!' said Edmund Peacock. 'I was never *in* danger. You and my wife are in a conspiracy to make an old woman of me. As for the wind, it's shifted, or I'm a Dutchman. And anyhow there's not enough of it to fill a paper bag.'

The advice, however, was not unwelcome: in no great hurry to get back to the office he was glad of the excuse to spend Saturday, as well as much of Sunday, pottering about the farm in breeches and gaiters and an old tweed jacket. So clad, so occupied, he felt more himself than in his sleek town-going gear, interviewing clients, drawing up wills, executing conveyances, and dissuading hotheads from litigation. All those activities represented not only

34

another life but another personality. This was recognized by the whole family: it was one of his favourite
jokes, of which they never wearied. 'You're a shameless woman, Emily,' he would say. 'You have two
husbands.' And Emily, pretending to be shocked, would
answer complacently: 'What a way to talk, and in front
of the girls too!' He did in fact sometimes shock her
with his more audacious pleasantries, but she enjoyed the
sensation and was perhaps obscurely gratified that though
he would often defer to her judgment, more especially in
matters that did not greatly concern him, he was a
genially masterful person with a will of his own. His
visible presence in the house—a large vigorous man, with
long chestnut-brown moustaches and copious side-
whiskers adorning a broad red face—made a subtly
different woman of her, younger, more placid, a wife as
well as a mother. For that reason alone, had there been
no other, his daughters would have adored him. The
family atmosphere was never so serene as when Papa was
at home.

Sunday morning was dedicated to churchgoing. The
Peacocks, a full muster, occupied the family pew, the
maids, following at a discreet distance, disposing themselves elsewhere, near enough to show that they belonged
but not so near as to seem presuming. Cook, who was
regrettably but perhaps conveniently a Dissenter, deferred
her devotions till the evening, for the hot Sunday dinner
at one o'clock—roast sirloin of beef with two vegetables,
followed by a fruit tart—was an institution only one
degree less sacred than divine service itself: it was an
indispensable part of Sunday observance. In the evening,

after Evensong, they would settle down to enjoy the lees of the day in whatever fashion their collective fancy suggested: desultory talk, reading aloud, or music. In earlier years, when the children were little, the Bible and Bunyan had been almost the only permitted Sunday reading, but recently Mr Tennyson's *In Memoriam* had been added to the list. The music, too, had to be appropriate to the day, Handel or Mendelssohn in their more solemn moods—though with Handel, indeed, a certain liveliness was always apt to break in.

Sometimes Mrs Peacock was prevailed on to sing, to her own accompaniment, *Oh rest in the Lord*. She did so this evening, and Edmund, who never failed to be surprised by her rich contralto, so unexpectedly different from her speaking voice, was transported in memory to the occasion of his first hearing it, twenty-six years ago, in her mother's house. Here was the same yellow-keyed rosewood piano, the same girl seated at it, and the same alien deep voice suddenly proceeding from her—the voice, it seemed, of another and secret woman, mature, alluring, intimidating. It was that that had startled the young man into first noticing her. He had been by no means sure that he enjoyed her singing, but it excited him, it hinted at unimaginable possibilities, it was the sign of a mystery that must, at whatever risk, be explored.

And now she was a woman of forty-six, and the mother of his three daughters.

'Thank you, my dear,' he said, as she left the piano. 'That was wonderful.' Meeting her oddly shy glance he grinned. 'I never thought to be married to a trombone.'

'Really, Edmund! You do say the oddest things!'

'Now, what's next?' said Edmund. 'Come along, Catherine.' His eyebrows shot up. He pulled excitedly at his moustaches. 'Give us the Harmonious Blacksmith.'

'But is it suitable, Papa?' asked Sarah mischievously. 'Is it sacred enough?'

'All good music is sacred, my love,' he answered with a wink.

'And is all sacred music good, Papa?'

'As to that, you must ask your mother.' Conscious that she was in danger of being teased by these two, Mrs Peacock refused to be drawn. 'Perhaps,' her husband continued, 'Julia has some ideas on the subject?'

'I do not see,' said Julia, 'how music that is written to good words, words from the Scriptures, can be anything but good. Am I not right, Mama?'

'Yes, dear. Perfectly right. Your father knows that quite well. He was only joking, you know. He is feeling much stronger this evening,' she added with an indulgent smile, 'and that makes him inclined to be a little naughty.'

'Naughty on Sunday!' said Sarah. 'Oh, Papa!'

The Harmonious Blacksmith was a favourite with Mr Peacock. He liked it less for its musical than for its descriptive quality, and during Catherine's performance kept up a running commentary, by whispered word and animated gesture calling attention to this and that illustrative feature that he fancied he detected—the sound of the forge, the strokes of the blacksmith's hammer —and to the simple homely theme persisting through all the variations. Mrs Peacock uttered no protest, for

Handel, even in his lighter moods, was still Handel, invested with an aura of sanctity by virtue of his *Messiah*. Before Catherine had reached the last bars, her father was hovering by the piano, fingering the music sheets on its lid and ready to be persuaded to oblige the company with one of his songs. Everyone applauded the prospect, and with scarcely an interval Catherine addressed herself to the joyous task of accompanying him. Even the most sanctimonious pieces acquired a robust heartiness, a resolute jollity, in his rendering, so that smiles and laughter, which he did not in the least resent, were apt to mingle with the eventual applause. He enjoyed singing, it let something out of him, gave him a sense of fulfilment; and his family, even the more critical among them, enjoyed his enjoyment.

They went to bed happy, all five. Next morning Mr Peacock got into urban uniform and resumed his career as a solicitor. The girls, as usual, between breakfast and luncheon did as their mother ordained, each also as usual loyally playing up to her pretence—or was it an illusion? —that they were perfectly free agents, suffering no shadow of compulsion. And in the afternoon Mr Pardew paid them a call.

He was shown into the 'garden room', so called to distinguish it from the other and larger drawing-room, to which it was a comparatively recent supplement.

Designed in an earlier century as a farmhouse, not as a gentleman's residence, the general layout of Peacock Place had features that would have discontented a prouder, less sensible man than Edmund: he, because it had been his father's and grandfather's before him,

found no fault with it. The house faced west, fronting
the prevailing wind, the slanting rain, the glory of sunset.
At the north end, flanking the house, was the farmyard,
accessible equally from road and from dairy; and beyond
the yard, to the east, lay the orchard and all that now
remained to the Peacocks of the once-extensive farmlands.
The garden, with its lawns and shrubberies, its winding
paths and green arbours, its distant spinney of tall trees
and its frequent hedges that by dividing it into many
rooms, as it were, made it full of happy surprises, was
situated not at the back of the house but on the south side,
shut off from the street by a mellow brick wall. The
windows of the drawing-room, which was sometimes
called the music room out of compliment to the piano,
looked to the east, and so were flooded with sunshine
only in the mornings, when the room was unoccupied;
and the adjacent garden room, which Mr Peacock had
supplied with two wide windows and a double glass-
panelled door giving on to the nearer lawn, represented
his retort to that inconvenient circumstance. The
alterations had been planned primarily with a view to
his wife's comfort, that she might enjoy the benefit of
sunshine from the southern sky whenever that commodity
was available; but in practice she used the room less often
than did her younger daughters, and it was to Sarah and
Catherine that Mr Pardew made his bow on this Monday
afternoon.

Catherine, curled up in an easy chair with a book in
her lap, raised her head reluctantly and looked at the
intruder with dazed eyes, hardly recognizing him, unable
or unwilling to rally her romance-enchanted wits.

Sarah, with a nicer sense of the proprieties, put down her sewing and got up.

'Mr Pardew! How nice!'

'Good afternoon, Miss Sarah.' He bowed over her extended hand. 'Good afternoon, Miss Catherine. Pray don't let me disturb you.' But Catherine, blushing for her bad manners, was now on her feet, ready for the ceremonial handshake. 'Good afternoon,' he said again. 'And *what* a good afternoon it is!' He smiled wistfully, as at some secret solemn joke. 'One only wishes one deserved it.'

'Do sit down, won't you?' said Sarah. 'I don't know where my mother is. I'll go and find her, if you'll excuse me.'

'No, no. Please not. Anything but. Delighted though I should be,' he added hastily, 'I would not dream of troubling her.'

'I fancy she may be resting,' said Catherine, longing to get back to her book and knowing that Mama, if she appeared, would insist on his prolonging the visit and staying to tea.

'Quite so. Quite so. I hope she is in good health, your dear mother? Splendid. Splendid. I need not ask whether *you* are,' he said, with a glance at Catherine and a longer glance at Sarah. 'Your looks, if I may say so, proclaim it.'

He punctuated his remarks with a series of little nervous laughs. Breaking the awkward silence that followed, Sarah said:

'Is this a pastoral visit, Mr Pardew, or merely a social call?'

'The latter, my dear Miss Sarah. Most emphatically the latter.' He laughed again, more happily, recognizing the banter. 'I'm sure you're in no need of my professional services.'

'That,' retorted Sarah, 'is a very rash statement. Really, Mr Pardew, I'm surprised at you. I cannot answer for my little sister,' she continued with mock-gravity, provoking a grimace from Catherine, 'but as for myself, I assure you I sometimes have thoughts that would surprise you.'

'That I can well believe,' said Mr Pardew gallantly. 'And how privileged I should be if you would share them with me.' With a sudden change of tone, his smile giving place to a look of ingenuous admiration, 'I know you are exceedingly clever,' he said, 'as well as . . .' Seeking for a word less daring than the one he had in mind, he failed to find it, so left the sentence unfinished.

Mr Pardew was a tall young man, stalwart, athletic, with well-modelled regular features, a head of vigorous fair hair, and an unblemished complexion. The startling cleanliness of his appearance, a cleanliness that was some-how moral as well as physical, suggested to Sarah a diet of cold baths and carbolic soap. But for his bovine eyes, and an excess of earnestness in his manner, he would have been—and by many, indeed, was—accounted handsome. Sarah, though she laughed at him, was more kindly disposed towards him than she would have admitted. Her sense of his absurdity, which often amused but sometimes exasperated her, was at war with her recognition of his masculine attractions. The exasperation was perhaps significant, though not to her. She felt it to be

a wicked waste that good looks should have been bestowed
on a young man whom it was impossible to take seriously.

'You are very polite,' said Sarah, helping him out,
'though I'm not sure you mean it as a compliment.'
She wished he would go, and to prevent his perceiving
the wish went on talking. 'Have you brought us some
nice tit-bits of gossip from the village? It must be so
interesting to be a clergyman and have everyone tell you
their secrets. But of course you wouldn't tell us, it
wouldn't be proper. Your lips are sealed, like my
father's. And we shouldn't listen if you did, should we,
Kitty?'

'Of course not,' said Catherine. 'We should stop our
ears and run from the room.'

Studying their grave faces, 'I rather think you're
making fun of me,' said Mr Pardew, with a puzzled,
inquiring smile. 'I hope so, I'm sure,' he went on
earnestly. 'Because, you know, we don't normally hear
confessions in our Anglican Communion. That is a
Roman practice.'

If his simplicity was sometimes embarrassing, his good
nature was disarming. Sarah repented of her well-
meant frivolity, and finding nothing unfrivolous to say
merely murmured assent and waited, hoping that some
more fruitful subject would turn up. Catherine's eyes,
in the silence that followed, strayed back to her book,
furtively desirous. She contrived to read a line or two
in a detached manner, as if by accident, while still main-
taining an attitude of polite attention.

Mr Pardew cleared his throat. He shifted a little in
his chair. Meeting Sarah's glance of inquiry he smiled

painfully and remarked, for the second time, on the beauty of the day.

'It's almost,' he said, 'a shame to be indoors, don't you think, Miss Sarah?'

'Would you like to take a turn in the garden?' Sarah asked.

'Indeed yes. I should enjoy that.' He rose eagerly and stood hovering at Sarah's elbow. 'I wondered, I half-wondered, Miss Sarah, if I might venture to propose a game of croquet?'

'Of course, if you like,' said Sarah, dissembling her surprise.

'But perhaps it is a little cold for you?' he said, on an anxious afterthought.

'Not in the least. It's quite warm.' She moved towards the glass doors, and he darted ahead and flung them open for her. 'The grass may be a little damp,' she said, 'but that won't hurt us.' She stepped out, spreading her hands wide as if to catch the sunshine. 'Coming, Kitty?'

Before Catherine could respond, which she was in no hurry to do, he saved her the trouble by saying: 'Miss Catherine, I fancy, is inseparable from her book. What book is it, Miss Catherine, if I may ask?' She exhibited the volume. 'A novel? I see.'

'Do you disapprove?' said Catherine.

'Not necessarily. By no means. There are novels *and* novels.'

'Which is this, I wonder?' she murmured, but expected no answer, seeing with a sigh of contentment that he was gone.

Sarah, though surprised at his boldness, was pleased

with Mr Pardew for suggesting croquet, a pastime which, though now played annually at Wimbledon and well established in popular favour, had still not entirely lost the charm of novelty, the distinction of being 'modern'. She could still vividly remember the joyous excitement, some years ago, of lifting the lid of a long box delivered by carrier from Newtonbury and seeing for the first time the strange, beautiful implements. She remembered little Catherine's squeals of delight, dear Papa's boyish enthusiasm, and all the solemn business of measuring and marking the lawn. Even now, she not only enjoyed playing the game, but took a childlike sensuous delight in everything associated with it: the brightly painted wooden balls, blue, red, black, yellow; the long-handled mallets, so good to grip, so glorious to swing; the two upstanding varnished pegs or posts; the six white-enamelled hoops; and the four coloured clips which, shifted from hoop to hoop, recorded the progress of the match. All these, today, had to be fetched from a garden shed and carried to the sunk lawn just beyond sight of the garden room window, a rectangle of level sward, newly mown, recently rained upon, surrounded on all four sides by a smooth grass bank and approached by three stone steps. It was a green and private place, sheltered from the April breezes, open only to the bright sky.

'What a good idea of yours, Mr Pardew,' said Sarah, when all was ready. 'It'll be the first game of the year.'

'I'm glad,' said Mr Pardew. 'It will be something that I shall always remember. Always.' He coughed nervously. 'My name, Miss Sarah, is Hugh. Could you perhaps do me the honour of using it?'

'Would that be quite proper, do you think,' she countered, 'and you a clergyman?'

He smiled uncertainly. 'But I am not, you know, so very old.'

'Well, shall we begin?' said Sarah, with nervous briskness. 'There ought to be four of us really. Perhaps Catherine and Julia would join us. Shall I go and ask them?'

'Not on my account,' he answered quickly. 'By no means. Far from it. I am more than content. Two, if I may say so, is the perfect number. Just you and I.'

'Very well. Which colours will you have?'

But no, he said: *she* must choose. The choice must always be the lady's. To choose in such matters, nay to command, was the undoubted prerogative of the fair sex. By 'such matters', she retorted, he meant trivial matters she supposed, flustered by his excess of politeness into arguing with him. In everything else women were expected only to obey.

'Oh no,' he protested. 'Where there is love, a true union of hearts, no question of obedience can arise. Guidance, yes. A little gentle guidance. *Strong to protect and resolute to serve*, as the poet says. But not . . . but not . . . how shall I put it?'

'Don't trouble to put it at all,' Sarah said. 'We've come here to play croquet, you know, not to talk about love.'

'I rather hoped,' he said meaningly, 'that we might do both.'

'Since I'm to choose,' said Sarah, 'I shall take the red and the yellow. That means you begin.'

'Must I?' he said unhappily.

'Certainly you must. It's laid down in the rules. Blue, red, black, yellow: that's the order of play.'

'Well . . . if you insist.'

The game began. It proceeded in an uneasy silence, punctuated by brief conventional exclamations. Mr Pardew played well. He had a good eye and wielded the mallet with grace and precision. It was impossible to deny that he was a personable young man. His lithe athletic figure showed to great advantage in this agreeable exercise, and Sarah could have admired it without stint or afterthought but for knowing that his mind, like her own, was elsewhere, not on the game. Even so, she could not help enjoying the sunshine, the scent of the grass, the delicious moment of contact between her mallet and the ball; but an uneasy suspicion of his intentions weighed upon her spirit, making these pleasures of the senses fitful and precarious. She knew, all too well, what was hatching in his mind. She could already hear in imagination the prepared phrases, the sentimental sighs, the quotations from the poets. It was flattering, disturbing, totally unexpected. It was also, for reasons she could not stop to analyse, profoundly unwelcome. Had she liked him less she could have laughed at his ridiculous plan: had she liked him much, much more, she might have been tempted to entertain it.

She won the game by a narrow margin. Her opponent was radiant with satisfaction.

'Splendid, splendid,' he cried, clapping his hands. '*Ave, victrix!* A most enjoyable game and the happiest possible ending.'

'If you talk like that,' she said tartly, 'I shall think you weren't trying.'

'Oh, but I was, I do assure you,' he protested. 'Nevertheless, since justice has been vindicated, I rejoice.'

'I'm not sure that I approve of that,' said Sarah, belabouring the theme in the hope of avoiding seriousness. 'To be a good loser is quite the thing, I know. But unless you can contrive to seem just a little mortified, you cheat me, don't you see, of my triumph.'

Puzzled, contrite, anxious to please, 'But . . . but surely . . .' he stammered.

'Dear Mr Pardew, don't look so worried,' she cut in. 'I was only joking. It's a bad habit of mine.' She despaired of him: how could one talk to a man so obtuse? 'Shall we go in now? Or would you like another game, so that you can take your revenge?'

'Thank you, but no. I've no wish for revenge. Far from it. Far from it indeed.' Weighting his words with solemn unction, holding her in the leash of his soulful gaze, 'I am more, more than content to be conquered, Miss Sarah,' he said, 'by you.'

'That you've already made plain,' she answered, turning away. 'It's very disobliging of you, Mr Pardew. One should always play to win, else there's no game. Come along, we'd better go in. You'll stay to tea, won't you?'

'But *have* I?' he said eagerly. 'Have I made my meaning plain? I fear not. Give me another moment or two, dear Miss Sarah. Hear me out.'

Seeing no way of escape, short of impossible rudeness, she faced him again, saying earnestly: 'I do assure you, Mr Pardew, the subject is not worth pursuing.'

'How can you say that, before I have spoken?   May I tell you what is in my heart?'

'Truly,' she said, 'I would rather you didn't.   I think it would embarrass us both.'

'I'm sorry,' he said simply.   'I'm desolated.'   He stood very straight and stalwart before her, suddenly invested, it seemed to her, with a new stern dignity. 'But I've said too much not to say more.   It is my dearest wish that you will one day consent to be my wife.'

The grave pronouncement, though so utterly foreseen, shocked, gratified, and dismayed her.   Because it was without precedent it marked an epoch in her life.   She was desired.   Can this be happening to *me*, she thought incredulously.   It was a situation which, though hitherto outside her experience, she had often enough read about in the romances she and Catherine so much enjoyed; and it was they that provided her with the right, the inevitable answer.

'I am deeply sensible, Mr Pardew, of the great honour you do me.   I wish I felt it possible to do as you ask.' No sooner had she uttered the stilted sentences than she was beset by an untimely temptation to laugh at them. But the sight of Mr Pardew's stricken eyes kept her sober, and with a sudden reversion to her natural self, she exclaimed impetuously: 'Oh, why did you have to say it? I tried to stop you.'

'You mean there's no hope for me?'

She shrank from saying yes, there was no hope: it seemed needlessly brutal.   And she dared say nothing that would encourage such hope.

'Let's forget this conversation,' she said, forcing a

smile, mutely inviting him to relax and be cheerful, 'and just be friends. Thank you for my game of croquet. I enjoyed it.'

§ 2

'HULLO,' said Catherine, looking up from her book. 'Have a good game? Who won?' Not listening to the answer, she stretched herself sinuously, like a cat, flushed and drowsy with her long literary seance. 'Where's Mr Pardew?'

'He's gone,' said Sarah. 'He couldn't stay for tea.'

'Gone!' cried Catherine. 'Without saying goodbye to *me*! I'm heartbroken.' She struck a tragic attitude. 'Alas, and I so young!'

The performance fell flat. Sarah did not even smile.

'Anything wrong, Sally?' Her eyes grew bright with suspicion. 'Did he make you an offer?'

'Don't be absurd,' said Sarah. Her discomfort was manifest.

'But did he? Come on! Tell!... I do believe he did,' Catherine persisted. 'You wouldn't be so serious else.'

Sarah said, turning away: 'I never heard such nonsense. Be quiet, do.'

'All right,' said Catherine sadly, her face clouding. It was a new thing for her to be shut out of Sarah's confidence. 'If you don't want to tell me, don't. I'm not inquisitive.'

'Of *course* you're not,' agreed Sarah, suddenly herself again. 'Politely interested, yes, but never inquisitive. Far from it, as Mr Pardew would say.' Unwilling to

D

leave it at that, seeing Catherine was hurt, 'But if you *must* know,' she continued, 'yes, he did.'

'Golly!' said Catherine, round-eyed. Paradoxically she was startled by this confirmation of her guess: startled and impressed. A proposal in the family, no matter from whom, was a tremendous event. 'What a lark!' she murmured, but with more of hope than conviction.

'But it's a secret, mind.' Sarah was quietly emphatic. 'Don't say a word to anyone, or I'll never speak to you again.' To soften this threat, 'It would be mean,' she explained, 'to give him away.'

'You like him, don't you?' said Catherine, appalled by the discovery. 'All right. I'm not a telltale tit.' After a pause she asked in a small anxious voice: 'Do you . . . *like* him, Sarah?'

'I don't think so. Not in the way you mean. But I will say this for him,' she went on in a cheerful tone. 'He plays a very good game of croquet. And what,' she inquired, in her mother's voice and manner, 'what have *you* been doing, child, this afternoon? Ruining your eyesight with a foolish book, when you might have been out in the sunshine?'

Jenny, in the doorway that led from the drawing-room, said breathlessly: 'Oh, you're here, Miss Sarah. I've been looking everywhere. Tea's ready and waiting, and the master's home.'

'Thank you, Jenny. We're coming.'

'How nice,' said Catherine, 'having Papa for tea.'

'Very nourishing,' said Sarah. 'But don't we always?'

'Yes. That's what's so nice.'

'Very well, donkey,' said Sarah. 'Very well, scratch-cat,' said Catherine. They grinned at each other, pleased with this echo from their nursery days.

Tea with the Peacocks was no elegant toying with thin bread-and-butter and exiguous ladylike pastries, but a noble spread, the last major meal of the day. It normally began at half-past five, when Papa got home from his office, and continued in a leisurely, talkative fashion for the best part of an hour. A huge loaf sat boldly on its trencher, waiting to be cut. Honey, homemade jam, Mama's best butter, a large fruit cake, and sometimes a bowl of thick cream, contributed their various colours to the scene. There would be ham on the sideboard for Papa, the breadwinner, the tired city man, and boiled eggs for anyone who chose to have them. A huge brown teapot—not the silver one: that was reserved for breakfast—dominated the table, with Mrs Peacock in proud command of it. It was a symbol of the maternal authority, untouchable, except by her permission expressed or implied, by any hands but hers. Teatime, because it marked the return after eight hours of absence of dear Papa, was a daily celebration, the hour of the family reunion, a feast of gossip and news at which all were tacitly expected to give an account of themselves. All except Mr Peacock himself. He, who had been out in the great world and must be supposed to have much to tell, made a great tantalizing point of never talking about his professional affairs. This reticence added to his other and more genial attractions an alluring air of mystery: his womenfolk liked to regard him as a man full of dark secrets.

'Well, girls, what have you all been doing with yourselves today?' He turned to his wife, teasingly. 'You
first, my dear.'

'I am no longer a girl, Edmund.'

'Certainly you are. And the prettiest of the bunch.'

'You must excuse your father,' said Mrs Peacock,
smiling at her three daughters. 'It's his first day back at
the office, remember, after his illness.'

'After my fiddlesticks!' he retorted. 'Never been ill in
my life.'

'What have *you* been doing, Papa?' said Sarah mischievously. 'That's more to the point. Who is going to
law with whom? And why? And when?'

'Simple drudgery, my love. The common round, the
daily task. Nothing could be more unexciting.'

'We had a visitor this afternoon,' said Catherine.
'Sarah and I.'

'A visitor? Who?' Mrs Peacock's tone was sharp.

'Ah, who?' said Catherine. 'Can't you guess, Mama?'

'Possibly. Possibly not. I prefer, however, that you
should tell me, Catherine.'

'It was only Mr Pardew,' said Sarah, with a warning
glance at her sister.

'Mr Pardew! Why wasn't I told?'

'We didn't quite know where you were, Mama. And
he begged us not to disturb you.'

'Very polite of him. He's a very well-mannered young
man. But I wasn't far away, you know that. Julia and
I were busy upstairs, with the linen. I hope you asked
him to tea?'

'Of course,' said Sarah. 'But he wouldn't stay. We

had a game of croquet. That was a great help. It saved the trouble of making conversation.' Her wish to make fun of Mr Pardew had mysteriously vanished, but it would look odd if she did not speak of him disdainfully. 'Besides,' she continued, glad to let her tongue run away with her, 'it was a kindness to Catherine. My dear little sister was able to go on with her book. I call it noble of me.'

'So you and Mr Pardew played croquet together? Is that how it was?'

'Yes, Mama. Was it improper of me? I do hope not. I suppose I could have got Jenny or Alice to chaperon me, but I didn't think of it. It *was* a risk, wasn't it? But all is well. I emerged from the ordeal quite unscathed.'

'That will do, Sarah. I don't enjoy that kind of joke.' But catching her husband's quizzical look—it was very nearly a wink—she blushed slightly and summoned up a smile. 'And you, Catherine, you chose to spend your afternoon with a foolish book, did you, when you might have been enjoying the sunshine.'

'Yes, Mama,' said Catherine. She dared not look at Sarah, but her eyes danced. 'Are all books foolish, would you say, or only the ones I read?'

Julia, softly intervening, remarked that Catherine knew very well what Mama meant. Nobody enjoyed a really good book better than Mama.

'What is it about, Catherine?' asked Mr Peacock. 'Let us all have the benefit of your abstruse studies.'

'It's beautifully silly, Papa. But nice too. I'm enjoying it hugely. I've just got up to where Lady Vera discovers that Millicent Brown is her half-sister. Millicent, you

know, is the mysterious beauty she met at the Debenhams'
dinner-party.'

'I didn't know,' said Mr Peacock, 'but I'm delighted to
hear it. Tell me more, dear child.'

'Well, what makes it so exciting is that they're both in
love with the young Earl.'

'Then his lordship is a very lucky man. He has only
to take his choice.'

'Yes, but the awkward thing is, he's already engaged
to be married, to a rather horrid woman that his mother,
the Dowager Lady Debenham, has forced on him. It
was really she who gave the dinner-party. The Dowager
I mean, not the horrid woman. *She* was there too,
keeping an eye on him. The horrid woman I mean, not
the Dowager. Though of course the Dowager kept an
eye on him too.'

'You relieve my mind,' said Mr Peacock. 'I was in
danger of envying the young gentleman. But don't
excite me too much, my dear. My condition won't stand
it. Your mother, remember, insists that I've been ill.'

'When I've finished the book I'll tell you how it goes
on,' Catherine promised, with an air of mock-gravity.
'By then, Papa, you'll have got back your strength.'

'Thank you, child. That will be very kind. I can see,
by what you've told me already, that it's a most talented
and distinguished piece of work.'

'*But*, dear Papa,' said Sarah, wrinkling her brow, 'is it,
do you think, quite suitable reading for the young? Is
not my little sister in danger of being led astray?'

'That is very true, Sarah,' said Mrs Peacock. 'A true
word spoken in jest. I never interfere. Catherine knows

that. But if she *must* fill her head with novels I wish she would choose them with more discrimination. So does her father,' she added firmly, challenging contradiction.

'Do you, Papa?' inquired Catherine with specious innocence.

'I do not need to give you my opinion,' Mr Peacock answered. 'Your mother saves me that trouble.' He smiled on his daughters with complacent affection. 'You're all wonderfully silly girls, but I daresay you'll come to no harm. Eh, mother?'

'In *my* young days,' said Mrs Peacock severely, 'we read Sir Walter and poor Mr Thackeray.' Sir Walter had died during her childhood but was still Sir Walter. Poor Mr Thackeray's death was a comparatively recent event: hence the epithet.

'You cannot include Julia in your strictures, Papa,' said Sarah. 'She sets me and Kitty *such* a good example. We can never go wrong if we model our behaviour on hers.'

'Me?' said Julia. 'Oh no.' She rebutted the charge indignantly, refusing to be excluded from the communion of sisters. 'I'm sure I'm as silly as either of you. But I have at least one virtue,' she declared. 'I never mind being laughed at. Which is just as well,' she sensibly added, 'for I get plenty of *that.*'

'So do we all, my dear,' said Mrs Peacock, 'with Sarah and your father about. They encourage each other.'

'I think *I* shall write a novel for Kitty,' said Sarah, 'and see that she reads nothing else. Julia will help me with the pious bits. I shall model it on *Ministering Children.* Or that book about the little motherless girl whose father was in India, and her kind auntie wouldn't let her open his letter because it came on Sunday.   Do you remember, Mama?   Something like that will be wonderfully good for Kitty.   It's just what she needs, poor child, to set her in the right path.'

'Why must you talk about me as if I were not here?' Catherine complained.   'But perhaps you didn't notice I was?   This is me, this beautiful young girl with red hair.'

'When you two have finished talking nonsense,' remarked Mrs Peacock, 'perhaps one of you will spare time to cut your mother some bread?'

Julia, jumping up from her seat, flung herself upon the loaf.   'Poor starving Mama!' she cried, infected by the general gaiety.   'How cruel we are to you!'

When the meal was over, and the family dispersed, Mr Pardew came creeping back into Sarah's thoughts.   And now, in his absence, she was drawn to him, remembering his good looks, his good nature, his unhappiness, and thinking she had perhaps been unkind.   Painful and absurd as the situation was, there was something of secret gratification to be derived from it: her vanity, little catered for hitherto, could not lightly dismiss the tribute of a man's desire, even such a man as Mr Pardew, who was, when all was said, an eminently respectable, well-bred, eligible person.   Nor, though it embarrassed her, did his devotion diminish for her his personal attractions, such as they were.   He was good and he was kind, manly in appearance and graceful in his movements; and if only he would consent never to open his mouth, except to put food into it, she half-believed she could have loved him. It could not be denied that marriage would be a triumph, a solace to self-esteem, and that this first chance might also be her last. In pursuit of the idea that she had perhaps done him some injustice, by being perversely over-critical, her daydreaming imagination, lacking the corrective of his presence, began wilfully endowing him not only with the virtues he might be supposed to possess, sincerity, loyalty, resolute good intentions, but with qualities that bore no relation to what she knew of him. Not wit: she drew the line there. He would never sparkle. He would never set the table in a roar. But humour, yes: she was determined to give him at least a modicum of humour. A man in love, or thinking himself in love, was never, she supposed, at his brightest; but, once his prayer were granted, his ambition achieved, he would surely be bolder, less dog-eyed, more capable of taking a point, or seeing a joke, without having it explained to him. Marriage could not fail to effect that much.

She began to see that her former judgment had been hasty, superficial. He had, after all, shown unusual enterprise. It was greatly to his credit that he had approached her direct, defying convention by not first asking her parents' permission. Though infinitely respectful, endearingly modest, he had been impetuous and brave. He knew what he wanted and was resolved to get it. Behind that mask of diffidence and excessive gravity lived a mature resolute spirit and a mind that refused to be deflected from its purpose by her evasive flippancies. Having thus created a new Mr Pardew, patient, masterful, and of wisdom and irony all compact, she proceeded to endow him with learning and saintliness for good measure: no sense in scamping the job. He was, she knew, a university man, with an honours degree, and might one day be a bishop. She grew hot and cold remembering how lightly she had dismissed him.

The truth is, she said, I'm frivolous, too fond of making fun. At my age I ought to be more serious, like Julia. Why doesn't he marry *her*? It would be just the thing. As a brother-in-law he would be nearly perfect. Yet, oddly, the idea did not entirely please her. Already she had certain property rights in the lover she did not want. She did not want him, but was not yet quite ready to let him go; and, though she half-dreaded the prospect, she was impatient to see him again.

§ 3

No woman since the world began—nor man either—has received with perfect indifference a declaration of love, no matter from what source; and even though disdain or repulsion or fear be her dominant emotion, mingling with it, in greater or less degree, is gratification, the response of a caressed vanity of which she may be unaware. Being young and inexperienced, neither Miss Sarah nor Mr Pardew was possessed of this universal truth of human nature. He did not, could not know, that by exposing his desire for her he had made himself for the moment the most interesting person in the world, nor she that her being desired had unsettled her judgment and half-persuaded her that she was fond of him. The seed he had sown, unregarded at the time, blossomed into a gratitude —mingled with compassion—that was dangerously akin to love, or at least could easily be mistaken for it if she were not careful. Unknowingly, he had added to her stature, transformed her conception of herself, given her a blissful sense of her own value: never again could she think of herself, without qualification, as the ordinary homely one, outshone by her beautiful sisters, with nothing but a lively sense of the ludicrous to offset her unremarkable appearance. Looking at herself in the glass, she tried to see what Mr Pardew presumably saw in her, and though the endeavour was unsuccessful she was more than ready to defer to his masculine and therefore (in this matter) superior judgment. There was, perceptibly, a new sparkle in her eyes, and with the hair done a little differently perhaps something might be made of her, in spite of the comic nose and dumpy figure. It was, at any rate, worth trying.

Catherine, who still shared with her the big bedroom that had once been the night nursery for all three, was more conscious than Sarah herself of the outward change in her. She had noticed uneasily that except at mealtimes, when the family was fully mustered and a special effort was called for, this volatile sister of hers was strangely unlike herself: silent and self-absorbed. The comfortable bedtime chatter which they had enjoyed together all their lives, their voices, disembodied by the darkness, growing drowsier and drowsier till sleep at last supervened, had become, as the days went by, more and more abbreviated.

'Sarah! . . . Are you awake?'

'No,' said Sarah. 'I'm fast asleep.'

'Will you promise not to be cross if I ask you something?'

'Cross? I'm never cross.'

'You are, you know, sometimes. You have been, lately. Not cross exactly. But sort of.'

'It's news to me. Since when, pray?' Regretting the incautious question Sarah hastened to add: 'Can a person be cross without knowing it? I shouldn't have thought so.' There was safety in generalities.

'Will you promise then?' Catherine persisted.

'All right. I'm not a dragon, Kitty. What is it?'

'It's since that game of croquet,' said Catherine, 'with Mr Pardew.' Her clear young voice, urgent and oddly shy, seemed to hover suspended in the warm darkness. Silence engulfed the words, a long palpitating silence in which their implications echoed and re-echoed. 'You're not thinking seriously of him, are you?'

'Why?' said Sarah. 'What if I were?'

'Oh, nothing. I only wanted to know.'

'Does it matter to you so much?'

'Not,' said Catherine bravely, 'if you really want him.'

'Well, you needn't worry, donkey. I said No. Nothing could have been plainer. He won't ask me again.'

'What on earth makes you think that? Of *course* he will. Men always do.'

'Not he though,' said Sarah. 'He hasn't been near us since. It's nearly a fortnight.'

'And you're disappointed, aren't you?' It was an accusation.

'Not at all. Why should I be? He's had his answer. It's only logical to keep out of the way.'

'If you ask me,' said Catherine resentfully, 'I think it's rather clever of him.'

'Clever? No, he's not clever. Not in that way.'

'He's getting you into a state. And then, in his own good time, *you*'ll see, back he'll come.'

'Will he? I don't think so.'

'Don't you? I do. I'm sure of it. So if you really don't mean to have him, you'd better be prepared.'

'Thank you for the warning, Kitty. Out of the mouths of babes and sucklings . . . Shall we go to sleep now?'

But sleep tonight did not come quickly to Sarah. The conversation had disturbed her more than she would admit. If he *did* ask her again, what would she say? That she could not confidently answer that question frightened her. She had had only one sight of him since the day of the proposal: in church, tall, unapproachable, priestly, reading the Lessons in a loud, polite, prefectorial voice. To see him so, a public figure, remote and impersonal in cassock and surplice, to hear him enunciating sentences too familiar to engage her thought, gave her the queerest sensation. The contrast between now and then was exciting: she could not forget that between this stranger and herself, whether she would or no, there now existed an intimate relationship, an invisible bond. How strange that a few unwelcome words could have effected so much, and all in a moment of time. Even now, in her fancy, he was thinking of her, as she of him. They shared a secret of which no one else in this crowded church, except Catherine, had any inkling. Except Catherine, sitting next to her. From time to time, waking from a dream, she became conscious of Catherine's curious, wondering, speculative glance.

Another Sunday came and went. At Evensong Mr Pardew occupied the pulpit.

'Did it make you laugh, the sermon?' Catherine asked, when they were alone again.

'Not particularly.'

'I thought not,' said Catherine sadly. Trying again, she ventured: 'But it was very churchified, wasn't it?'

'Naturally,' said Sarah. 'What else could it be? He's not a good preacher. We've always known that.'

'Never mind. I'm sure you'll brighten him up when you're married.'

'Are you, donkey?' said Sarah. 'Then that's all right, isn't it?'

Next day, exactly a fortnight after his former visit, he presented himself at the house half an hour before teatime. Mrs Peacock received him with her customary graciousness. He shook hands with the girls, letting his glance linger for only a moment on Sarah, and after some careful desultory conversation, in which he and Mrs Peacock did most of the talking, took his place at table, smiling gratefully on all the company. At Mr Peacock's entry, a moment later, he leapt to his feet.

'Good afternoon, sir. The bad penny again.' He laughed selfconsciously, baring white teeth.

'Afternoon, Pardew. Delighted to see you.'

'Most kind. Most kind. I'm afraid the ladies spoil me. It's so nice to be made welcome. I do hope you're fully recovered, Mr Peacock?'

'Recovered? What's this?'

'Last time I had the pleasure of visiting here,' said Mr Pardew, blushing and beaming, 'you had recently been ill.'

'Nonsense, my dear fellow! An idle rumour. A

zealously propagated myth. You mustn't believe all my wife tells you.'

'*Really*, Edmund!'

'There,' said Mr Pardew, 'I must venture, with all respect, to disagree with you, sir. Mrs Peacock, I am sure, would never deviate by a hair's breadth from the strict truth. And that, in this lax modern age, is so very important, don't you think? It's a thing I'm always trying to impress on my children at Sunday School. Speak the truth, children, I say, and shame the . . .' He hesitated, glancing at the ladies. 'And shame the, er, Evil One.'

'Very sound advice,' said Mr Peacock politely, with a covert glance at Sarah.

'How is the Sunday School shaping?' asked Mrs Peacock. '*Such* a good idea. Such a wholesome influence in the village. The little boys are *so* much better-behaved and respectful since you started it, Mr Pardew. It was a thing sadly needed.'

'Very kind of you to say so, Mrs Peacock. Most kind. Most kind. The Vicar approves too, I'm glad to say. Prayers, a few hymns, and a short, frank talk. Just a simple service. It would never do, I told him, to let the chapel folk get ahead of us.'

'Indeed no,' said Mr Peacock. 'Can't have them getting to heaven before us.'

'And you do it all by yourself?' asked Julia. 'That *is* good of you.'

'At the moment, yes. But when our numbers grow, as I hope and pray they will, perhaps you, Miss Julia, or you, Miss Sarah, will be so kind as to come and help in the good work? That would be a great blessing, especially for the little ones. They need, after all, a lady's guidance. Though as a mere man,' he ended modestly, 'one does what one can.'

It needed only this, thought Sarah. The balloon of her fortnight's eager imagining was pricked. She watched its collapse with regret but also with a sense of release. The dream was over: the waking, though painful, was salutary, liberating. Even now she strove to be just. The young man was sincere and well-meaning. She did not doubt that he did good and useful work. He deserved better than to be laughed at. But . . .

The conversation went on and on, till the meal reached its end. Sarah, rising from the table with the others, became aware that Mr Pardew was angling for her private attention.

'Before I go,' he murmured, sidling up to her, 'I wonder if you would be so kind as to show me the rose garden, Miss Sarah?'

'Certainly, if you like. But it's too early for roses.'

'So it is. How forgetful of me. But the buds, don't you think,' he confided softly, bending towards her as she led the way into the garden, '*fast-folded buds, the sleeping babes of Spring*, as the poet says, are even more appealing?'

'It depends on what one is looking for,' answered Sarah. 'Old Piggott wouldn't agree with you. He takes a sort of angry pride in his roses, but only when they're in full bloom and because he wins prizes with them. His chief interest is potatoes. We've persuaded him at last to spare a little space for asparagus, but he only does it to oblige, with much grumbling. It's a wonder to me that things grow at all in the kitchen garden, with that comic old misery for ever scowling and sneering at them. I'm sure I shouldn't. My meaning, miss, he says, if it beant one thing tis another. Never rain when we wants it and then a methuselah downpour, as the saying is, and they dratted creeping lilies everywhere. Ay, the weeds'll grow fast enough, trust *them*: tis ten men's funeral to keep pace with 'em. He's always called Old Piggott,' she rattled on, 'even to his face, because there's another Piggott in the village, Young Piggott, aged about fifty. Everyone knows he's his nephew, son of poor naughty old Lizzie, his sister——'

'Dear me!' said Mr Pardew, blushing. 'How sad!'

'But Old Piggott'—she hurried on—'won't admit the relationship. He be none of mine, miss, nor his mother neither. I don't hold with ungodliness. Quaint, don't you think, after half a century? You'd think he would have got used to it by now. The village isn't usually so unforgiving.'

'Forgive us our trespasses, yes,' said Mr Pardew. 'But repentance must come first.'

His discomfort was manifest. Sarah realized that in her anxiety to keep his ardour at bay she had let her tongue run away with her. How shocked Mama would have been, could she have heard her!

A silence fell between them. She could think of nothing to say.

'What a lovely evening,' sighed Mr Pardew. 'So golden. So serene.'

'Yes, isn't it. But I shouldn't be surprised if we had rain before morning.'

E

'Almost too lovely,' said Mr Pardew. 'Sometimes, do you know, the beauty of the world is almost more than I can bear.'

'How very inconvenient for you!'

'And when I am with you, Miss Sarah, it's . . . it's as if the gates of paradise itself were opening.'

'I'm sorry,' said Sarah firmly. 'Because they aren't, you know.'

'You haven't forgotten our last conversation? May I hope that you've given some thought to it?'

'Yes, but——'

'Perhaps you feel I was too bold, too hasty? That I should have addressed myself first to your dear parents? That would indeed have been more proper. But, forgive me, I was carried away.'

'Not at all,' said Sarah. 'I thought no such thing. You've nothing to reproach yourself with. I assure you I shouldn't have enjoyed being discussed behind my back. It was *my* affair, and yours. No one else's.'

'Then perhaps . . .' he said, seizing her hand. She released herself quickly. 'No, do not answer me yet. Give yourself time, and let me at least hope.'

'No, Mr Pardew. I've had plenty of time. I've had a whole fortnight.' To reject him, she found, was easier than she had feared. She was more than ever sorry for him, but she hardened her heart against pity, seeing now with clear eyes that only in his absence could she come within sight of loving him. 'Forgive me, please, but my answer is still the same, and always will be. I hope,' she added gently, 'we need never speak of this again.'

'If that is your wish, Miss Sarah, I will try to obey you. Your wish is my law. But——'

'There is no *but*,' she said impatiently. 'I'm . . . I'm . . . grateful for your kind proposal, but what you ask is quite, quite impossible. I cannot see myself in such a position. I should never do justice to it.'

'My dear Sarah, if *that* is your only reason——'

'But it's not, it's not,' she burst out, angry to find that she had set a trap for herself. 'It's the least of reasons. The true reason must be obvious, even to you. It's simply,' she said, driven to desperation, 'that I don't *love* you, Mr Pardew. Surely that's sufficient? And don't say that I might learn to love you, because it isn't true, it's quite out of the question.'

'Very well.' He was pale with mortification. 'I have exposed myself to no purpose.'

'I don't know what you mean by exposing yourself,' she said coldly. 'But you needn't imagine I shall boast of the honour you have done me. I propose to forget it.'

She turned, and left him standing.

Arrived back in the house she encountered a battery of curious eyes.

'Well, my Sarah?' said Mrs Peacock. 'What have you done with your young man?'

'If you mean Mr Pardew, Mama, he's gone. He begs you will accept his most humble apologies for not taking leave of you. He has another visit to pay.'

'Did you have a nice talk?'

'Quite tolerable, thank you. Not exactly scintillating. You know what he is.'

'I know he's a very amiable young man, Sarah. I hope you weren't rude to him.'

'I hope not too, Mama. But he wouldn't have noticed if I had been. His chief contribution, I recall, was that repentance must precede forgiveness.'

'And who, I wonder, is in need of forgiveness?' inquired Mr Peacock urbanely.

'Old Lizzie Piggott, Papa, who went astray fifty years ago.'

'Really, Sarah!' exclaimed her mother. 'I'm surprised at you! Catherine, you may leave us.'

'Thank you, Mama,' said Catherine, making no move. Her eyes were on Sarah, trying desperately to read her mind.

CHAPTER THREE

Midsummer Revels

§ 1

SARAH kept her word. Except to Catherine, who knew too much not to be told more, she said nothing of what had passed between herself and Mr Pardew. It was a little unkind in her, she sometimes felt, to deprive her family of such a gigantic plum of gossip, argument, and fun; it would have kept their tongues busy for days and been remembered ever afterwards as marking an epoch in the family history; but for her own sake, as well as his, she preferred to be silent. She had no wish to be the centre of discussion, to be argued with and perhaps disapproved of. Papa, she thought, would have been sorry to lose her, and would have raised his eyebrows at her choice; but of Mrs Peacock she was unsure. Silence therefore was best on all counts; and Catherine, sworn to secrecy, loyally resisted the temptation to chatter. Then by what mysterious process did Julia and Mama acquire some inkling of the situation, so that during the weeks that followed any mention of Mr Pardew's name gave rise to meaning looks and expectant silences? Perhaps it was because Sarah no longer indulged her wit at his expense, and because on his subsequent visits—for he manfully continued to call—he had the air of cherishing a secret sorrow and could not refrain from angling for sympathy.

Mr Pardew's irruption into the family consciousness

had turned the thoughts of all three girls in the direction of matrimony. Even Julia, cheerfully resigned to eternal maidenhood, looked with new eyes at every male visitor that came near them, half-consciously asking herself whether this one or that might 'do' for one or the other of her sisters. Dr Witherby, who with undeviating regularity came once a month to play chess with Mr Peacock, was clearly too old, probably not less than forty, and a confirmed bachelor to boot. Mr Garnish, the vicar, though a widower and sadly in need of someone to look after him and keep a busy eye on the parish, was older still: moreover, it was notorious that his house-keeper, Mrs Budge, imported from the county town of Mercester, was busy making herself indispensable and would never let him out of her clutches. Mrs Budge won't budge, said the village, slapping its knee and roaring with laughter at the subtle pun. She, with the help of a fourteen-year-old daughter, and an overgrown lad from the village who was nominally the gardener but spent much of his time scrubbing floors and carrying coals, did all the work of the large half-empty vicarage. Several unmarried ladies of suitable age were suspected of aspiring to the position of vicaress, but had to content themselves with humbler offices: running the Bible class and the sewing guild, organizing 'sales of work' for the relief of the deserving poor, and decorating the church at harvest festivals. Julia herself, with no ulterior motive, took part in these activities; and the time could not be far distant when her sisters would be drawn into them.

Dr Witherby, a comparative newcomer to the district,

was a tall man but from the habit of much courteous
bending had acquired a slight stoop. The effect of his
large aquiline features was softened by a nimbus of red
beard surrounding them from ear to ear, chin and upper
lip being clean-shaven, and by a pair of bushy and
extremely mobile and expressive eyebrows which, had he
been deprived of the power of speech, would alone have
been adequate for all emotional occasions: in his chess-
sessions with Mr Peacock they came much into play,
sometimes rising so high as to threaten contact with his
mass of brown, unkempt hair. He did not however rely
on them exclusively for the expression of his varying
moods: in moments of unprofessional relaxation he had
a vein of sardonic talk that was highly congenial to Mr
Peacock. It was characteristic of him, whether to call it
tact or cunning is a moot point, that with Mrs Peacock
and her like his manner was more ceremonious, lacking
nothing of the sober, smiling gravity expected of a
physician: he had in fact, it might almost be said, as
many manners as he had patients, from Colonel Beckoning's lady, of Manor Park, to old Mrs Bateson in her
cottage. Despite his eccentric appearance, which suggested a tragic actor rather than a medical man, he was
well regarded by rich and poor alike. And perhaps,
thought Julia in her new role of matchmaker, he was not
too old after all: Sarah would be all the better for a
steadying influence.

The Vicar was quite another story. He had held his
office from time immemorial, had christened them, all
three, prepared them for confirmation, and was now
rapidly declining into senility. His conduct of the church

services had become a nervous embarrassment to the more percipient among his congregation. His speech grew more slow and uncertain with every week that passed, and at any moment, they felt, he might forget what he was at and precipitate a minor scandal in God's house. Only stubbornness, and a bitter resolve not to be ousted by Mr Pardew whose youth and vigour he resented, prevented his retiring. It was whispered in the village that the curate had much to put up with in the way of sulks and snubs from his vicar, even to the indignity of having to receive his salary from the hands of Mrs Budge. This was unproven, but everyone remembered that dreadful Sunday morning when Mr Pardew, mounting the pulpit sermon in hand, had been silently but testily recalled and displaced by the feeble formidable old man, who then proceeded to preach for forty weary minutes on the virtues of faith, hope, and charity. *And the greatest of these is charity.* Was it malice or mere absentmindedness? Mr Pardew himself would admit to no doubt on the point. An unfortunate misunderstanding, he insisted. Distressing, yes; but he, not the Vicar, was to blame. It is possible that he had profited from the sermon, though like others he had heard it often enough before. It is equally possible that he knew that no one would believe him. This episode, though not consciously recalled, was part of the background of Julia's reflections. It was manifest that the Vicar, greatly as he needed a wife, if only to rescue him from Mrs Budge, was not a marriageable proposition.

This attempt on Julia's part to dispose of her sisters was no more than a game which she played in idle moments, when there was nothing more serious to occupy her. Mr Pardew had set it going, and it was to him, coupled in her fancy with Sarah, that her speculations always returned. She could not believe that his frequent visits, his delicately pointed attentions, his parade of a melancholy bravely borne under a mask of resolute cheerfulness, could ultimately fail of their purpose. At times she was tempted to take him aside and urge him to speak plainly, feeling it to be almost her duty, as the eldest in the family, to do what she could to ease his heart of its burden and promote her sister's happiness. Nor was there any lack of opportunity, for she now, and she alone, helped him in the Sunday School. While he dealt with the bigger children, she got into a huddle with the little ones, telling them moral stories from the Old Testament, such as the Infant Samuel and Joseph and his Brethren, and explaining gently that if they were rude to old gentlemen, like the children who mocked Elisha ('Go up, thou bald head!'), a she-bear would come down from the mountain and eat them up. Mountains, it was true, were conspicuously lacking in this midland shire, and bears not plentiful; but no doubt the lesson went home. Mr Pardew, however, gave her no opening, and she reluctantly decided not to interfere, at any rate for the present. Meanwhile it would be as well to sound Catherine.

'Whatever shall we do, Kitty,' she said one day, 'when Sarah's gone? We shall miss her dreadfully.'

Catherine stared. 'Do you mean when she goes to Aunt Druid's? Perhaps they won't ask her. And it won't be till the autumn anyhow. It never is.'

Aunt Druid, Mrs Peacock's sister, was the wife of a

prosperous farmer in a neighbouring county, a long slow train-journey away, involving two changes. It was her habit to have one of her nieces to stay with her for a few weeks every year. She would gladly have had all three, but it was understood that only one could be spared. This year it was Sarah's turn. Catherine, disliking the prospect of losing her, did her best to pretend that it might not happen, but knew in her heart that nothing was more certain that that the invitation would punctually arrive.

'I didn't mean that, silly,' said Julia. 'I mean when she's married.'

'What *are* you talking about, Julia? Is she going to be married? But how exciting! Who to, pray?'

'Well, it looks like it, doesn't it? I mean . . .'

'Yes? *What* do you mean?'

Julia flushed, but was not to be put off. Her scrutiny on occasions could be as keen and shrewd as Mama's.

'I think there's no doubt that she's . . . liked a good deal, by a certain gentleman. You must have noticed that.'

'Not I,' said Catherine coolly. 'I'm too busy to concern myself with other people's likings.'

'Don't you think it's true then?'

'How should I know? I'm not in your certain gentleman's confidence.'

'No, but you *are* in Sarah's,' said Julia quickly. 'She tells you everything.'

'Does she? I wonder. Not everything. No one tells everything. Still, I think she'd have told me, and you too, and Mama, if she were thinking of getting married.

We'd have to know, wouldn't we, sooner or later?   I
mean, she wouldn't just elope, leaving a letter pinned to
her pillow confessing all and begging forgiveness.   That
wouldn't be a bit like her, so you really needn't worry,
dear Julia.'

'Now you're just being foolish,' sighed Julia.   'All
the same, I'm sure he likes her.'

'Who does?'

'Can't you guess?'

Catherine put on a considering air.   'Well, it can
hardly be Dr Witherby.   And I don't think it's Mr
Crabbe.   The only other gentleman who comes to see us
regularly is poor Mr Pardew.'

'Exactly,' said Julia.   'So you *have* noticed something!'

'As for his liking her,' said Catherine airily, 'I daresay
he likes all of us.   I shall never marry, shall you?   But
it would be fun to collect a few proposals.   I haven't had
one yet—isn't it a shame?   I shall write them all down
in my diary and cry over them when I'm an old woman,
like poor dear Miss Fotheringay in *Tried in the Fire, or The
Gold and the Dross*.   But of course that was different,
because she was in love with fascinating Guy Chevenix,
who jilted her and broke her heart.   She had dozens of
offers after that, but always said No, and promised to be
a sister to them, because she never forgot Guy, he was the
one love of her life.   Where shall I begin, Julia?   There's
not much time left.   Do you think the Claybrook boys
would do?   Not very exciting, but one has to start somewhere, and I think I could bring them to the point if I
set my mind to it.   First Jack, then Will.   With any luck
I might get them quarrelling about me.   A duel or

something. Wouldn't that be a triumph?' Before Julia could think of a suitable answer, Sarah came into the room. 'Hullo, Sally, you're just in time. I'm planning to make Jack Claybrook propose to me. Julia thinks it's a capital idea. I do hope you agree?'

'Certainly,' said Sarah. 'Will you accept him?'

'Oh no. Will must have a turn too. I shan't accept him either.'

Divided between laughter and impatience, 'I must say,' said Julia, 'I've never listened to a more ridiculous conversation.'

'Let the dear child prattle while she can,' said Sarah. 'When she comes to my age, she'll sober down. Won't you, Kitty?'

Catherine grinned. 'Yes, granny.' She put out her tongue.

'Don't ever let Mama see you do that,' Julia begged. 'She'd think it most unladylike. Oughtn't you to be busy with your needles, you two? It's only four weeks to the Midsummer Ball.'

'And why not you, Julia?' Sarah asked.

'I'm not sure I shall go. It depends on whether Mama can spare me.'

'We'll make her go too,' said Catherine. 'And Papa, why not? I think I shall wear green satin,' she went on, looking forward as much to the bustle of preparation, the measuring, the pinning-up, even the fine stitching, as to the dance itself. 'Papa will buy it for me; Miss Jenkinson will cut it out, she's so clever; and I shall help her with the sewing. What will you go in, Sarah?'

'Pink, I expect, to match my maiden blushes. Or

mustard yellow, to match my freckles. I wish it were
going to be a masked ball. It would be so nice not
knowing anyone, and having to guess. Besides, it would
give one's own face a holiday.'

'Don't you like your face?' asked Catherine. 'I do.'

'I don't mind it,' said Sarah. 'I don't mind it at all.
It's quite a useful face for eating and talking with.'

'I wonder if Mr Pardew will go to the ball?' said Julia,
in what she imagined was a casual tone. 'And if he does,
who he'll dance with?'

'Why not ask him?' Sarah suggested. 'I'm sure he'd
be flattered by your interest.'

§ 2

COLONEL BECKONING of Manor Park was a legendary
figure, regarded by the village with admiring awe but
seldom seen in the flesh. With his young second wife,
four children, an aged aunt, and numerous servants, he
lived two miles away, in a white-stone eighteenth-century
house of many windows, surrounded by a hundred acres
of undulating parkland. Whether or not he was in law
as well as in fact the lord of that domain, or merely the
heir and deputy of his aunt, Lady Mallard, relict of the
late Sir Godfrey, was known only to themselves, to
Messrs Peacock and Crabbe their solicitors, and possibly
to the agent, Mr Prickett, who managed the estate and
kept a sharp eye on the various rights and properties that
went with it. Thirty years of soldiering in India had left
the Colonel short of an arm and with a white scar running
across his lean left cheek. His infrequent appearance in
the village, mounted on a white horse and looking like an

elderly Saint George in languid pursuit of the dragon, was always a nine days' wonder and the occasion of much bobbing and bowing and touching of forelocks. But though he was apt to look stern and fierce he was not unduly proud. Hidden within him was a fund of geniality, carefully saved up and stored away for use at that joyous annual event, the Midsummer Night's Ball at Manor Park, to which all the gentry and near-gentry of the neighbourhood were invited. The villagers had their own revels of which singing and dancing formed only a part.

This year the Peacocks went in force. Since the girls could not go unescorted, and their next neighbours who farmed the contiguous acres (once Peacock property) had a bunch of female cousins to transport, Papa and Mama, after putting up a token resistance, allowed themselves to be persuaded.

'Your father and I,' said Mrs Peacock insincerely, 'are getting too old for dancing. I'm sure the Claybrook boys will oblige us, as they did last year.'

'We do not care to be obliged, Mama,' said Sarah. 'Besides, they have their own party. There'll be no room for us. You would not have us sit on their knees?'

'Not in front of the cousins,' said Catherine with a giggle. 'They'd scratch our eyes out.'

'Jack and Will Claybrook,' Mrs Peacock reminded them, 'have known you all since you were children. They're like brothers.'

'They *are* brothers,' said Sarah. 'But to each other, not to us.'

'We shan't enjoy it half so much,' murmured Julia, tactfully interposing, 'without you and Papa.'

'If that is so, Emily my love,' said Mr Peacock, 'we must try, don't you think, to forget our grey hairs, our dwindling blood, our palsied limbs, and indulge the girls?'

Julia had never quite outgrown the feeling that to be up and about at an hour long after bedtime was a kind of wickedness, and some echo of a childish guilt came back to her on this midsummer evening as with parents and sisters she took her seat in the seldom-used carriage, sank back against the warm-smelling leather upholstery, and felt herself riding, sailing, floating to adventure, on an invisible road that slipped away under the turning wheels. It was strange and exhilarating, dashing and daring, to be setting out at so late an hour with the prospect of turning night into day. Harry Dawkins, scrubbed and polished for the occasion and wearing a smart green livery that reeked of camphor, handled the reins; her sisters, wonderful to relate, were dumb with expectancy; Mama and Papa were wearing their most polite, benign, party-going faces; and nothing was lacking that could make her heart beat quicker and her dark eyes sparkle.

Their progress, despite Harry Dawkins's cajoling grumbles and readiness with the whip, could not be rapid. Manor Park, as was only proper, was at a slightly higher elevation than the village. To reach it one must ascend a winding and gently rising hill flanked on either side by fields of young corn, alternating with lush meadows where ruminating cattle stood at gaze. Trees cast a lengthening shadow and the colours of sunset were draining from the inverted bowl of the sky as the carriage turned in at the Park gates. Ten minutes later the house came into view. Cool and mellow in the afterglow of day, solid embodiment of elegance and good sense, it seemed to Julia at this distance both beautiful and unreal, a harmonious incident in an imaginary landscape.

But the mood of wonder very soon gave place to more practical considerations. For now they had arrived, and there were things to worry about: their reception by host and hostess, the disposal of the horses, the meeting with old acquaintances and the being introduced to strangers. For one nervous moment she wished herself home again. The moment, however, passed quickly. No sooner had the carriage come to a halt than servants were at hand to help the ladies to alight and to take charge not only of the horses but of Harry Dawkins as well. He, having received his instructions from Mr Peacock about the return journey, quickly made himself scarce and was seen no more.

Though brightness had gone from the air, dusk was not yet come; but already, in the great ballroom, the five central candelabra and the many wall-sconces held minims of flame whose every movement was reflected in hanging lustres and surrounding mirrors. In the middle of the upper lawn, just beyond the open french windows, stood an ancient cedar, its lower branches hung with variously-coloured Chinese lanterns soon to be lit. The sound of the fiddlers tuning up wove a pattern of expectancy against a background of chattering voices and rustling shimmering silks. Julia awoke to the alarming consciousness of having lost sight of her family, but before she had time to despair a voice at her elbow said, with elderly courtesy: 'Miss Peacock, may I present my son? Captain Arthur Beckoning. Miss Peacock.'

A tall figure, resplendent in scarlet dress-uniform, stood at attention before her.

'Your servant, ma'am.' He bowed stiffly. Julia, speechless with timidity, sketched a curtsey. 'May I have the honour of the first dance?'

Murmuring assent, and vexed with herself for feeling frightened, she surrendered her card. Having signed it, with the little pencil attached, he retained it for a moment in his left hand, while the other delicately stroked his long moustaches. He gazed down at her, frankly admiring.

'By Jove, Miss Peacock, I *am* a lucky fellow! Shall we take a turn on the lawn?'

Her answer was interrupted by the Master of Ceremonies. 'Take your partners, ladies and gentlemen, for the waltz.' The fiddles struck up; and the next moment she found herself in the respectful embrace of this gallant middle-aged gentleman—he could hardly be less than thirty-five—and surrendering happily to his expert guidance, the hypnotic dancing rhythm, and the magical half-melancholy charm of *Greensleeves*. Her eyes modestly downcast, she was but vaguely aware of his ardent gaze, the firm pressure of his clasp on her waist; and when presently he manœuvred her, still dancing, through the french windows into the open air, she woke with a start of surprise as from a dream.

'Cooler out here,' he explained. 'More room, don't you know. Quite a crush, what?'

Preoccupied by the difference between a ballroom floor and even the smoothest lawn, she made no answer. She and her partner were but one of a dozen couples who had had the same idea and were enjoying the fresh air, the

F

fragrant grass, and the sense of a vast overarching sky in which dusk was fast gathering. The sprays of the cedar rustled faintly in the light breeze. The Chinese lanterns glowed pink and blue and green, like luminous fruits. Up here on this green eminence, with the valley below growing ever more dim and conjectural, a miniature patchwork of cultivation dotted by tiny buildings in which here and there a light fitfully sparkled, Julia could imagine she was dancing on the top of a visibly round world.

But suddenly the music ceased, and at once self-consciousness returned to her. The couples on the lawn began drifting back to the ballroom, in search of their next partners.

'Shall we go in, Captain Beckoning?' said Julia. She felt it her duty to be rid of him.

'And dance again? Yes, by Jove! Unless you will give me the pleasure of showing you the garden?'

'Thank you, but it's rather too late for that, don't you think? Besides,' she reminded him, 'you have other guests.'

He laughed, a hearty guffaw. 'You mean the little stepmater will be after me, what? She's a tartar, and no mistake, for keeping a fellow in order. But tell me, Miss Peacock, why haven't we met before? I've been wasting my time until now, I find.'

'Surely not? You've been serving your country,' she answered hurriedly. 'Have you seen much action, Captain Beckoning, against those terrible black people?'

'All in the day's work, ma'am. They're uncommonly troublesome at times.'

'I've no doubt you're very brave,' she said.

'Terrified, I assure you,' he answered with a grin. 'But one doesn't let the men know. That would never do.'

'I'm afraid I don't believe you,' said Julia. 'And now I really think we must go in.'

Instead of offering his arm he seized her hand. 'I say . . . By Jove, Miss Peacock!'

Snatching the hand away, she asked forbiddingly: 'What am I to understand by that remark, Captain Beckoning?'

'By Jove, Miss Peacock, I've never met a girl like you before.'

'Then let us hope it will be a lesson to you.'

She began walking away. He followed, full of contrition.

'I say! Don't be hard on a fellow. High spirits and all that, don't you know. I'd cut my right arm off rather than offend you.'

'That won't be necessary,' said Julia. 'I am not offended. Only a little surprised.' A formal speech, but not far from the truth. She was surprised not only by his freedom, but still more by her failure to resent it.

'Aren't you really? I say! That *is* good of you. Will you dance the next with me, to show there's no ill feeling?'

Preceding him through the french windows, 'Certainly not!' she said severely, over her shoulder. 'You must dance with someone else, and so must I.'

The second dance was already beginning, but no sooner had she entered the room than an unattached male presented himself.

'Come along, Julia,' said Jack Claybrook. 'Off we go!'

'That's not the way to ask. Where are your manners, pray?'

He made a profound obeisance. 'May I have the honour, Miss Peacock?'

'With pleasure, Mr Claybrook. Little as you deserve it.'

He stared, in amusement and surprise. This was a Julia he had not seen before.

As they joined the dance, 'Something's happened to you, Julia,' he accused her. 'Come on now. Tell your old uncle.'

'My uncles aren't here,' she retorted. 'Where are your cousins? Are they nice?'

'Not bad, when they're washed. I believe you're enjoying this party.'

'Of course. Aren't you?'

Conversation was suspended while they gave themselves to the pleasure of the dance. But Julia, in part of her mind, was still turning over the astonishing fact that someone, for the first time in her life, had tried to flirt with her. After a second dance with Jack Claybrook she pleaded fatigue and sat out the third with him in a quiet corner, from which they could idly watch the couples floating past.

Fearful lest he should read her thoughts, 'I like the old dances best, don't you?' she remarked. 'Like *Tolly-polly* and *All in a Garden Green*.'

'Me, I don't care what it is,' said Jack Claybrook. Anything for a romp.'

She examined him thoughtfully, with a sidelong glance.

The elder of 'the Claybrook boys'—an affectionate mis-
nomer, for they were both past thirty—was a large
creature, discreetly whiskered, broad-shouldered, with a
long gaunt face, prominent ears, and a jutting, clean-
shaven chin. The surprising thing about him was his
voice, which, though he could roar like a bull on occasion,
was in ordinary conversation quiet and gentle, with a hint
of shyness, and his manner in general oddly at variance
with his somewhat bucolic appearance. He walked with
the gait of a man accustomed to striding across ploughed
fields; his talk was mainly of crops and his humour
primitive; yet he danced, Julia thought, like an angel,
and looked wonderfully nice in his unaccustomed evening
clothes. She was now relaxed, fortified by his uninspiring
but goodnatured company, so restful after suffering the
attentions of Captain Beckoning with his meaning looks
and loud nervous guffaws. She could not remember a
time when Jack Claybrook and his brother Will had not
been a familiar part of her environment. They had
teased and petted her as a child, and now treated her with
an easy intimacy tempered only by respect for her years
and elegance. It was a most satisfying relationship, to
which she had never until now given a moment's thought.

'That's not true,' she said. 'You're no romper. You
dance very well.'

'Thank you, miss. May I have that in writing?'

'You don't need any testimonials from me. I wonder
what Sarah and Catherine are up to. With such a
crowd there's no finding anyone. I saw them both a
minute ago. Sarah was dancing with Papa of all people.'

'So she is still. Look! Is there to be an interval for

supper, do you suppose? Or do we go and help ourselves as the spirit moves us? It's all laid out in the next
room. Enough for an army. I had a peep.'

Julia did not answer. Her glance had strayed to the
french windows, through which, coming in from the
garden, stepped a tall figure in scarlet uniform.

'There she is.'

'Who?'

'Catherine.'

His eyes followed hers. 'So she is, with your soldier
man in tow. The son and heir.'

'Are you getting hungry, Jack?' said Julia. 'How
prosaic of you.'

'What is he like, that fellow?' Jack asked, eyeing her
curiously.

'Shshsh!' Though her eyes were now averted she was
aware that the fellow in question had arrived within a few
yards of where they were sitting. 'Keep on talking,' she
said hurriedly, 'but about something else. Did I tell you?
Blossom has a heifer calf. She's a beauty, with a white
star on her forehead. We're all so glad it's a heifer.'

At that moment the music of the fiddles died away, and
the dance was over. In the momentary silence, before
general chatter broke out, a drawling masculine voice, as
of one in a trance of admiration, was heard to exclaim:

'By Jove, Miss Catherine! . . . By Jove, what!'

Julia, to her dismay, felt herself colouring. She did
not care two straws for Captain Beckoning, was resolved
to avoid him, and yet . . . she was conscious of being
shocked and disappointed. It would be Sarah's turn
next, she supposed; and then every other young woman

in the room. Embarrassed by his proximity she hoped he would not see her, he having no eyes but for Catherine; but Catherine herself put an end to the hope by turning from him with a toss of the head, an amused shrug of slim shoulders, to say 'Hullo' to Jack Claybrook, who, rising and taking her ingenuously outstretched hands, promptly asked her for a dance. How pretty she looks, thought Julia in surprise, and how young!—envying Catherine her cornflower-blue eyes, her red-gold hair, her lily-and-roses complexion: all so much more attractive, she imagined, than her own dark enchantment, notwithstanding that the gallant Captain, with no visible effort, had instantly transferred his look of adoration to herself.

'By Jove, Miss Peacock! We meet again. May I have the honour . . . ?'

Miss Peacock, with cold civility, prayed he would excuse her, and while he was obtusely arguing the point a commanding voice announced that the supper interval had arrived: whereupon the communicating doors were flung open and all the company began surging into the next room, each face concealing its eagerness under a mask of perfect indifference to anything so gross as food.

'Good idea,' said the Captain. 'Deuced peckish, between ourselves. Let's put on the nosebag together, Miss Peacock, shall we?' He smiled at her possessively, twirling his moustaches in high satisfaction.

There being no escape, she suffered herself to be guided, with his hand on her elbow, into the supper-room, while contriving to keep as near as possible to Catherine and Jack. Supper proved to be an informal, go-as-you-please affair, a glittering, chattering scene. Footmen and maidservants, with countrified accents and the manners of dukes and duchesses, were in watchful attendance. There was not seating enough for so large a company: a proportion of the gentlemen had to eat and drink standing, or wait their turn at the long table. This happy circumstance absolved Julia from the necessity of talking to her escort, but did not prevent his hovering. He did not trouble her with much conversation: it was only in a tête-à-tête that his genius fully blossomed. He had to content his ardour with seeing that she was plentifully supplied with cold chicken, jellies, and claret-cup. But she was conscious of his near presence, knew that as soon as supper was over he would renew his petition for another dance, and for a reason obscure to her was determined to disappoint him.

To leave the table without ceremony, making room for someone else, was in these special circumstances a virtue. Julia did so as soon as chance offered, choosing a moment when Captain Beckoning's vigilance was relaxed; but before she had taken many steps he turned his head, in mid-munch, saw her, and at once bore down upon her, sandwich in hand, with long purposeful strides. Her irritation became fury; consciousness of fury, and of the scene it might lead to unless she took hold of herself, dissolved into panic. She moved swiftly, almost running, to the nearest door, and the next moment found herself not in the ballroom but in a part of the house that was foreign territory to her.

The situation was desperate. She would not go back and risk capture. She could not stay where she was, lest he should follow her, perhaps—scandalous, humiliating

thought!—taking her flight for an invitation. She was
committed to the unseemly adventure of exploring a
strange house in search of a temporary hiding-place.
Reason whispered that such conduct was unworthy of
her mother's daughter, that she was behaving like an
hysterical child; but anger and the stubborn resolve to
escape made her deaf to its voice.

She ran down a corridor, ascended a broad flight of
stairs, and plunged into the first room that offered,
shutting the door behind her. She stood breathless, her
heart racing, slowly assimilating a shock of astonishment
to which at first she could ascribe no cause. Subcon-
sciously she had expected the room to be in darkness: the
sight of a lamp, glowing like a harvest moon, made her eyes
widen in wonder and nameless alarm. It took her some
seconds, measured in a beating pulse, to realize that she was
not alone, that from the shadows beyond, from a half-seen
sedentary figure beyond the lamplight's glow, a pair of steely
eyes, under raised eyebrows, were intently regarding her.

A gasp of terror escaped Julia. No words would come.
Her impulse was to turn and run. She could not move.

'Who are you? What do you want?'

The voice had neither warmth nor colour. It was dry,
toneless, mechanical, a clockwork voice: as though a
skeleton had spoken, or a giant insect, all legs and staring
eyes.

Julia stammered: 'I beg your pardon. I am so sorry.
I didn't know.'

'Ah! So you have a tongue. Come here, girl. Let
me look at you.'

Reluctant, but waking from her nightmare, for the note

of irascibility was at least human, Julia obeyed. The two stared at each other for a long silent moment, the girl meekly standing, her inquisitor, a small cadaverous aged lady, sitting very erect and still in a high invalid-chair, one gaunt hand folded over the handle of an ebony stick, the other lying in her lap. Her grey face, the skin tightly stretched over jutting bones, seemed to be balanced precariously on the collar of a beaded black bodice that held her frame together: at any moment, in Julia's fancy, she might disintegrate and decompose.

'That's better. Take a good look, child. I am Gwendolen Mallard. Who are you?'

'Julia Peacock, ma'am.'

'Peacock? Peacock? Ah, the lawyer's daughter. Why aren't you dancing with the others?'

'I beg you will forgive the intrusion, Lady Mallard. I didn't know anyone was here.'

'Never mind. Never mind. Take a good look at me while you've the chance. You don't see a corpse every day. Yes, I'm dead. Don't interrupt me. I've been dead for three years, all but this useless body, this beating heart. Gwendolen Mallard, made perfect by suffering. And to this you must all come, my dear, every Jack and Jill of you. Have you a lover?'

'I don't understand you,' said Julia, half-affronted.

'Fiddlesticks! You're a young, ripe girl. Have you a lover, I say?'

'No, madam. I have not.'

'Then get you one, while you still can. You haven't much time, let me tell you. Only fifty years or so. And when they're gone they'll seem no more than a day.'

The eyelids came down, over the staring eyes. 'You may go now. Go and enjoy yourself.' The mouth shut tight.

§3

'WELL, my dears, did you enjoy yourselves?' asked Mrs Peacock, on the way home.

'Yes, thank you, Mama,' said Sarah sleepily.

'It was delicious,' murmured Catherine, smiling to herself.

'And my Julia? Has she nothing to say?'

'It was a lovely ball,' said Julia, 'especially after supper. What a nice old gentleman the Colonel is. I danced with him twice. So clever of him, with only one arm, poor man. It's wonderful how he manages. Don't you think so, Papa?'

'Yes, my dear. But we old gentlemen *are* wonderful. You have only to look at me. Here I am, still awake, at two o'clock in the morning.' He yawned prodigiously. 'The countryside looks good, doesn't it, in moonlight. A pity we've got to go home. How would it be if we spent the rest of the night in the fields and watched the dawn in. What do you say, Emily?'

'Do let's, Papa,' cried Catherine. 'I'm sure I don't want to go to bed. I shan't sleep a wink.'

'You're all tired out,' said Mrs Peacock, in a tone of great satisfaction, 'and tomorrow you'll be fit for nothing. Your father and I had such a nice talk with young Mrs Beckoning. Didn't we, Edmund?'

'Did we, my dear? Yes, I expect we did.'

'So polite and unassuming. You'd never guess she was related to the peerage.'

'Why, Mama? Is the peerage always rude?' asked Catherine.

'So devoted to her children,' said Mrs Peacock. 'It was pretty to see. And to the Colonel too, of course.'

'Nice of her to include him in her regard,' remarked Mr Peacock, 'seeing he's only her husband.'

'Don't be naughty, Edmund. You know very well there must be nearly thirty years between them.'

'Is that too much, Mama?' Catherine asked.

'That,' said Mrs Peacock, primming her lips, 'is not for us to say. If the Colonel chooses to have a second family, it is no one's business but his.'

'Except, perhaps, his wife's,' suggested Edmund. 'The Colonel, I hazard, is of Shakespeare's opinion, that a man should take a younger than himself so that he can shape her to his liking.'

'How old, do you imagine, is Mr Crabbe, Papa?'

'My imagination, Kitty, has not been engaged by that question. Why do you ask?'

'Would you believe it,' said Catherine, 'he danced three times running with that Mrs Stapleton. Is she, do you think, setting her widow's cap at him?'

'Why not ask her, my love? I'm sure she would be happy to confide in you.'

Sarah, jerking awake, said drowsily: 'Am I dreaming? Or are the horses really running away with us?'

The same idea had occurred to her father. He had been every moment expecting a protest from his wife. They were going downhill at a brisk pace, and the carriage swayed alarmingly. It had been evident, at the setting out, that Harry Dawkins's entertainment in the servants' quarters had lacked nothing that could make a man merry while his betters were enjoying the ball; and now, but half way home, snatches of tuneless song put the matter beyond doubt.

Mr Peacock shouted to him to stop. It took some time for the command to penetrate his understanding, but at last he pulled hard on the reins and flung himself back, lifting the horses' forelegs three feet from the ground.

'Sit tight, girls,' said Mr Peacock, alighting. 'I'll handle this . . . Harry, what's come over you? Do you want to break all our necks?'

Harry met the inquiry with a beatific grin. He yammered a little but uttered no word.

'Get down, man. I'll drive.'

'All good fellows,' said Harry. 'All jolly good fellows.' His eyes closed. His mouth hung open. His head drooped.

'Disgraceful!' Mrs Peacock had joined her husband on the road. 'I do believe the man's drunk.'

'Your conjecture, my love, has much to commend it. Hi! Wake up. You're not in bed yet.' Prodding and shaking, he pulled the delinquent driver off his perch and set him, swaying precariously, on the ground. 'Shall we have him inside?'

'With the girls! Certainly not.'

'Come along,' said Mr Peacock, taking his arm.

A glimmer of reason appeared in the fuddled eyes. 'I dursn't, master. Not with the ladies. Twouldn't be right, look.'

'Very proper sentiment, Harry. It does you credit,' said Mr Peacock. He led him to the grass verge and persuaded him, with less than no difficulty, to lie down 'Sleep it off, boy. It's a warm night. You'll come to no harm.'

Seeing his wife safely bestowed again, he picked up the reins and got into the driver's seat.

'Poor Harry,' said Sarah, as they drove off. 'What a surprise he'll get when he wakes up!'

'It's a very shocking thing to happen,' Mrs Peacock declared. 'I shall ask your father to dismiss him.'

'Oh, Mama,' protested Catherine, 'would that be fair? We've had our fun. Why shouldn't he have his?'

'I am not in the habit of arguing with you, Catherine. You know that.'

'Yes,' agreed Sarah. 'Kitty knows that, Mama.'

The journey continued in silence and without further incident. A quarter of an hour later they were home and on their way to bed. At the head of the stairs, after the parents had gone to their room, the three girls lingered for a moment, all but overcome with sleepiness yet too excited to part without a few last words.

'How did you get on with Captain Beckoning, Catherine?' Julia asked.

'Oh, him!' Catherine made a grimace. 'He kissed me, under the cedar. But you needn't worry,' she added, answering Julia's horrified look. 'I didn't much care about it.'

CHAPTER FOUR

Catherine in Action

§ 1

MR PEACOCK was not so uninterested in Robert Crabbe's personal life as it suited him to pretend. He had been surprised to see Mrs Stapleton at Manor Park and suspected that Robert had somehow contrived her invitation. He was not in the habit of minding other people's business —he left that, he would have told you, to the women— but here he felt himself to be professionally as well as personally concerned. Liking Robert Crabbe, he would be sorry to see him make a fool of himself. Nor did he relish the possibility of a scandal that might in the public mind become associated with his eminently respectable firm. He had therefore observed the growing friendship with misgiving, the more so because Robert maintained an impenetrable reserve about it. That the dear fellow should think of marrying again was natural enough. He had perhaps forty years ahead of him and could hardly be expected to remain a disconsolate widower for the rest of his life, living over the office and resorting to restaurants for all his major meals. But it was a moot point whether marriage was now in question; and if it were, thought Mr Peacock, no good could come of it with such a person as Mrs Stapleton.

He could not have said why, for it was a matter o
principle with him to discount gossip and reject innuendo
but the fact remained that there was something abou
Olive Stapleton that attracted the wrong kind of man and
made women in general fight shy of her. How then
since Robert was *not* the wrong kind of man, had she
succeeded in attaching him? She lived, with two
servants and a large-eyed little boy, in a small house on
the outskirts of Newtonbury, having arrived there from
nowhere a year or two ago. Mr Peacock, unlike some
resolutely believed her to be the widow she professed to
be, and that the elderly gentleman of military aspect who
visited her from time to time was her uncle. The ground
of his distrust of her owed nothing, he told himself, to
uncharitable rumours. It was simply that he did not like
her face. Yet it was not an unhandsome face: all the
constituents of beauty were there, except gentleness: in
default of which she had developed, in early middle age
a boldly ingratiating manner and with men a cooing
comehitherness that passed for playful. But though the
lips smiled, with an effect of childish candour, the eyes
remained cold, shrewd, watchful.

Robert Crabbe, in tribute to his bachelor condition
had a standing invitation to take Sunday luncheon with
the Peacocks; and it had become an established routine
that he should resort to them at least once a month. He
was not a favourite with Mrs Peacock, his manner with
her was too reserved, he was always the polite visitor; but
this much attention was due to him as her husband's
partner. She thought him deficient in small talk
resented Edmund's regard for him, was irritated by his

enthusiasm for Browning, that so difficult poet, so difficult and so different from dear Mr Tennyson, and suspected him of entertaining unsound opinions on religion, for he had once at luncheon mentioned the name Huxley without visible distaste. He was, in short, a somewhat mysterious character, and Mrs Peacock did not like what she did not understand. She discerned certain merits in him, allowed him intelligence and good manners, accepted her husband's judgment of his professional capacity, and saw that her younger daughters, if not Julia, found his conversation stimulating. Whether she liked it or not, he was an established friend of the family; and she resigned herself with a good grace to being unable to fit him into a pigeonhole.

It was the accepted thing that after luncheon the two men would take themselves off, to stroll round the farm together, it being out of the question that Edmund should forgo that weekly pleasure, and Robert being always eager to indulge him. Mrs Peacock, rising, would always say: 'We shall meet again at teatime, I hope, Mr Crabbe?' And he, with a bow, would answer: 'Thank you, Mrs Peacock. You are most kind.' But today, his first Sunday after the Manor Park affair, the ritual question evoked a different, an unprecedented response.

'Forgive me, but I fear not. So very sorry. I have to be back at Newtonbury by four o'clock.'

Five pairs of astonished eyes were turned upon him, seeming to demand an explanation. He offered none. Edmund, cutting in on his wife's polite protest, said quickly: 'Very well, my dear Robert. But you needn't go for half an hour. Come into my study and have a talk.' He shepherded his womenfolk into the drawing-room and left them there.

The two men left behind them a speculative silence, which Catherine was the first to break.

'I wonder if Papa will get it out of him,' she said: half to herself, half to Sarah.

'Get what out of him?' asked Sarah.

'Where he's going. Who he's going to see.'

'Your father,' said Mrs Peacock, 'is too much the gentleman to be inquisitive. I wish his daughters may take after him.'

'Would you wish us to be gentlemen too, Mama?'

'I would wish you to be ladies, Sarah, and not trouble your heads about what doesn't concern you. Mr Crabbe is not our property, remember. He comes and goes as he pleases.'

'But he *always* stays for tea, Mama,' said Catherine. 'Ever since I can remember, he has.'

'You're young, my dear. Your memory is short. And why this sudden interest in Mr Crabbe, pray? You realize, I hope, that he's old enough to be your father?'

'Is he really, Mama?' asked Sarah, who knew he was not. 'And ought that to make him less interesting to us? Kitty's like me. She prefers old gentlemen. Young men are so insipid, aren't they, Kitty?'

'I said nothing about old gentlemen, Sarah. You deliberately twist my words.'

'I didn't mean to, Mama. For my part I like Mr Crabbe, however old he is. Why don't you marry him, Kitty? I daresay he'll have you if you ask him. He'll read Browning to you in the long winter evenings.

Think of that.' Seeing with astonishment the beginnings of a blush in Catherine's cheeks she hastened to add: 'Or perhaps Julia ought to, as she's the eldest.'

'That's enough, Sarah. Your jokes go too far. They are very unsuitable, especially on the Lord's Day.'

'I'm sorry, Mama.' Sarah refrained from asking whether the Lord had no sense of humour. It was a question that sometimes seriously exercised her.

Catherine contrived to be out of the room when Mr Crabbe returned to take formal leave of Mrs Peacock: a circumstance that made it imperative, she argued, that she should join him and her father in the yard, watch him mount, and wave good-bye to him. He looked well on a horse: easy, upright, quietly masterful. His hired nag was restive almost to friskiness, but he handled her expertly and with style. 'Steady, girl! Steady!' His long grave face relaxed into a smile. His voice was dark and gentle.

But for her father's presence Catherine would have spoken to him, to make him aware of her. She wanted to ask him if he would lend her a book, one of his many books, whether Browning or another, that she might learn to share his interests and improve her butterfly mind. A month ago, had such an impulse moved her, she would not have hesitated to announce her request in full view and hearing of the whole family. What had happened to her that she should shy away from so simple a thing? And what made her, in the total absence of evidence, so sure that it was Olive Stapleton's steel-bright eyes and avid mouth that were drawing him untimely back to Newtonbury? As he rode away, transfigured by her fancy into the semblance of a dashing cavalier, she was glad that he had chosen that form of locomotion in preference to his newly acquired boneshaker, ingenious amusing but unromantic machine, and that he had refrained from disturbing her mother by using the railway. Railway-travel on Sunday, because it involved human labour, was a thing Mrs Peacock disapproved of (horses, having no souls, did not matter), and Catherine, for no conscious reason, was anxious that he should do nothing to incur the maternal displeasure.

'Why did he have to go so early, Papa?' asked Catherine, as they turned towards the house.

'I can only suppose, my dear, that he had another engagement.'

'Didn't you ask him?' said Catherine, artfully artless.

'No, Catherine. I did not. One doesn't catechize one's friends.'

'I do,' said Catherine lightly. 'Specially my friends. With others it would be rude, but not with friends. Not catechize exactly, but I ask questions if I want to know something. It seems the simplest way to find out. Is that wrong, Papa?'

'I don't say it's wrong, but it may sometimes be inconsiderate, tactless, and therefore hardly polite.'

'People don't mind being asked, unless it's something they're ashamed of. And it couldn't be that, with Robert . . . with Mr Crabbe. Could it?'

'Of course not.' Mr Peacock laughed shortly. 'But it's time you outgrew these nursery notions, my dear child. Civilized life isn't quite so simple as you seem to imagine. I do declare!' he exclaimed, halting and looking back. 'That fellow Harry is asleep again already by the look of him! Did you ever see such a drowsihead? Why doesn't he go home, since it's Sunday?'

'Because his mother would find him a job to do,' said Catherine. 'He knows where he's well off, does our Harry.'

She knew better than to pursue the subject of Robert Crabbe. To do so might provoke an awkward question. They rejoined the rest of the family; nothing more to the point was said; and it was not until some hours later that she inadvertently, but conveniently, overheard a scrap of dialogue not meant for her ears.

'You must speak to him, Edmund.'

'I can hardly do that, my love.'

'It's your duty. She's a notorious person.'

Catherine tiptoed guiltily away. She had heard enough—too much. It was time to take action.

§ 2

ACTION, but how? It was more easily said than done. The first step was obvious: since in the ordinary course of events she would not see him again for four weeks, during which time anything disastrous might happen, she must begin by writing him a letter. That in itself would surprise him, mark an epoch in their relationship, and remind him pointedly of her existence; for she had never had occasion to write to him before. Moreover she would address him, boldly, as 'Dear Robert'; yet not too boldly, for to sharpen the point, and at the same time hint at shyness, she would first put 'Mr Crabbe' and then cross it out and write 'Robert' above it. What to say was the next problem, and how to combine decorum with the necessary secrecy. A dawning enthusiasm for literature was the answer. Books, apart from Mrs Stapleton, were his chief preoccupation, so books provided the easiest and most innocent form of approach. Dear Robert (she began in her mind), Will you be very kind and lend me a book, please. Mama does not know I am writing to you, I fear she would disapprove! If you can spare it for a week or two I would so much like to read that poem you told us about, Persian I think you said, about grasping the sorry scheme of things entire, it sounded very nice and rather original. Now I must bring this letter to a close. Yours very sincerely, Catherine.

Dispatching this letter, marked *Private* to prevent its being confused with business communications, involved stealing a postage stamp from Mama's davenport and then making a secret trip to the village : she accomplished both crimes without scruple. When the book arrived, *if* it arrived, there would be questions and explanations; but in her eagerness to open the campaign she refused to think about that. She had but the vaguest notion of what 'the sorry scheme of things' referred to : the only scheme she wished to shatter to bits was the one she attributed, rightly or wrongly, to Mrs Stapleton. She could not doubt that whatever was afoot between those two was Mrs Stapleton's doing, not Robert's : he was the innocent predestined victim, like poor Henry Maltravers in *Lovers' Rue, or The Ways of Woman*. For Robert was not, like silly Captain Beckoning, a flirt. He was serious and good and full of deep thoughts, no gay deceiver. She remembered, with a belated thrill, the ceremonial hand-kissing in the office three months ago. A perplexing episode, but nothing could have been less alarming or more utterly respectful than that grave salute.

Not till she stood, letter in hand, confronting the wide mouth of the pillar-box, did she hesitate; and then only to savour more deliberately the high drama of the moment, the delicious frightening sensation of standing on the brink of an irrevocable act of which the consequences could not be foreseen. Her fingers released the letter. It fell, light as a whisper, into the box, and was gone beyond recall. In imagination she went with it on its journey and watched Robert's face—surprised, gentle, gravely sympathetic—as he read it.

'Hullo! Where have you been?' asked Sarah, on her return.

'Why? Has there been a hue and cry?'

'Mama was asking for you. Something about doing the flowers.'

'What, again? They've been done once today. Have they disarranged themselves, the clever things?' Catherine brooded for a moment on her wrongs. 'Of course it had to be *me*—just because I wasn't here. Flowers indeed! She might have thought of something more likely.'

'Don't excite yourself, donkey,' said Sarah. 'It was the best she could manage on the spur of the moment.'

'I'm not in the least excited. But I *am* rather tired of being on a lead. Aren't you? Sometimes I feel like running away.' Uneasy in her conscience, she was still rattled, her sense of humour in abeyance.

'Good idea,' said Sarah, dissembling her surprise at

this uncharacteristic outburst. 'Let's go together. You can be Rosalind, you'd make a pretty young man, and I'll be your Celia. And we'll take Harry Dawkins with us for our Touchstone. But where shall we go? There aren't any suitable forests hereabouts.'

The Shakespeare allusion, by reminding her of school, gave Catherine an idea.

'Why can't we go and stay with Ellen Skimmer for a few days? She's invited us often enough.'

'You, not me,' Sarah objected. 'She was *your* bosom friend, after I'd left. I hardly knew her.'

'At school you didn't, but you quite liked her when she was here last summer. It was fun having her. I can't imagine how we came to lose touch. It would be nice to see her again.' And highly convenient to be domiciled in Newtonbury for a while. The sooner the better if Olive Stapleton's design was to be frustrated. It was, in fact, she suddenly perceived, the only way.

Sarah remembered Ellen Skimmer as a plump, cheerful, ordinary girl with nervous ultra-ladylike manners in the presence of her elders and a disposition at other times to excessive enthusiasm and loud laughter. She had accepted her serenely as Catherine's friend; the visit, though unrewarding, had been accounted a success; but neither Sarah nor Catherine herself had been greatly grieved when it came to an end. Ellen's chief virtue in Sarah's eyes, apart from a general amiability, was her evident devotion to Catherine; but it was as much Catherine's lack of eagerness as Mrs Peacock's gentle obstructiveness that had made the reciprocal invitation abortive. During the twelve months that had passed

since then there had been an occasional exchange of
letters between the two girls, but Ellen's name had
occurred but seldom in the family conversation, and she
herself had become a shadowy, almost forgotten figure.
Her sudden emergence from that semi-oblivion, her
promotion to the status of urgently desired companion,
was therefore a surprise to Sarah. It was a case of any
port in a storm, she supposed; but, being unaware of any
storm, of its nature and origin she could have no inkling.

'If that's how you feel, my child, you'd better go.
Why not? If Mama will let you.'

'She'll never let me go alone,' said Catherine, frowning.
'You'd have to come too, to keep an eye on me.' Seeing
a satirical gleam in Sarah's eye she added quickly:
'Besides, it would be more fun.'

Sooner or later it might be necessary to confide in
Sarah, who could, if she would, play a useful part in the
work of rescue by occupying Ellen's attention while she,
Catherine, was elsewhere. But not yet. Her secret was too
new and too precious to be divulged lightly, even to Sarah.
She quivered, in an ecstasy of embarrassment, at the thought
of exposing herself, of being argued with and perhaps,
however gently, laughed at. Moreover, to 'listen to reason',
to be 'sensible', was the last thing she intended.

'Here she comes,' said Sarah, recognizing their mother's
step. 'Why not ask her and see?'

'Ah, Catherine, so you're back. Where did you get to,
my dear? We've been looking for you everywhere.'

'I'm so sorry, Mama. Did you look in the doubleyou?
I might have been there, you know. Or in the garden.
Or anywhere. Does it matter?' Before her affronted

parent could answer this impertinence she went on: 'Or perhaps I was taking the dog for a run. Poor old Gruff! He deserves a treat now and again.' By this transparent evasion, and by re-airing an old grievance, she hoped to confuse the issue and escape an inquisition. The only dog about the place was a sheepdog who was not allowed in the house and whom it was forbidden to make a pet of.

'Very well, Catherine,' said Mrs Peacock, in a tone of offended dignity. 'If that is your attitude there is no more to be said. You must try to forgive your mother for taking an interest in your doings,' she continued with heavy irony. 'She never interferes with her girls. She is content for them to enjoy a wonderful freedom. But she does like to know that they are at hand, within call, ready to render any little service she may ask of them.'

An uncomfortable silence followed.

'Well, Catherine?'

'Yes, Mama?'

'I shall not ask you again where you've been.'

'Thank you, Mama.'

Mrs Peacock retired defeated, but, as her daughters knew, more formidable in defeat than in victory. Catherine, with a defensive sub-smile on her lips that made her look even younger than she was, a stubborn pretty child, kept her eyes averted, refusing the challenge of Sarah's half ironical, half sympathetic glance. Conscious of having blundered, and interpreting Sarah's tactful silence as disapproval, she felt lonely, defiant, and a little frightened, yet still resisted the temptation to explain herself to this one person in the world who would understand. Sarah was the first to speak.

'I'm on your side, Kitty. You know that. But I'm afraid Mama is hurt.'

'Angry, you mean.'

'It's the same thing,' said Sarah. 'Very tiresome for you, but you'll have to say you're sorry, you know.'

'I'm not sorry. I can't tell a lie.'

'Can't you? I can. It's quite easy with a little practice.'

'I must say,' said Catherine, 'it's a pretty fine thing if one can't go for a walk without being put in the dock.'

She knew now, but would not admit it, that her tactics had been wrong from the start. It would have been far better had she boldly left her letter with the others, on the hall table, to be collected by the postman when he came with the morning's delivery: there were even chances that it would never have been noticed, and if it had its innocence would have been apparent for very lack of concealment. Instead, by a piece of childish secretiveness, she had invested a simple action with an appearance of shamefaced guilt which could not but be remembered against her when the moment of revelation arrived, And arrive it must, unless Robert failed to reply: a contingency too painful to contemplate.

'Yes,' agreed Sarah, 'but it was a pity, don't you think, to make a mystery of it?'

The voicing of her own thought was almost more than Catherine could bear.

'Oh, Sarah! Why are you always so *sensible*?'

'I know,' said Sarah. 'It *is* annoying, isn't it. But something will have to be done about it, you know. We can't leave poor Mama immured in High Dudgeon. Miffy is coming tomorrow, don't forget.'

'Good gracious, so she is!' exclaimed Catherine. After a frowning contemplation of the prospect, her brow cleared. 'But what a lucky thing! Don't you see, Mama will *have* to come out of her castle, whether she wants to or not.' She smiled triumphantly, confirmed in her unfilial resolve to offer no apology.

'Will she? Perhaps.' Sarah was dubious. 'But there's the rest of today to get through.'

'I shan't say I'm sorry,' declared Catherine, 'because I'm not. But don't fret: I'll be as sweet as honey to her, all smiles and girlish chatter.'

This plan, suddenly conceived, had all the attractiveness of a new discovery: that by seeming serenely unaware of being in disgrace she could make her mother's minatory attitude ridiculous and untenable. So, in the sequel, it proved. At teatime, still unappeased, Mrs Peacock began by pointedly ignoring her errant daughter; but Catherine, aided by Sarah, and unwittingly by their father who was in his usual high spirits, succeeded before the meal was done in coaxing her into at least a semblance of good humour. This happy result, because achieved without the ritual of apology, constituted a great and unprecedented victory. It was the beginning of a new era in the family history.

§ 3

UPLIFTED and heart-softened by success, and eager to reinstate herself in Mama's affection by a pointed recognition of her authority, Catherine, all sweet submission, begged to be allowed to meet their visitor with the pony and trap: a tacit plea for reconciliation to which Mrs

Peacock, kind as well as possessive, instantly responded. The asking and the giving gave comfort to both. Hurt feelings were forgotten: the lamb was back in the fold. For the pony's sake, since Miss Smith was sure to bring heavy luggage with her, both Julia and Sarah elected to stay at home and forgo the rapture of seeing their one-time governess alight from the train and break into smiles at sight of them. Catherine, gratefully conscious of her privilege and half-ashamed of having snatched it, went to the station alone.

The railway station at Lutterfield, which her father used most days of the week, had never quite lost for Catherine the romantic charm with which she had en-dowed it in childhood, that morning of the world when the most ordinary object of sense—bird, flower, milk-jug, newel-post, Mama's silver thimble, a pattern of sunlight on the nursery floor—was seen in its essential character, uniquely and miraculously itself. The tiny booking-office resembled a child's toy; the brief stretch of plat-form, set in the midst of flat green country under a wide arch of sky, was divided from the lane that flanked it by a low white-painted fence; the rails this afternoon, still wet for a magical moment from a recent shower, gleamed with a startling brilliance. Catherine, with five minutes to wait, had time to savour the delight of her situation: the sense of adventure, the fragrance of half-conscious memories, the expectation of presently seeing the train appear in the far distance, creeping like a snake nearer and nearer and growing every moment bigger in the process, like a gradually realized thought, till at last it should come puffing its way into the station, a plump tall-funnelled engine so friendly and familiar as to be almost a person, dragging importantly behind him a load of maroon-coloured carriages, in one of which Miss Smith, Miff-Miff, Miffy—she answered with equal composure to all three names—would be primly seated, ticket in hand, pretending to be quite calm.

The five minutes passed, and then five more. Mr Flack, stationmaster, porter, ticket-collector, signalman, and diligent cultivator of marigolds and carnations in the narrow strip of garden that ran beside the up-platform, joined Catherine where she stood waiting.

'Don't fret, missy. He won't be long now.' He fished a plump silver watch from his pocket, laid it snugly in his palm, and stared at it meditatively. 'Another ten minutes maybe. He's not often later than that.'

Catherine smiled. 'I've plenty of time,' she assured him.

'That's right. Hurry's a bad workman, not worth his wages. All well at home, Miss Catherine? A nice lady is Miss Mary Smith, always the pleasant word. And a longish time since we've seen her in these parts.'

'Nearly three years,' agreed Catherine, amused but not surprised at his knowing who was expected. 'She lives with a family not far from London now.'

'Ah,' said Mr Flack. 'That'll be a place called High-gate. And coming to you for a week's holiday, I fancy, welcomed by one and all. . . . Dash my brass buttons, just look at that! The signal's against her. If you'll excuse me, miss. . . .'

He sauntered off, to put that matter right. The fall of the great wooden arm, sudden and dramatic even though expected, delighted Catherine as of old, renewing for a moment her childish persuasion of its being not merely a sign, but the compelling cause, of the train's arrival; and, sure enough, a few minutes later her time of waiting came to a climax and was dissolved in the sight of a woman's face staring eagerly from a carriage window as the train slowed to a standstill, of a door swinging open, and a trim spinsterly figure stepping cautiously out on to the platform. Not seeing Catherine, she stood for a moment as if lost, standing guard over her large leather bag, and looking around uncertainly, as though surprised to find herself the only alighting passenger. Catherine, shy and excited, ran to her rescue.

'Hullo, Miffy!'

'*Well!*' cried Miss Smith, wide-eyed with pretended astonishment. 'Now who can this be, I wonder?'

'Don't you know me?'

'I do believe it's my little Catherine!' They leaned towards each other and exchanged a peck, then drew back to resume their mutual scrutiny. 'But how you've grown, my dear. Quite a young lady.'

'Lovely to see you, Miffy.'

Lovely, yes, and strange. The queerest sensation, as recognition always is. The image one carries in long absence is shadowy, nebulous, fluid, and its correction by reality brings a momentary shock of surprise. As every parting of lovers or intimate friends is a little death, prefiguring the final inevitable cutting-off, so every meeting after long absence is a resurrection, a re-discovery that is in part a new creation. Miffy, Catherine found, was at once different and the same; but by the time Mr Flack

with a flow of genial gossip had carried the luggage to
the waiting trap and seen them safely on their way the
difference was already in process of diminishing. As she
became gradually used to Miffy's presence at her side she
saw that there was little if any outward change in her
She was not visibly older; her eyes were still the same
innocent blue, her thin cheeks pale and unlined, the coi
of hair projecting under her bonnet a warm brown like
beech-leaves in autumn; and her voice had the same
slightly exaggerated gentleness, as of one accustomed to
dealing with children. Mary Smith in her early thirtie
was neither young nor old. She was ageless, placid, and
in Catherine's conception unalterable, like a character
in fiction. She it was who had taught the sisters their
alphabet, persuaded them each in turn to interest themselves in a cat that sat on a mat and caught a rat, took
them for walks, told them pretty edifying stories, guided
their infant steps in arithmetic, read to them carefully
selected passages from *Little Arthur's History of England*, and
showed them how to draw pictures and work samplers
Since then she had performed the same office for other
children, and would continue to do so, if her luck held,
until Called Up Higher.

'I hope your father and mother are well, dear? And
Julia? And dear Sarah?'

'Quite well, thank you.'

'It's so kind of you to have me. A real joy.'

'We've been looking forward to it for weeks,' said
Catherine. 'All of us. Me especially.' And but for
the distraction of the Robert affair it would have been
true.

'*I* especially,' murmured Miss Smith. 'And how is Jumbo getting on? Do you still take him to bed with you?'

'Oh Miffy! Of course not! I'm not a child now.'

'Dear me, no. I can see that. But you were such a funny little girl. It was a sad day for me when I had to leave you. Never mind. Children have to grow up. It's only right,' she admonished herself, 'that they should. The next thing, you'll be getting married and have children of your own, God willing.'

'If I do, Miffy, will you come and governess them?'

'May I, dear? That would be a wonderful happiness. But your husband will have something to say about that, I expect.' Catherine smiled, but made no answer. Sensing a mystery in her manner Miffy said archly: 'Is he nice, Catherine?'

'But of course,' said Catherine, laughing. 'You don't think I'd marry a nasty man, do you? He hasn't turned up yet, you know, but I can promise you he'll be nice. It's so important in a husband, I always think. He'll be tall, and dark, and not too young. Not old either, but young men are so impudent and conceited, or else cow-eyed—that's Sarah's word—and sentimental. I hate flirts, don't you?'

'I don't know that I've met any, dear. But no doubt I should have disliked them if I had. Yes, to be sure!'

'Didn't you when you were young . . . when you were a girl?' said Catherine, correcting herself. 'Meet any, I mean?' The idea of Miffy's having once been young, really young, was new to her, a sudden surprising insight; and it seemed a little sad if she had never enjoyed

H

the nuisance of being dallied with by impudent young men.

'None that I can recall,' answered Miss Smith, with an indulgent smile. 'My walk in life was rather different from yours, Catherine. We were never well off, and when my dear father died—he was a clergyman, you know—there was only just enough for mother in her last few years.'

'Poor you! So you had to be a governess and teach brats like us. But did you never, in one of your posts, encounter a wicked baronet or something, like the young woman in *Pomeroy Towers*? She was a clergyman's daughter too. It was dreadful for her,' said Catherine blithely. 'What are your present children like, Miffy?'

This was a subject on which Miffy had much to say. It occupied her for the rest of the short drive, and she returned to it again and again during the days that followed. All the Peacocks made much of her, and but that she had no function in the house, no lessons to impart, to have her with them again was like old times. The absence of specific duties, however, was a continual small worry to her. To be of service to others had become second nature: only so could she justify her existence to herself and placate her embarrassed sense of the high privilege of being a guest in this house, where she had once earned her bread. She had to be almost forcibly restrained from scandalizing Alice and Jenny by making the beds and clearing the table after meals, and nothing could prevent her joining the sisters in the various daily tasks that their mother, as was her inflexible habit, found for them. To all their protests, that she was supposed to

be having a holiday, she would answer disarmingly:
'It's holiday enough, my dears, to be with you again.
And anyhow I can't sit in idleness. It was never my way.'

Of Mary Smith's many virtues, which everyone learnt
to appreciate anew as the days went by, one of the most
important in Catherine's estimation was her talent for
attracting letters. A serene humour, a gentle manner, an
extravagant delight in the simplest pleasures and a total
incapacity for being bored, these in themselves would have
sufficed to make her an ideal guest; but that she was also,
in spite of her lack of near relatives, an industrious letter-
writer who looked eagerly for the postman's coming and
loved reading to her breakfast companions what dear
little Claud and darling Vera had written to her, perhaps
with 'just a tiny bit of help from their mother', seemed to
Catherine the crowning mercy; for it was possible, she
thought, that under cover of some such amiable commotion, Miffy performing, the audience fixed in a polite
paralysis of attention, Mr Crabbe's anxiously awaited
reply might pass unnoticed. This, however, was only
her second line of defence, contingent on her failure to be
first at the door, and unobserved, when the postman
arrived.

Twice every day, for four days, she contrived to do that.
But the letter she looked for did not come. Nothing
came for her but an enthusiastic invitation from Ellen
Skimmer, to whom, without consulting Mama, she had
sent a carefully garrulous epistle the point of which was
concealed in a casual-seeming postscript. If Ellen could
answer so promptly, why not Robert? His silence
unnerved her. It was unlike him. It could only mean

that he had no time for her, or, worse, that he thought her
a forward miss and was resolved to ignore her simple
request. But this she could not in her heart believe: it
was impossible that she should have been so mistaken in
him. Each disappointment plunged her into despair,
but always, within a few minutes, she emerged again, full
of hope. It will come this afternoon, it will come
tomorrow, she told herself, arguing that every time it did
not come made it the more not the less probable that the
next postal delivery would bring it. At moments she
paused to chide herself for making so great a fuss about a
small matter, and especially for having embarked on this
tiresome campaign of secrecy. She, Catherine, who had
never before hesitated to announce her intentions to the
world, confident of provoking nothing worse than
laughter, what had possessed her that she must labour to
hide so innocent a thing as borrowing a book from an
old friend of the family? The question was rhetorical:
the answer, though she refused to formulate it, made her
tremble.

The fifth day dawned. The post arrived. Still
nothing. Sadly, angrily, she went back to the breakfast-
room and distributed the letters, then resumed her seat
at the table. Two minutes later a rat-a-tat-tat at the
front door made everyone look up.

'Who can that be,' said Mrs Peacock, 'at this hour?'

'No, Miffy,' exclaimed Sarah, 'don't disturb yourself.
Jenny will answer it. That's what we pay her for.'

'Do you, Sarah?' inquired Mr Peacock, with an air of
courteous interest. 'Do you indeed? I was under the
impression that I did.'

The door opened silently. Jenny came in.

'A packet for Miss Catherine, m'm. The postman forgot it.'

'Thank you, Jenny.' Mrs Peacock extended a hand.

Catherine, half-rising, said quickly: 'Thank you, Jenny. Will you bring it to me, please?'

The loudness of her voice startled her. She felt slightly sick. The noise of her hurrying pulse filled the room. Everyone except Mama was looking at her, friendly, inquisitive, eager to share her pleasure in this unwonted event. Mama, the packet in her hand, was looking at the postmark, examining the writing on the label, before passing it back to the hovering Jenny for delivery to the dear child, who received it without remark, gave it no more than a glance, and let it lie unopened beside her plate. The blush draining from her cheeks, she helped herself to marmalade, waiting for the interest around her either to die down or to explode into questions. She no longer cared which: the defeat of her ill-conceived unnecessary plan had released her from all anxiety. Let them say or think what they pleased, it was all one: the silly little secret, so soon to be exposed, had become subtly distasteful to her.

'Well, Catherine?' said Mrs Peacock. 'Aren't you going to open your nice parcel?'

She answered with specious calm: 'It can wait. After breakfast will do. It's only a book I'm borrowing ... From Mr Crabbe.'

'Fancy that! I'm sure it's very kind of him.'

'Yes, isn't it? Are you going to let us go to Ellen's,

Mama, me and Sarah? If not,' said Catherine belliger-
ently, 'I shall have to think of an excuse.'

No more was said of Mr Crabbe. The anti-climax left
her feeling curiously flat. And even his letter, kind but
brief, which she read in the seclusion of her bedroom half
an hour later, failed at first to reinvigorate her. The
book he sent was a new copy, and he had written her
name in it. What more had she expected? Not so
much. Yet she was unreasonably disappointed; and
only gradually, as the day grew older, did her spirits rise
and her dream resume its dominion.

§ 4

THE Skimmers, lamentably, were in trade, and retail
trade at that. Was this why Mrs Peacock had hesitated
so long over Ellen's invitation? If so, she never admitted
it, so must be given the benefit of the doubt. Snobbery,
to do her justice, played as a rule little conscious part in
her mind: in a social order where class distinctions were
taken for granted, and everyone 'knew his place', it was
(or could be) an innocent and unaggressive folly; and she
thought too well of her own situation to be either timid
with her social superiors or overbearing with humbler
folk. Though excessively confident in the rightness of
her own judgments, and an incorrigible manager of her
daughters, she was by no means entirely lacking in
common sense: it was perhaps because events so often
proved her to be right that she found it difficult to
imagine she could ever be wrong. If she did in fact
question whether the Skimmers were a suitable family
for her daughters to be intimate with, it was no doubt the

shop that gave her pause: the shop, and the recollection
of having seen a little old man in shirtsleeves sitting in a
corner of the shop-window, his back to the light, bending
over his work of watch-mending.   But to offset his being
a shopkeeper, and somewhat rustic in his speech, was his
craftsmanship, for which she had an instinctive respect.
Much of what he offered for sale, which included jewelry
as well as chronometers, was the work of his own hands,
as she knew.   His daughter Ellen, moreover, she knew
to be a presentable ladylike young person.   The unknown
factor was his wife, who might, alas, be anything.   But
even so, she may have argued, the risk was small, and for
the girls' sake, Catherine's especially, it had best be taken.
Catherine was restive, difficult: it would perhaps do her
good to be away from home for a little.

Mr Skimmer, with his alert brown eyes, oval face, and
neat exiguous figure, suggested to Sarah's fancy a dor-
mouse.   His bald dome was fringed with silky grey hair;
and his cheeks, clean-shaven, were smooth and sleek as a
child's.   When, at their entry, he left his bench and
stood behind the counter with his head cocked on one
side and his little hairy paws confidently clasping each
other across his stomach, Catherine and Sarah were
delighted with him.   They had arrived earlier than was
expected, leaving their luggage at the station to be
fetched.

He stood awaiting their pleasure.   'Good afternoon!'

'Don't you know us?' said Catherine.   'We know you,
Mr Skimmer.   We're the Peacocks.'

'Mercy me, so you are!   What a privilege!   What a
pleasure!   But did no one meet you at the station,

young ladies? What can Ellen be dreaming of? Dear
me. Dear me.'

'It's our own fault,' Sarah explained. 'We caught an
early train. We couldn't wait, you see.'

'Well, well, well,' said Mr Skimmer. ''Tis a sad
welcome, to be sure; but we must try to make amends.
You'll have tried the house-door, I fancy, and got no
answer?'

'No. Should we have done? We wanted to see you
first,' said Catherine guilefully. 'It's nice in here.'
The dark little shop, filled with the small busy voices of
time, was like something in a fairytale. She stood with
half-closed eyes, listening entranced to the ticking of
many clocks, like the sussuration of a thousand grass-
hoppers. 'What were you doing when we came in, Mr
Skimmer? Mending a watch? I think it's so clever.
Will you teach *me* how to?' she said irrepressibly, careless
of Sarah's ironic glance.

'Not mending, cleaning,' said Mr Skimmer. 'He's
got the moth in him, like so many.'

'The moth, did you say?'

'Yes indeed,' said Mr Skimmer gravely, making big
eyes. 'And a pair of nesting moorhens. Handsome
birds they are. 'Tis a pity to disturb them.'

His air of seriousness was so convincing that Catherine
dared not laugh: she felt more than ever that she was
living in a fairytale. But Sarah, with a gravity equal to
his own, said:

'Is that all, Mr Skimmer? No lions or tigers?'

'Dear me, no, young madam. Not in an English
lever.' He seemed slightly shocked. 'But we mustn't

keep you standing, all weary and worn with your travel. I'll just step out with you, shall I, and show you the way in? We live upstairs, don't you see, over the shop.'

They lived not only over the shop but behind it. Kitchen and parlour, where Mrs Skimmer, with one servant to help her, spent much of her time, were on the ground floor; above, in the second and third storeys, were seven other rooms, four of them bedrooms. With two extras to accommodate it was a tight fit, but cosy, like living in a dolls' house. The room that Catherine and Sarah shared was a bedroom only in emergencies. Its floor was covered with a worn red carpet; two of the beflowered walls, from floor to ceiling, were lined with books; the two narrow beds occupied so large a proportion of the space that the girls had to take it in turns to dress and undress; the white-enamelled washstand in the corner, under a framed engraving of the Parthenon, looked sadly out of place. Two days after their arrival they realized, with some dismay, that this was Mr Skimmer's private sanctum, to which he retired when he wanted to be alone with his books.

'Ought we to have come, Kitty? They can't have much money, poor things.'

'I know. But they don't seem to mind, so why should we? I like Mr Skimmer, don't you? But he does say the most extraordinary things. Do you think he knows how funny he is? Or is he a little bit . . . you know, queer? Fancy having all these books! You'd never guess it to look at him.'

'I wonder if he's acquainted with Mr Crabbe,' said Sarah.

Catherine was instantly on the alert. 'Why?'

'Oh, I just wondered. Mr Crabbe's a great reader too, isn't he? Has he lent you any more books?'

'Not yet.' Catherine was silent for a moment, then said in a casually reflective tone: 'I *might* perhaps go and see him while we're here.'

'So you might,' agreed Sarah placidly. 'Shall I come too?'

'Of course, if you like.'

Sarah smiled. 'Somehow I don't think I will. I'll stay behind and keep dear Ellen company.'

'I think literature's tremendously important, don't you? I mean, one *ought* to read books. Good books, I mean, not novels.'

'I'm sure it's an excellent plan, Kitty. Let's hope it succeeds.'

'Succeeds?'

'That's what I said.'

'I don't know what you mean.'

'Don't you? I thought perhaps you would.'

Catherine let that go. She was sorely tempted to confide in Sarah. It was not secretiveness but shyness that held her back, and an instinctive unreasoned fear that by trying to articulate the dream that possessed her she would expose it not only to Sarah's critical scrutiny but to her own as well, and so destroy it. Besides, what was there to tell? That she intended to rescue Robert Crabbe from Mrs Stapleton's clutches? But how?—and why? Put into words and spoken aloud, it would sound too absurdly presumptuous. She shied away from the subject.

'He's really very sensible and nice. He's teaching himself Greek, did you know?'

'Who? Robert Crabbe?'

'No, donkey. Mr Skimmer. He showed me his copy of the Iliad yesterday, proud as a little boy. I said how clever of him to be able to read it. Read it? he said. Not a word. It's all Greek to me, I haven't mastered the alphabet yet, but what a beautiful page!' quoted Catherine, imitating his warm gentle voice. Then, having created a diversion, she could not refrain from running back into danger by saying with a touch of complacency: 'Robert, of course, knows Greek. Like Papa.'

'You haven't forgotten, by the way,' said Sarah, 'that if you do pay Robert a call, Papa will be there too?'

'Yes. How nice. But not in the evening he won't.'

Mrs Skimmer, though not tall, was two inches taller than her husband, a rather silent but amiable woman; and the bouncing ebullient Ellen, their one ewe lamb, daughter of their middle age, over-topped them both, making them look like a pair of gnomes. They had never ceased to wonder at the belated miracle of her birth, had stinted themselves of many comforts in order to give her an expensive schooling, with the daughters of gentlemen, and humbly rejoiced in what they conceived to be her surpassing cleverness. She could sing; she could play the piano; she was studying to become a fully-fledged teacher in an infants' school, where already she did duty five mornings a week as a wiper of small noses and a sponger of bruised knees; and it was much to the credit of her good nature and common sense that though

cheerfully basking in her parents' admiration she was not
unduly puffed up by it. The Peacocks found her
pleasant if not very interesting company. It was agreeable to chatter about old times, to exchange remini-
scences of their long-departed schooldays and vie with
each other in lifelike impersonations of this or that
mistress; and Ellen's noisy enthusiasm—she had changed
scarcely at all in two years—made the sisters feel very
mature, tolerant, and wise.

The visit, in fine, gave every promise of being worth-
while for its own sake. All that remained to be discovered, for Catherine, was whether its ulterior motive
would be justified in the event. That, she decided
should be put to the proof on Monday evening. Meanwhile there was Sunday to be got through. The Skimmers were chapel-folk, and the two girls, always ready
for new experience, elected to accompany them to their
place of worship. Its exterior was plain and forbidding
suggesting a penitentiary; but inside, though the interior
too was bare and unadorned, was an atmosphere of
warmth and enthusiasm very different from the stained-
glass solemnity to which the Peacocks were accustomed.
Never before had they heard such hearty hymn-singing
such impassioned reading of the Lessons, or listened to a
man so familiarly addressing the Almighty in prayer
'As though,' said Sarah afterwards, 'he were a kind of
caretaker, who needed to be reminded of his duties.'
The minister, with a wealth of dramatic gesture, preached
a rousing hell-fire sermon which seemed to give everyone
the greatest possible satisfaction, except Mr Skimmer,
who at lunchtime, carvers in hand, apologized for it

remarking that though of course he didn't disbelieve in hell he was quite sure no one would be sent there.

'So unkind,' he said. 'And besides, what good would it do? He's got more sense than that: it stands to reason.'

'That's not for the likes of us to say, Father,' said Mrs Skimmer, with an anxious look at the young ladies. 'And what about your old Dante?' she demanded.

'That's different,' said Mr Skimmer. 'That's literature.'

It soon became evident that he was no sabbatarian, for in the afternoon he produced for the entertainment of his guests a 'magic lantern', an ingenious novelty which filled the darkened room (its window heavily shrouded) with a warm oily smell and projected a series of coloured pictures, of a distinctly secular and even comic character, on a white sheet hung on the wall. This marvel provoked much laughter and admiring astonishment. Particularly diverting was the sequence that showed a man escaping the attentions of a lioness by fastening a barrel to her tail, and finding her, on a subsequent visit to the scene, surrounded by numerous cubs, all similarly furnished. The Skimmers enjoyed simple jokes, and this one lasted into teatime and beyond. And then, after evening chapel, a number of their cronies came in, to sit round the room and read aloud with them, turn by turn, from Mr Skimmer's book of the moment. Catherine, though she thought the book both difficult and 'funny', enjoyed them all very much, especially Mr Skimmer himself.

Next day she and Sarah, while Ellen was at work in her school, spent the morning sauntering about the town,

savouring the unaccustomed pleasure of being surrounded
by shops. They were delighted with their freedom,
interested in everything they saw, and tempted again and
again by something seen in a window. They bought a
few trifles—ribbons, embroidery silks, a bottle of scent—
pausing after each purchase, pleasurably guilty, to re-
count their money and discuss what presents they should
take back for Julia and the parents. Strangely, because
of an obstinate unexplained notion of Catherine's, they
paid no call on Papa.

'Why not, Kitty?'

'I don't want to. I'm going there this evening.'

'That's no reason.'

But it was reason enough for Catherine, and Sarah did
not persist.

'Look, Sarah. Ellen will think it funny, my going out
by myself. I shall say I want to leave a message at the
office for Papa.'

'Why didn't you go during the daytime, when your
father was there? That's what Ellen will ask.'

'Because I forgot,' said Catherine.

'From Skimmer's in North Street to Messrs Peacock
and Crabbe's premises in the more stately and dignified
East Street was a fifteen-minutes walk, and a pleasant one
on a fine August evening. Business was over for the day,
the scavengers had done their work, the shop-fronts
gleamed in the late sunlight, and the sound of her shoes
on the pavement was loud in Catherine's ears. Very
conscious of her daring she glanced nervously about her
in a kind of stage-fright, resisting with some difficulty the
temptation to proceed stealthily, on tiptoe; for now that

the moment of meeting was so near she felt a little sick, being equally divided between eagerness and dread. The town, to her senses, was unnaturally quiet: yet vigilant, as though eyes were watching her from upper windows: quiet and empty, but for a diminutive street-arab armed with shovel and pan and scanning the scene for treasure, last-lingering member of his tribe that all day long had been darting in and out of the traffic like mayflies, at imminent risk of their lives, collecting the horse-manure as it fell. She stopped to watch him for a moment, glad of a pretext for delay.

Mr Skimmer, as we have seen, lived over a shop. Mr Crabbe, a professional man, lived over his office: which, of course, is quite a different thing. The two were in some sense neighbours, and had, if they but knew it, interests in common; but Catherine was uneasily aware that though they had undoubtedly seen each other many times they had never 'met', moving as they did in different spheres.

Her first ringing of the bell brought no response. Having never in all her previsions of this moment allowed for the possibility of Robert's being not at home, she was at first ingenuously astonished, then indignant, and finally reduced to despair. On the way here she had half-hoped for an excuse to abandon her project, but now, confronted by the shut door, she felt angry and desolate. So this was the end! Never, never, would she come again! Having thus resolved she pulled again at the bell, and presently, straining her ears, she heard the bump-bump of someone descending the stairs.

'Good evening, Mr Crabbe.'

'Why, hullo, Catherine!' His surprise was manifest
She searched in vain for a sign of pleasure. 'Is anything
wrong?'

'Wrong? No. Why should it be? Being so near, I
thought I'd come and see you, that's all. I wanted . .
I wanted . . .' What did she want? 'I wanted to
thank you again for that book.'

'Not at all. Very glad you liked it.' He stood
anxiously regarding her, obviously at a loss. 'Forgive
me, Catherine, I'm afraid I can't ask you to come in
I'm alone, you see.'

Blood burned in her cheeks. She felt like a child
rebuked. But I'm not a child, she thought angrily. I
won't put up with it. Instinct told her that only boldness
could serve her now.

'Pray don't apologize, Robert,' she said coldly, but
using his name for the first time. 'Are you afraid for
your reputation?'

'No, my dear. For yours. We have to think, you
know, of what people would say. Your father, for
example.'

'I'm not a child,' she retorted angrily.

'No, Catherine. That's precisely the point.'

The intentness of his look, eloquent of more than
admiration, appeased her; but she would not let him
know it.

'I see that it was foolish of me to come. And improper
too. Thank you for telling me. Good night.' She
turned away.

'Please don't go!'

'Perhaps I ought to have explained,' said Catherine

over her shoulder, 'that Sarah and I are staying with the Skimmers, in North Street. But I imagined Papa would have mentioned it.'

'He did mention it,' Robert earnestly assured her.

'But evidently you weren't interested. And why indeed should you be?'

Coming nearer he put a restraining hand on her arm.

'If we're to quarrel, Kitty, let's do it in comfort. We might walk a little way, don't you think? Will you wait while I get my hat?'

She raised her eyes to his, silently assenting. He had never called her Kitty before.

At the junction of the four main roads of Newtonbury stood the Market Cross, a noble octagonal structure stained and mellowed by five centuries of time. Except for the church, All Saints, it was the most ancient building in a town predominantly Regency in style; and the paved open court at the base, with its stone seats round a central pillar, provided the perfect venue for an ingenuous young lady and a gentlemen bent on correct behaviour. Here, in this public place, they could sit and talk freely, and even intimately, while advertising their innocence to any passers-by who might chance to see them.

'What a lovely evening,' said Robert. 'The best time of the day.'

'Yes,' said Catherine.

Now that she had at least part of her wish, and need struggle no more, peace descended on her. She gazed at the gilded street, a river of brightness intersected by long, clean-cut, patches of shade. Soon she must resume her

I

campaign, but for the moment it was enough to be with Robert, enjoying the shared silence, the occasional word, the illusion—if it were no more—of intimacy. But the quietness she had won was not absolute: it was quickened by her sense of his physical presence, as of something long imagined and dwelt upon and now miraculously actual.

'Are you staying long in Newtonbury?'

'Only ten days, I think. With the Skimmers.'

'Ah yes. The watchmaker.'

'Do you know him, Robert?'

'Not socially, of course. But I've been to his shop.'

'Why of course? Don't you like him?'

'Oh, quite. An odd but amiable character, I imagine.'

'He's really, you know, rather clever in his way. Much cleverer than Ellen, though she's nice too, and *they* think she's marvellous, poor dears. He's got any number of books, Robert. I know, because I sleep with them.'

'You *what*?'

'Sleep with them,' she repeated, laughing. 'They've put up beds for us in his library. I'm sorry you don't like him much, because they have a sort of reading circle every Sunday after Evensong, and I was wondering if you could come. They'd be very pleased and flattered if you did. They're reading Dante or something, but I'm sure they'd change over to Omar Khayyám if you'd rather. Just a few neighbours,' she finished breathlessly, echoing Mrs Skimmer's words, 'and a cup of coffee.'

'I'm afraid it's not possible. I have an engagement for next Sunday.'

'What a shame.'

'But there are other evenings, aren't there?' he said quickly. 'Would you and Sarah do me the honour of letting me drive you to Crowle Hill to see the Ruins one evening this week? And your friend Miss Skimmer too, of course, if she cares to come.'

'Thank you. How very polite of you. Would you take us on your machine?'

He laughed, glad of the chance. 'No difficulty about that. I'm sure Jobson will hire me a carriage. We might, don't you think, make a picnic of it?'

'What fun,' said Catherine flatly. 'I shall be well chaperoned, shan't I? Don't you think Mr and Mrs Skimmer ought to come too, just to make sure?'

'Certainly.' He ignored the irony. 'If we can squeeze them in.'

Silence fell between them. The proposal was left in the air. It had served its purpose of carrying them past an awkward moment, and whether or not it would be put into effect was a matter of almost indifference to Catherine, so remote was it from what she had hoped for. Normally the prospect of an outing would make her heart leap, but a party of four, three women and a man, would bring her, she thought despairingly, no nearer to Robert. It would leave him, moreover, free to follow his own dangerous devices on the Sunday. She ached to know the truth of that situation.

The silence lengthened. The precious minutes dragged by. She sat broodingly, staring at the ground, only half aware of the eyes anxiously watching her averted profile. In a few moments she must get up and go back to North Street. With nothing said to the purpose? The idea was intolerable. Yet how, without shocking and repelling him, could she expose herself, men being so proper, so conventional, so stupid?

Anger came to her rescue. 'Will you tell me something, Robert?'

'Of course, if I can.'

'Are you as careful of Mrs Stapleton's reputation as you are of mine?'

He did not answer.

Turning to him, searching his face, she said tragically: 'Now, I suppose, I've offended you. You'll never speak to me again.'

A queer smile visited his severe features. It vanished instantly, giving place to a gentle gravity that made her heart turn over.

'No, Catherine. I'm not offended.'

'Aren't you?' she said eagerly. 'Do you promise?'

'Nothing you say could offend me,' he said, lightly touching her hand. 'But . . . well, never mind.'

'Tell me then. Are you very fond of her?'

'Why? Why do you ask? Is it so important?'

'Yes,' said Catherine. 'Yes. Yes. You know it is.'

'But why, my dear? What can it matter?'

'Don't call me your dear,' she exclaimed angrily. 'You don't mean it. Else you wouldn't be so blind.'

'Am I blind? I didn't know.'

'It's not fair. I can't help being young.'

'It's not such a bad thing to be, you know.'

'Can't you see she's not your sort?' asked Catherine in a tone of wonder. 'Besides, she's too old for you.'

He smiled. 'I've no doubt she must seem very mature

to you. But you forget: I'm not so young myself. At least fifteen years older than you.'

'I know that,' said Catherine. 'It's nice. Just the right difference.' Embarrassed by his sudden, startled comprehension, she got up. 'I must go now. Good-bye.'

'May I not see you home?'

'Of course, if you wish.'

The walk to North Street was accomplished in all but silence: a silence on her part full of a tremulous happiness, shot through with doubts and fears; and on his part, what?

§ 5

IN this flat country, enclosed on all sides by uninterrupted sky, Crowle Hill was a curiosity and an excrescence: no soaring eminence, but a sudden round bump, smooth and green, that looked as though it had been turned out of a gigantic pudding-basin. It was one of the recognized 'sights' of the county, and a favourite resort of picnickers. Coupled with it, by the accident of propinquity, were 'the Ruins', a broken geometrical pattern of walls, open to the sky, which were all that remained of Newtonbury Abbey where centuries ago generations of monks had lived and died, holy and aloof, taking no part in the busy life of the town three miles away. The thing to do was to ascend the obscuring hill and on reaching its rounded summit exclaim in wonder and delight at the expected yet always surprising sight spread out below, and then descend on the other side to make its nearer acquaintance and perhaps, if one had a taste for such experiences, imagine oneself to be living for a moment in that bygone age.

Robert Crabbe, by virtue of his temperamental bias,

was able to do just that: standing in the long grass full of nettles and willowherb, and surrounded by the walls of what had once been the Abbot's Kitchen, he assumed in fancy a monk's habit, feeling the sun warm on his bare, tonsured head, and under his sandalled feet the hard brick floor that was in fact buried under centuries of accretion. Not so his two young ladies (Ellen had elected to stay at home): to them the ruin was a ruin and no more, the past remote and unreal, the present, the living moment, everything. It was nice to be here; it was fun; but the mystery of time did not engage them. It was enough for them, Catherine and Sarah, that they were alive *now*, now and for ever, in an endlessly exciting and amusing world.

'Here we are,' said Robert, 'in the Abbot's Kitchen. The external shape, you see, was a square; but the interior was octagonal, with fireplaces and chimneys filling in the four corners.'

'Why the Abbot's?' asked Sarah. 'Did the poor man have to do his own cooking?'

'Hardly,' said Robert, smiling but serious. 'He was an important person. His authority was absolute. The work of the place, I imagine, was done by lay brothers, men whose vocation was for the humbler forms of service. Hewers of wood and drawers of water, as the phrase goes.'

'Poor things,' said Catherine. 'It doesn't sound much fun. What did the rest do, Robert?'

'They would be engaged in spiritual exercises, don't you see? Prayer and meditation.'

'What, all day long? I think I'd rather have been a what-d'you-call-it, a lay brother.'

'Me too,' said Sarah.

'Well, yes, perhaps you would. But we must remember they also produced some beautiful works of art. Illuminated missals and so on. Let's go and see the chapel, shall we? What's left of it. Actually, it's the best preserved of all the ruins.'

They picked their way through the rank grass and emerging from the kitchen resumed their exploration in an easterly direction, along a lane enclosed by low ivy-clad walls. Three parts of the chapel, and even a section of its roof, were still intact. Nave and chancel were buried under soil and grass, the sediment of the ages giving ground for new growth; the odour of incense lingered only in imagination; and where prayer and praise had once ascended, invisible exhalation of piety, was now the haunt of wayfaring or roosting birds. A whirr of wings startled the silence as they approached. Suddenly alert, they came to a standstill.

'Where we're standing now,' said Robert, 'were the cloisters. The floor, it's supposed, is some three feet below the present ground level. How do we know that? Not by digging, though that would be a good way to make sure. But no. It's because on moonlit nights, at a certain time of the year, a ghost has been seen, perhaps the old Abbot himself, gliding along the cloister, head sunk in meditation. I say gliding because only the upper half of him is visible, the rest of him, from the waist downwards, being submerged. That means, don't you see, that he's walking on the original flagstones: which, of course, is what one would expect, isn't it?'

Catherine shivered. 'How gruesome!' But Sarah,

eyeing him curiously, said: 'Do you really believe that?'

'Not quite, my dear Sarah. But it's a good story.'

Catherine, clutching at his arm, said urgently: 'Look, Robert! There's someone there now—in the chapel!'

'Dear me! So there is. How very——'

He left his comment uncompleted, embarrassed by what he read in Catherine's face.

'Don't worry, Kitty,' said Sarah equably. '*She's* not a ghost.'

'So I see,' remarked Catherine. The toss of her head, the look she flashed at Robert, were an accusation.

'How very extraordinary,' said Robert, 'and unexpected.'

She averted her eyes from him, burning with the consciousness of having been seen and watched by the interloper, perhaps for some minutes. How hateful, she thought. How shameless. She's come to look after her property. Not for a moment did she doubt who the woman was; nor did she ask how she knew that Robert was to be here this evening. He had told her. He had told her everything. She, Catherine, had been the subject of an amused conversation. Her first impulse was to escape, but a counter impulse resolved her to stand and give fight.

Olive Stapleton, elegantly posed, awaited the party's approach with an air of polite indifference tempered by amusement.

'Good evening, Mrs Stapleton,' said Robert, raising his hat. 'This is an unexpected pleasure.'

'Is it?' She offered her hand. 'But why so formal, dear Robert? Won't you introduce your young friends?'

'I was on the point of doing so. Miss Sarah Peacock. Miss Catherine Peacock.'

'Ah! So we meet at last, my dears. I've heard so much about you. Haven't I, Robert?'

'Have you? I don't recollect——'

'But yes indeed. The Peacock sisters are famous. He talks of you day and night, and always, I assure you, in the most flattering terms. How odd that we should chance to meet here. A chance in a thousand.'

'A remarkable coincidence,' said Catherine.

'Yes, isn't it, Miss Catherine? Yet perhaps not so remarkable. I so often come here. It provides, you know, an objective for one's evening walk.'

'You're fond of walking, Mrs Stapleton?'

'I dote on it, Miss Sarah. And I dote on these dear ruins. So quaint. So old.'

'Age, I imagine, is a feature of most ruins,' remarked Sarah. 'You must be fond indeed of walking to have come so far.'

'Ah, but one's little house is only half an hour away. I make nothing of the distance. Something less than two miles, wouldn't you say, Robert?'

'We shall believe you,' said Catherine, 'without Mr Crabbe's corroboration.'

'Dear me! What long words for a young girl!' drawled Olive Stapleton.

Robert said, tactfully intervening: 'Too far, I suppose, for Harold's small legs? Mrs Stapleton, Catherine, has a charming little boy.'

It could not be denied, even by Catherine, that she was handsome in a bold, exotic fashion: high-arching

eyebrows, regular features, brilliant colouring, an elegant
sinuous figure. Her voice was warm and caressing, her
every movement had a feline grace. Worst of all, she
was mature without being old. Her self-assurance was
impregnable: the sight of it made Catherine feel like a
schoolgirl battling against impossible odds, a schoolgirl
whose crudeness and rudeness were no match for the subtle
insolence that gleamed in her rival's eyes and sat like a
predatory cat in the curve of her sleek full lips. Catherine perceived that this scene had been carefully staged
by Mrs Stapleton with the sole view of demonstrating that
she was the woman in possession.

The desultory unmeaning conversation went on, and
Catherine, retired into herself, let it flow past her unheeded, till something that Robert was saying stabbed
her resentment into quivering life.

'We came in a hired carriage. You must let us drive
you back.'

Catherine said: 'If you don't mind, Mr Crabbe, I
prefer to walk. Shall we go, Sarah?'

'Very polite of you, Robert.' The voice was velvet,
the smile at once bland and satirical. 'But, thank you,
I shall not join your party. Something tells me I should
be *de trop*. I wonder what?' Her glance, like a pointing
finger, indicated Catherine, and coming back to Robert
presented the absurd child for his derision. 'Good-bye
for the present, Robert. I must be on my way. I shall
see you on Sunday, no doubt, if by then you are released
from your nursemaid duties. Good-bye, Miss Peacock.
Good-bye, little Miss Catherine. So delighted to have
made your acquaintance.'

Almost before she was out of earshot Sarah remarked, fixing her candid gaze on Robert Crabbe: 'So that's the notorious Mrs Stapleton! Quite a pretty performance. Is she always like that, Mr Crabbe?'

His brow was dark, whether with anger or discomfort she could only surmise. Painfully aware of Catherine's condition, the burning cheeks, the sullen eyes, the puckered, trembling lips, she refrained from looking her way and resisted, though with difficulty, the impulse to offer comfort. She got no answer to her question: it was doubtful whether he had heard it.

'I think I'll go back to the carriage now,' she announced, 'and have a talk with that nice horse. He must be tired of being tied to the gate, poor thing. Come when you're ready, you two. But not too soon, or we shall overtake her on the way back. That would be too much happiness for one evening.'

So far, since Olive Stapleton's departure, neither Robert nor Catherine had uttered a word. Nor did they evince any sign of having heard Sarah's careful speech. Her going found them still silent.

But presently, without looking at him, Catherine said: 'I apologize, Mr Crabbe, for being rude to your friend.' He made a deprecating gesture. 'It was childish, unpardonable,' she continued, pale and cold.

'No, no,' said Robert, avoiding her eyes. 'Don't be angry, Catherine. Only give me time.'

'Give you time?' she echoed. Then, suddenly reverting to her natural self, 'Why did you have to tell her, Robert?' she burst out.

'Tell her? I didn't tell her. Well, yes. I may have

mentioned in passing that we were coming here. But I never dreamt——'

'Didn't you? More fool you. Anyone but a baby would have known what she'd do.'

'I'm sorry, Catherine. I'm more than sorry. Shall we not discuss Mrs Stapleton any more?'

'Certainly we won't, since the subject is so sacred to you.'

'You misunderstand me.'

'On the contrary. I understand everything. Everything. It's all too hatefully clear to me. Shall we go back now? There's no more to be said.'

'I think perhaps there is. Much more. But . . . I have no right. Be patient, Catherine. Give me time.'

Time? Time for what? A flicker of hope kindled in her heart, but she could not bring herself to ask the question. In silence they made their way to where Sarah awaited them, on the broad grass verge of the road; and drove back to Newtonbury at a careful walking-pace.

CHAPTER FIVE

Sarah: Julia: Sarah

§ 1

In the home-going train on Monday evening, 'Well, my children, have you enjoyed your stay at Newtonbury?' asked Mr Peacock.

'Yes, thank you, Papa,' they answered in chorus. And Catherine said: 'But we shall be glad to be home again.'

It was true of both, but especially of Catherine. The two days that had passed since their visit to the Ruins had been a weariness, and to Catherine a torment. It had been a comfort on Friday night to join with Sarah in caustic remarks about Mrs Stapleton, and to ask again and again what Robert could see in her that attracted him; but the question was rhetorical, insincere, for Catherine, who had read many a lush contemporary novel about simplehearted gentlemen and predatory charmers, fancied she knew the answer all too well. Conscious of her inexperience, her deplorable youngness, she felt sadly at a disadvantage in this duel with an expert man-catcher. Saturday found her in a fever of hope and fear: she spent it with Sarah and Ellen, chattering and laughing but hearing only half they said. It was maddening to be so near Robert and not see him; yet to visit him in his office, on some specious excuse, would have been worse than useless. It would have been impolitic, it would have

looked 'forward', and it would have told her nothing of
his state of mind. Sunday evening, she decided, would
be crucial: against all reason she cherished the crazy hope
that despite his previous engagement he might, he just
might, turn up at the Skimmers'. Obsessed by her dream
she found it difficult to believe him indifferent: how was
it possible that her own feelings should evoke no response
in him? He is mine, mine, her heart said stubbornly;
but cold reason told another story. He is kind, com-
passionate, brotherly; but he doesn't want me; he wants
someone cleverer, older, more artful in the ways of love;
I've embarrassed him to no purpose. Looking in her
glass she despaired, wishing herself ten years older.

Sunday dawned, bright with delusive promise. Once
again there was the chapel-going, the hearty luncheon,
the aimless afternoon walk filled with Ellen's incessant
prattle about the children she ministered to and the
prospect of becoming a fully-fledged teacher. The day,
with enormous sloth, dragged on; the crisis of evening
loomed ahead; and in due time the same hobnobbery of
neighbours arrived, bursting with solemn expectation of
improving their minds, in a godly, intellectual fashion,
by reading Cary's Dante together: Mr and Mrs Iron-
monger Grigg, Mr Purbeck the long-nosed chemist, old
Mr Jolly the saddler, and a dried-up spinsterish person,
Miss Latti, at whose shop one could buy hosiery, glass-
ware, letter-paper, string, yesterday's newspapers, and
honey from her own hives. These came, but no Robert.
True, he had said, or implied, that he would not, could
not come; but Catherine in her heart of hearts could not
quite believe he would be as bad as his word.

'So you girls have been out gallivanting with my excellent partner, I find,' said Mr Peacock.

'He took us to see the Ruins,' said Sarah. 'Wasn't it good of him? We hadn't visited them since we were at school, all those years ago. I'd quite forgotten how dull they were.'

'Did you mention that to your escort, by any chance? He must have been highly gratified.'

'When Sarah says dull she doesn't mean dull in a *dull* way,' said Catherine. 'She means historical. We liked it very much and were *most* polite. You'd have been proud of us, Papa. He told us about the monks and their spiritual exercises, and how all the work was done by the unspiritual ones. Would you have been a monk, Papa, if you'd lived in those days? Think how nice it would have been not having any daughters to worry about.'

'Very true, my love. A blissful thought. But let's not dwell on it. Tell me more.'

'There's no more to tell,' said Sarah. 'Not really. Except that—would you believe it?—the fascinating Mrs Stapleton was there, lying in wait for him.'

'Ready to pounce,' said Catherine.

'Like a cat at a mousehole,' said Sarah.

'Or a scorpion,' Catherine suggested. 'Or a giant spider.'

'A versatile lady,' said Mr Peacock. 'And *did* she pounce?'

'Not exactly, did she, Sarah? She just waited for him to walk into her parlour. Do you think she means to gobble him up, Papa?'

'She hasn't acquainted me with any such intention, my dear Kitty. Would you like me to inquire for you?'

'Well, yes,' Catherine confessed. 'It would be nice to know.'

'This passion for knowledge is very commendable in you, my child. Does it extend to other spheres, or only to Mrs Stapleton?'

'We want to know everything,' Sarah assured him. 'Don't we, Kitty? What's been happening while we've been away?'

'Life has gone on,' said her father, 'in spite of your regretted absence. The sun has risen punctually every morning, much to its credit. The cows have been milked and the pigs fed.'

'And Mama?'

'Yes, Sarah, she too has been fed, and she continues to enjoy good health.'

'What a tease you are, Papa!' cried Catherine. 'Haven't you any *news* for us?'

'If by news you mean news of scandal or disaster, as of course you do, I'm afraid I must disappoint you, Kitty. We at Lutterfield, you know, live in a quiet corner of the world, minding our business, and growing a little older every day. But yes,' he went on, in a brighter tone, 'there *is* one little item. The poor old Vicar has taken to his bed, and young Pardew now conducts the services. That's the best I can do for you, but it's something, you'll admit.'

'Poor Mr Garnish! Is he very ill?'

'Julia will tell you all about it. She's been several times to see him. She's a good girl, your sister, and a brave one.'

'Brave, Papa?'

'Yes, and needs to be, with the formidable Mrs Budge to tackle. She's a dragon, that woman, by all accounts.'

Catherine's eyes sparkled: with excitement, compassion, and the light of battle. Robert Crabbe for the moment was forgotten in the exhilaration of homecoming, the prospect of family gossip. She found it difficult to imagine that Julia, dear mild Julia, could be a match for the Budge; and as the train slowed to a standstill at Lutterfield station it was more difficult still, for there she was on the platform waiting to welcome them, prim, serious, elegant, her lips slightly parted, her dark eyes full of watchful affection.

'Well, my dears!' she said, almost in Mama's manner. Her sisters flung themselves upon her. 'Goodness, you're smothering me!' The kisses over, the laughter and excitement subsiding, 'There's a letter from Aunt Druid,' she announced. 'An invitation for Sarah. You'll like that, won't you, Sarah?'

'Shall I?' said Sarah. 'I don't know.'

'But you're not to go till September, thank goodness,' said Julia. 'We've missed you both dreadfully, Mama and I.'

'And what about me?' demanded Mr Peacock. 'Haven't I missed them, the baggages?'

'Have you really, Papa?' said Catherine, gratified.

'Well, my dear, I *am* your father, you know. Or so I have been led to believe. It's at least a plausible hypothesis,' he added judicially.

K

§ 2

THAT Aunt Druid should be visited was a family obligation, and this year it was Sarah's turn.   The prospect did
not allure her; she expected little pleasure from it; but
short of making a fuss and displeasing Mama there was
nothing she could do about it.   To make a fuss was not
in her character: to be placid and sensible and do what
was required of her was apparently her destiny; and her
trick of detachment, her capacity for extracting amusement from little things, and especially from the oddities of
her fellow-creatures, made it easier to comply than to rebel.
Yet of late, ever since her rejection of Mr Pardew, she had
been conscious at intervals of a vague discontent, a half-
formed wish that something, she didn't know what, might
happen to *her*.   Time was passing, life was drifting away,
and to be an amused spectator was not, was not always,
quite enough. Boredom was an experience unknown to her,
but now, at moments, it hovered, a threatening shadow.

Meonthorpe, they said, would be 'a nice change' for
her.   She   assented   to   the   proposition,   but   without
believing it.   No sooner, however, had she said good-bye
and boarded the slow-going cross-country train, taking
care, as commanded, to choose a compartment containing
other female passengers who would protect her from rape,
than her mood changed.   The unaccustomed sensation
of being alone, with no one but herself to consider, was
exhilarating, and the journey that had been embarked
upon reluctantly began to assume the aspect of adventure.
It was two years since she had seen her Meonthorpe
relations: by now they would be almost strangers to her.

But Aunt Druid—whom to her face one must remember to call Aunt Bertha—was after all Mama's sister, and therefore worth studying. That she *was* Mama's sister, that the two had been girls together, was a truth stranger than fiction : only by an effort of the imagination could it be believed.

The warmth of her welcome left nothing to be desired.

'How you've grown, my dear!' said Aunt Druid admiringly. 'And what nice plump, rosy cheeks!'

'It's hardly likely, Aunt Bertha. I stopped growing years ago.'

'Oh, but you have! Hasn't she, Father?'

'Youth's the time for growth,' said Uncle Druid, earnestly regarding his niece and carefully weighing every word. 'My meaning, if a body doesn't grow when he's young he never will, nor she neither, if you follow me.' Opening his eyes wider, 'It stand to reason,' he urged, with the air of one imparting an important discovery. 'Let me put it another way, young lady. The seed falls to the ground. And presently, what happens? The soil nur-ridges it, so to say; the rain gives it moisture; the sun gives it warmth; and it begins to grow. Am I right? Very well then. But mark this : when it's finished growing it doesn't grow any more. There's a lesson for us there.'

'Yes, uncle,' agreed Sarah. 'I expect there is.'

'Ah, there's always a lesson,' remarked Aunt Bertha, 'if only we could find it. But come along, my dear, you'll be ready for your tea, *I'll* be bound.'

'So she will,' said Uncle Druid, 'and so she should be, seeing the perilous long way she's come, poor soul. After a train-journey, nurridgement. It's the law of nature.'

'That's very true, Father. You'll find your Cousin Patience in the kitchen, my dear. She'll have wetted the leaves by now, if I'm any judge. We won't wait for Barney. He'll come when he can from the milking.'

Aunt Bertha, unlike her sister, was short and plump. She had the kind of resolutely pious face that one sees in stained-glass windows: the conventional halo was all but visible. She was kind and earnest; spoke with an exaggerated gentleness, as to a backward child; and shared with her husband the habit of sententiousness. Which of them, Sarah wondered, had acquired from the other this talent for investing the obvious with moral glamour? Or had their common possession of it drawn them together? Aunt Bertha was older than Mama by several years. Her cheeks, though plump, were colourless, her eyes soulful, her hair sparse and peppery. Uncle Druid was broad and burly, with ferocious eyebrows, a ruddy complexion, and a forest of black beard. Such conversation as his came oddly from a man whom Nature had designed as a pirate, or a highwayman, but was in fact a working farmer. Out of the strong came forth triteness.

'A boiled egg will restore the tissues, as the saying goes, so long as it's not too hard nor yet too soft. Too soft is *too* soft, if you take my meaning, and too hard is harder than it should be. Lightly boiled is the rule, some say; but I say, *rightly* boiled.' He repeated the aphorism with solemn relish. 'Whether it's eggs or no matter what,' he continued, 'always do right, and you can't go wrong: that's my motto, isn't it, Mother? And that, you know, Sarah my dear, is the trouble with this modern world of ours. We live in an age of hurry and scurry, scamper and

rush, no time for this, no time for that, no time to get
anything *right*. But you can trust your aunt. You're
safe with her—eh, Mother? And with Patience too.
Patience by name and patience by nature, is our Patience.
Four and a half minutes, neither more nor less. There's
a time for everything, as the Good Book says. A time for
laughing and a time for weeping and a time for boiling
eggs. Do you follow me, niece?'

'Yes, uncle. I think I understand.'

'How many lumps, my dear?' asked Aunt Bertha,
sugar tongs in hand.

'One, please, Aunt Bertha.'

'Three score years and ten,' said Uncle Druid, rather
sternly. 'And honey from our own bees.'

He looked round the table in a knowing manner, with
the air of having clinched a difficult argument.

'How are they all at home?' asked Cousin Patience,
breaking a mystified silence.

'Quite well, thank you,' said Sarah.

'Uncle Edmund?'

'Yes, thank you.'

'Aunt Emily?'

'And Julia,' said Sarah, 'and Catherine. All well,
thank you, Cousin Patience.'

'I do hope dear Barney won't be long,' sighed Aunt
Bertha. 'The tea will be stewed.'

'That's another thing we can learn from,' said Uncle
Druid. 'The hive. Industry and per-sevverance. Service for others. Busy all day long gathering honey for us.'

'God's little husbandmen,' interpolated Aunt Bertha.

'For *us*, uncle? Surely not!'

'For you and me, Sarah. For your Aunt Bertha. For your Cousin Patience. Milk from the cow, honey from the bee. That's Providence, that is. Isn't it, Mother?'

'Yes, dear. All good things around us, as the hymn says.'

'In the comb,' said Uncle Druid. 'But not till we've finished our eggs.'

'I see what you mean,' said Sarah meekly, 'but all the same I'm glad I'm not a bee. For one thing they haven't any sex worth speaking of, except the queen and the poor drones. It seems rather an unfair arrangement.'

'My dear,' said Aunt Bertha, 'we don't talk of things like that.' She smiled forgivingly.

'Don't you, Aunt Bertha? We do,' answered Sarah. She glanced expectantly towards her uncle, hoping for a further instalment of wisdom. He did not disappoint her.

'Nature,' said Uncle Druid, announcing his new text. 'You can't go against Nature. Rain and sun. Seed-time and harvest. Take the bees, take the flowers, take anything you choose,' he added generously, 'and what have you got, what does it all amount to? Nature. Consider the lilies how they grow, said Our Lord. They toil not, neither do they spin. But they're there, there's no denying, and you may depend on it, they're there for a good reason. Why, you may ask. Why are they there? Why do they grow and grow and . . . in short, why do they grow? The flowers of the field. The poppies in the corn. The buttercups, the dandelions, the daisies. Every spring they appear, every summer they bloom, every autumn they shed their petals, every winter they die down. But they're there, Sarah, they're still there, biding their time, as you might say. Why? I'll tell you. Because of Nature.'

'And,' said Aunt Bertha, gently corrective, 'because it's
God's will.'

'Amen, Mother,' said Uncle Druid. Throwing back
his head he lifted his cup and poured its contents into a
small red gap in his beard. 'Ah, that's better. There's
nothing like a cup of tea.'

In the conversational lull that followed, Sarah had time
to take stock of her situation: the low ceiled red-tiled
kitchen, the open brick hearth, the chimneypiece with its
gleaming array of pots and pans, and the proximity, half-
seen, half-heard, of the cobbled yard. Through the
narrow sash-window, open three inches at the top, came
the rhythmic, resonant sound of warm milk spurting into
a pail. To her ears it was a familiar music, but here at
Meonthorpe the sense of farm was stronger, more per-
vasive, than at home. There it was an incidental accompaniment to a more elegant style of living: here it was the
prime business of life, to which all other activities were
subordinate. As she listened, lost in drowsy reflection,
the sound of milking ceased; there was a rattle of loosening
chains, a man's voice speaking, the slap of a broad
buttock, the soft thud of hooves as the cattle slowly
lumbered across the yard; and a few moments later, with
a great clatter of boots, Barnabas Druid burst into the
kitchen, a lean giant of a man, already going bald, with a
small, sharp-featured face, prominent ears, a straggling
wisp of sun-coloured moustache. He brought with him
a pungent suggestion of farmyard.

'Daisy's going dry, governor! What d'you make of
that?' He dragged a chair up to the table, sat himself
down, and began voraciously eating.

'There's manners for you!' said his mother fondly. 'Aren't you going to say how-d'you-do to your Cousin Sarah, dear?'

'Eh? Hullo, cousin! So you've arrived then? Pleasant journey?'

'Yes, thank you.' If a dog could talk, thought Sarah, it would talk like Cousin Barnabas.

'That's the style. What about a cup of tea, Mother?'

'Manners,' said Uncle Druid, 'are what you like to make of them. The way I look at it, there's good manners and there's bad manners, and what the eye doesn't see the heart doesn't grieve over, as my old father used to say. When he was alive, that is,' he explained, turning to Sarah. 'Dead and gone now this many a year, poor soul.'

He proceeded to embroider the theme, but Sarah, though she appeared to give him her full attention, was no longer listening. Fascinated though she was by the quality of her uncle's discourse, and longing for the time when she would be able to share him with Catherine, for the moment she could hold no more.

'Quite right, Father,' said Aunt Bertha. 'The important thing, for us all, is to set a good example.'

Patience took no part in the conversation. She attended diligently to the wants of the others, and for the rest sat in silence, munching, sipping, unsmiling: a woman of perhaps forty whose premature greyness and apathetic expression made her seem scarcely younger than her mother. As for Barnabas, he did not open his mouth again except to put food into it or to interrupt his father's flow of words with a curt remark about crops, market

prices, the weather. It was small wonder, Sarah reflected, that Uncle Druid's surviving children were
inclined to be taciturn: the three others she had vaguely
heard of had no doubt been talked to death in their
infancy. The wonder was, not that they were silent,
these two, but that dear Uncle Druid, with so much to
say, had ever found time to initiate them. Despite these
unuttered sarcasms, however, and though already she was
counting the days to her return, she did not regret having
come. Whether 'nice' or not, a change it certainly was,
to be living in a genuine farmhouse, with full-time
farmers, and surrounded by excitingly unfamiliar country.
She promised herself some good long walks; she might, it
was just possible, meet some new people to add to her
collection of human specimens; and there was always a
chance that something amusing might happen during the
next thirteen days.

§ 3

WHAT is a man to do when, having wilfully with resolute
folly involved himself with a bold-eyed, tenacious Cleo-
patra, he becomes aware of young Juliet, fair as the
morning and sweetly beckoning, and finds himself
distracted in his too-successful pursuit of the one by
inconvenient visions of the other? Leaving Robert
Crabbe to resolve this problem as best he can, for it will
take him some time, let us turn in parenthesis to another
theme, to Julia: who, like her young sister but from
motives more genuinely disinterested, was now engaging
in a work of rescue. Death was the adversary she had
set herself to circumvent, and Fear, his cunning lieutenant.

She had entered the battle without enthusiasm, animated by nothing but her unsleeping sense of duty, the unarguable necessity of doing the right, the neighbourly thing; but before many weeks were past she had found herself deeply, personally concerned, moving in a region of dark and palpitating mystery; and now, with her mother's consent and approval, she was visiting the vicarage almost every day, leaving Catherine to cope, willy nilly, with the various small household tasks that normally fell to the lot of Mama's Right Hand. That she, Julia, should have been willing to resign that proud office, even for a while, gives the measure of her new zeal.

Nearly every morning then, after breakfast, she set out for the village, a quarter of an hour's brisk walk, carrying with her such edible dainties as she thought might tempt the appetite of an invalid. The vicarage, hidden from the road by tall funereal fir-trees, stood some sixty or seventy yards back from the High Street, surrounded by two acres of neglected garden, a wilderness of rank grass, weed-infested flower-beds, decaying summerhouses, and overgrown laurels; for Roy Tupkin, since the beginning of his master's illness, had abandoned even the pretence of being a gardener, and now spent what time he could spare from more congenial pursuits, such as eating and sleeping and pursuing the village girls, in scrubbing floors and filling scuttles for the formidable Mrs Budge and her fourteen-year-old daughter Gladys. A stranger entering upon the desolate scene would have supposed the place to be uninhabited; nor would his first sight of the house itself, bleak, grimy, uncared-for, have contradicted that impression; but, though the interior too was comfortless

and forbidding, the wallpaper discoloured by damp, the
pictures slightly crooked, the upholstery dying of old age,
once inside, and confronted by Mrs Budge, no one could
doubt that inhabited it was, and by someone who would
not be easily dispossessed.

In appearance, as in some of her habits, Mrs Budge
resembled a plump, elderly hen; but there was cunning
as well as greed in her small, sharp eyes, and her manner,
an uneasy mixture of obsequiousness and self-assurance,
suggested that she entertained delusions of grandeur and
was determined to be taken at her own valuation.

'Most kind, I'm sure, miss,' she too-carefully articu-
lated, on Julia's first visit. 'Most kind.' The eyes
glittered. The thrusting beak hovered over the basket.
'Not but what dear Mr Garnish is being well looked after.
Anything he fancies. He has only to name it.'

'Quite so, Mrs Budge. And now, if you please, I should
like to see him.'

'Not today, miss, I fear, if you'll excuse me. It
wouldn't, you must understand, be quite convenient.'
She switched on a false, deprecating smile. 'The poor
gentleman's in bed.'

'So I suppose,' said Julia. 'All the more reason why I
should see him. Please tell him Miss Peacock is here.
Miss Julia Peacock.'

'Seeing he's so out of sorts, miss, I don't care to disturb
him. But I'll tell him you called. Good morning.'

Julia, on the doorstep, stood firm, refusing the hint. The
two stared at each other, the one gravely intent, the other
goatishly smiling. Then the face of Mrs Budge withdrew.
The door, so narrowly open, began closing. A spasm of

unwonted anger quickened Julia's pulse. Insolence, and from an inferior, was something her mother's daughter would not brook. She stepped quickly forward, put out a hand, and pushed her way into the house.

'I think perhaps you misunderstood me, Mrs Budge,' she said pleasantly. 'I wish to see the Vicar. Be so good as to announce me. I shall follow you.'

'Very good, Miss Peacock. No offence, I hope. I only want to do what's right.'

'I'm sure you do,' said Julia. 'Shall we go upstairs then?'

'And if harm comes of it,' said Mrs Budge, as she turned to lead the way, 'it can't be laid at *my* door.' Arrived within sight of the bedroom she darted forward and attached herself to the door-handle. 'I'll see if he's awake,' she said over her shoulder; then entered and shut herself in. Julia waited and listened, still utterly resolved, but fearful of intruding at an awkward moment. After an uncomfortable interval the door opened and Mrs Budge peered round its edge. 'The Vicar can spare you five minutes, I find.'

Pink-eyed, chap-fallen, and with a stubble of grey beard blunting the line of his jaw, the Reverend Mr Garnish was an unlovely sight. He sat, a picture of apathy and old age, in a large four-poster bed, wrapped in a dressing-gown, three pillows at his back, his hands lying limp on the coverlet. On a bedside table were a number of books, a candlestick, a nightcap, a dirty handkerchief, and a carafe of water. On the wall to his right, interrupting a cabbage-rose pattern in sage-green, hung a full-length portrait in oils of the late Mrs Garnish, dressed in the style of twenty years earlier: a tall, fair, elegant woman, leaning against an improbable tree, in a sunlit garden, and smiling fixedly at distance. Julia half-remembered having seen it before, in the drawing-room downstairs, a memory dating from the days, now long past, when she and her family were occasionally invited to tea at the vicarage. Its presence in the old man's bedroom struck her as pathetic.

'A lady to see you,' said Mrs Budge, rearranging the pillows. 'Now *isn't* that nice!'

He slowly turned his head, peering from screwed-up eyes.

'Good morning, Mr Garnish.'

'Eh?'

'It's Julia,' said his visitor. 'Julia Peacock.'

'H'm. So I see. Good morning, my dear.'

'I'm so sorry to hear you're not well.'

'Well? No, I'm not well. How should I be?'

Julia looked at Mrs Budge, who stood as it were on guard, at the bedhead. 'There's no need for you to stay, Mrs Budge. I won't take up any more of your time.'

'My time is the master's, miss, thank you.'

'Of course. But I'm sure Mr Garnish will excuse you.'

The woman made no move. Julia looked a question at Mr Garnish, but he seemed not to have noticed the exchange. Short of an unseemly brawl, there was nothing to be done. She decided to contain her indignation.

'What does the doctor say, Vicar?' she lamely asked.

'Doctors are no use to me. Too old for doctors.'

'But I'm sure Dr Witherby——'

'Ah, Witherby. Yes, he came once. Not been near

since, and good riddance. That's what *she* says.' He
jerked a nod in the direction of Mrs Budge. 'I'm at the
end of the road, eh Budge?'

'It's the Lord's will,' said Mrs Budge. 'Not but what
we don't hope you'll get better, I'm sure,' she hastily
added, meeting Julia's look. 'It'll be a sad day for
Gladys and I when you're taken.' She produced a wad
of handkerchief from her apron pocket and wiped an
imaginary tear from her eye.

'Could find nothing much wrong, the duffer. Bah!
Nothing but everything! Let's hope they've more
sense up above. Is your father still alive, girl?'

'Good gracious, yes!'

'So much the worse for him. It's a dreary business,
living.'

'Oh no!' protested Julia. 'It's wonderful. Think of
all the lovely things you'll soon be enjoying again.'

'Darkness and corruption, child. A convocation of
worms.' His eyes closed. His head sank back against
the pillow. 'Don't let that smart young curate come near
me,' he muttered. 'I can't do with him.'

Julia was dismayed, pity mingling with a sense of
revulsion of which, instantly, she was ashamed.

'You're tired,' she said soothingly. 'I'll leave you
now. Have a nice sleep.'

Reluctantly leaving Mrs Budge in possession, she tiptoed out of the room, ran downstairs, and let herself out.
What she had seen and heard, so different from her
sentimental expectations, had shocked and frightened
her: to emerge from that spiritual darkness into the strong
morning sunlight was a release almost unnerving in its

suddenness. She looked up and down the wide, gently sloping High Street, from the ancient church at the higher end, with its green copper spire pointing heavenwards, to the broad-based comeliness of Lutterfield's eighteenth-century alehouse, the Waggon and Horses, at the other; and was surprised and comforted to find everything placid and unchanged. The street at this mid-morning hour was empty of people, and at any other time she would have enjoyed the sunlit solitude, but now, after her glimpse of hell, she longed for the reassurance of a human contact. She resisted, however, the temptation to look in at the grocer's and for the sake of a chat with Mrs Salop make some small purchase; for with Sarah and Catherine away at Newtonbury there was no one but herself—apart from three capable domestic servants—to attend upon Mama. Indeed she must hurry home. But not, she suddenly decided, until she had seen Dr Witherby.

The idea reinvigorated her, and five minutes later she was knocking at the door of his house.

Ever so sorry, but the doctor was out on his rounds. Would Miss Peacock care to wait? Well, it might be an hour or it might be less: you could never tell with the doctor. But he'd be in for his dinner at one o'clock— unless he was kept unexpected.

While Julia stood hesitating, Dr Witherby and his dog-cart, drawn by a sturdy grey cob, came spanking down the road. He drew up at his house and alighted.

'Good morning, Miss Peacock.'

'Oh doctor, I'm so glad to see you!'

'My dear young lady, how gratifying! No one ill, I hope?'

'Indeed there is.   It's Mr Garnish.'

'Ah, the man of God.   He's a difficult customer, I find.'

'I know,' said Julia.   'But——'

'Between ourselves, Miss Peacock, he as good as showed me the door.   I'll look in again tomorrow, I said to him. No, you won't, said he, you'll wait till you're sent for—good morning.   Dr Witherby grinned at the recollection.' 'I'm a wicked fellow, don't you see?   I don't go to church.'

'Yes, that *is* wrong of you,' said Julia, in simple candour. 'But that's not why he's rude.   It's because he's old and ill and miserable.   You must know that quite well.' She gave him a straight, severe look.   'And you *will* go and see him, won't you, doctor?   There's something queer going on in that house.'   She shivered at the memory.   'That Mrs Budge, I don't like her.   She's up to no good.   I know it's difficult for you,' she went on, before he could answer.   'But if you can't go as a doctor surely you can go as a friend, a neighbour?'

'Ah,' said Dr Witherby, 'but the poor old gentleman doesn't regard me in that light.   To him I'm still a new-comer, an interloper, a fellow who doesn't belong.   Bless you, I don't mind his manners.   I don't mind his not liking my face.   Why should I?   I don't much care for it myself.   But if he's taken against me I can't be much help to him, you'll admit.'

'I've just come from the vicarage,' Julia said.   She was too intent on her purpose to argue with him.   'I don't trust her.   I believe she *wants* him to die.'   Her own words startled her.   'No, I oughtn't to say that. But we must do something, doctor.   Why wouldn't she leave me alone in the room with him?'

He looked at her appreciatively. There was irony in his eyes, but kindness too. She was suddenly conscious of liking him, in spite of his odd appearance, his sardonic manner. A fringe of beard enclosed his otherwise shaven face with a semi-circle of fire, like an inverted halo. His high-raised bushy eyebrows, very mobile and expressive, with a life of their own, seemed not to belong to him, as though stuck on, part of a comic disguise. But the man who looked out from the disguise, with his alert humorous eyes, square jaw, resolute nose, was a good man, she decided; was friendly; was a man she could trust. Moreover, Papa thought highly of him, played chess with him, enjoyed his company; and if Mama didn't . . . well, it was possible, just possible, that Mama was mistaken for once.

'What happened, Miss Peacock?' said Dr Witherby. 'Suppose you tell me the whole story.'

What she told him made him thoughtful. He listened in silence, and when the recital was over he made no promises beyond saying that he would see what he could do. His business at the moment was to get Mrs Bateson her pink medicine. It had to be pink, he explained; no other colour did her any good; and its pinkness was its only medicinal virtue.

Three days later he presented himself at Peacock Place to report progress. He had visited the Vicar and talked to him about everything under the sun except his health.

'I talked a good deal about you, Miss Peacock. Your name worked wonders. It's hardly too much to say that it's made a new friend for me. That, and our hearty contempt, his and mine, for doctors. Doctors are duffers, he said. Not only duffers, said I, but thieves as well.

L

They take your money and do nothing for it but look wise. You'll get, said the Vicar, no money from me, young Witherby. And you, my dear Vicar, will get no doctoring from me, if you don't mind your manners, I told him. So put out your tongue, man. It's a rude gesture. Just your style. Ah! As I thought. Filthy. Let's hope it's not an index of the state of your soul.'

'Oh, doctor!' cried Julia, delighted but a little shocked. 'Did he laugh?'

'I wouldn't say that, my dear. But he did as he was told, and he didn't throw me out, and I'm seeing him again tomorrow. That's something gained. As for your Mrs Budge, if I have any nonsense from her I'll frighten the life out of her.'

That was the beginning of Julia's campaign, an enterprise that now occupied much of her waking thought. Her visits to the vicarage grew more frequent as the weeks went by, and now she was going nearly every day.

§ 4

SARAH's hope of meeting some new people at Meonthorpe was quickly fulfilled. The very next day Cousin Patience, prompted by Aunt Bertha, put on her best bonnet and took their visitor to call on their nearest and most eminently presentable neighbours, Mr and Mrs Pluvius. Away from the house, and with no father to compete with, Patience Druid became a new woman, showing unexpected signs of animation. A hint of colour came into her cheeks as she spoke of the treat in store. To be on visiting terms with the Pluviuses, her manner suggested, was a privilege, but not an undeserved one.

They lived a quarter of a mile from the village street, in a large Queen Anne house, one might almost call it a mansion, surrounded by five acres of lawn, flower-beds, shrubbery, paddock, and playing-field. Here some thirty-five young gentlemen, their ages varying from twelve to eighteen, were being prepared by Mr Pluvius for the battle of life, with the help of Mrs Pluvius, five domestic servants, and Mrs Pluvius's nephew, young Edward Linton. The friendship between Mrs Pluvius and Aunt Bertha, who had discovered interests in common and enjoyed a good gossip, did credit to the broad-mindedness of both parties: Mrs Pluvius tactfully ignored the social difference implied in Mrs Druid's supplying the school with eggs, dairy produce, and boiling fowls; and Mrs Druid did not hold it against Mrs Pluvius that her husband was, or had formerly been, a nonconformist minister.

'The Reverend Pluvius,' said Patience, with a touch of defiance, 'thinks a lot of my father, too.'

'How nice,' said Sarah. 'Does my uncle give him good advice?'

Patience glanced suspiciously at her young cousin, but the look that met hers was all innocence.

'They don't meet very often. My father's too busy. But when they do there's always plenty to talk about.'

'I'm sure there is,' said Sarah, with simple veracity.

'He's got letters after his name,' said Patience. 'And quite a number of his boys go on to Oxford or Cambridge. But so did my Uncle Edmund, didn't he? So of course it's nothing to you.'

Except for a murmured disavowal of the implied grandeur, Sarah found no answer to that meekness.

There was a story told in the Peacock family of how a four-year-old Sarah, looking out of the window, had remarked in an interested, matter-of-fact tone : 'Here's Mr God coming down the street.' A dim echo of that forgotten moment accompanied her first encounter, these many years later, with Mr Pluvius, whose short legs and tubby figure supported—somewhat precariously, it seemed —a majestic head, high-domed and venerable, and whose features, all but the small bright eyes and eagle nose, were hidden behind a copious snow-white beard, which was still, however, in the region of the upper lip, stained with the mustard colour of his earlier years. His wife, a tall sandy woman, slim and erect, presided with a certain stateliness at the tea-table. The severity of her looks betokened no ill will: it was her habitual tribute to the importance of any social occasion that was graced by the presence of the headmaster.

'It's very kind of you, Mrs Pluvius, but we really didn't mean to stay to tea,' said Patience Druid nervously, continuing to worry a recent bone of civil contention. 'Did we, Sarah?'

'Nonsense, my dear. Two lumps or three? It's not every day we have the pleasure of seeing Miss Peacock.'

'Very true,' said Mr Pluvius, in a high reedy voice that would have seemed querulous but for the benign smile that accompanied it, 'and a notable example of meiosis, since in point of fact we have never had that pleasure before.'

'You know very well what I mean, headmaster.'

'Perfectly, Mrs Pluvius. And so, I am sure, does the young lady.'

Here in Highfield House, taking tea with the Pluviuses,

Sarah felt very remote from the Meonthorpe farm, which was only seven minutes away. But for her cousin's presence she could have forgotten that the place existed, or at any rate could not have supposed that there existed any connexion between the two so different worlds. It was this element of continual surprise that made life, the unfolding story, so unpredictable, so full of interest, so quick with expectancy. The coming here had been enjoyable: the walk down the village street and into Church Lane, the distant glimpse through trees of the ancient church itself standing lonely and aspiring in a three-cornered field, the turning into a narrow winding drive that was like a dark green tunnel: from which one emerged, with an effect of suddenness, into a region of wide sky and sunlit lawn, with the great white house, embodiment of dignity and good sense, in the middle distance. And now, in this cream-coloured drawing-room, lofty and spacious, hung with water-colours in gilt frames, and containing (above all) two persons never met before and therefore a challenge to curiosity, Sarah sat in smiling silence, bewildered for the moment by the riot of her new impressions. Conscious of being the youngest member of the party, and a stranger, she surrendered to her shyness and allowed Patience to do the talking, contenting herself with brief answers to the polite questions fired at her. How did she like Meonthorpe? Was she making a long stay? Had she found the journey tiring, and was it not very enterprising of her to come so far by herself?

'Ah,' said Mrs Pluvius, as the door opened. 'This will be our Mr Linton.' She looked at the young man with mock-severity. 'You are ten minutes late, Edward.'

'Yes, Mrs Pluvius.   I pray you will forgive me.'

'We have a visitor.   Two visitors.   Miss Peacock, this is Mr Edward Linton.'

'How do you do, Miss Peacock.   How do you do, Miss Druid.'

'He is not without virtues,' said Mrs Pluvius, 'but punctuality is not among them.   Eh, Edward?'

'I was kept by my duties, Mrs Pluvius,' said the young man, taking his seat at the table.   'I find that Jenkins minor has not yet mastered his Third Conjugation.   I had to tell him that without it he would infallibly end on the gallows.'

'Did he believe you, Mr Linton?' inquired the headmaster.

'Fortunately, no, sir.   But he got the general idea, I fancy.   He's not a bad boy.'

'Then let him be an example to you, Edward,' said his aunt.   'You will find, as you grow older, Miss Peacock, that men always have a plausible excuse for being late for meals.'

'Am I included in the indictment?' asked Mr Pluvius.

'I feel sure you are, sir,' said Edward Linton.   'One may put the point syllogistically.   All men are late for meals and make excuses.   Mr Pluvius is a man.   Therefore Mr Pluvius is late for meals and makes excuses.'

'In the present instance, however,' said Mr Pluvius, 'we must, I think, distinguish.   You, my dear boy, have pleaded duty.   Now duty is not an excuse: it is an explanation.'

'Thank you, sir.   Then I shall take my tea with a clear conscience.'

'Not only,' said Mrs Pluvius, 'do they make excuses.

They try to dazzle and confuse us with their cleverness, knowing us to be ignorant women.'

'Really, Mrs Pluvius!' protested Edward Linton. '*Ought* you to say that of your guests?'

He met Sarah's inscrutable look, smiled at her shyly, and looked quickly away, as though conscious of having talked too much.

'You are wondering, Miss Peacock,' said Mr Pluvius, 'why my sister's son addresses his aunt and uncle with so much ceremony. The answer may be given in the words of Seneca, which, should your Latin be rusty, Mr Linton himself will be happy to construe for us. Longum iter est per precepta, breve et efficax per exempla. Well, Edward?'

'Must I, sir? And at tea-time? What Seneca had in mind, Miss Peacock,' said the young man, gazing into his teacup, 'was that if I address my uncle as Uncle Ambrose on private occasions I may inadvertently do so in the presence of the boys, which would be bad for discipline. In short, I have to set them a good example. Will that do, sir?'

'The translation is somewhat free,' said Mr Pluvius. 'But never mind. It will serve.'

'But would it matter, Mr Pluvius,' asked Sarah, 'if the boys did call you Uncle Ambrose?'

Startled glances greeted this audacity. Mr Pluvius alone was unperturbed.

'Not to me, my dear young lady. But to them, yes. If I did not stand on the pedestal of my dignity I should deprive them of the unlawful joy of pushing me off when they talk about me among themselves. That would be unkind.'

'How noble of you,' said Sarah. 'You carry the burden of dignity, so that they may enjoy the pleasures of impudence.'

Oh dear, she thought, beginning to blush for herself, why must I show off? Who is it I want to impress? He's clever no doubt, but he's very young, and looks it in spite of his elegant starched linen and black tailcoat. To hide her preoccupation she began asking questions about the school. How many boys? How many classes? What time did they go to bed, and what games did they play? She hardly listened to the answers, but pricked up her ears, inwardly rejoicing, when Mrs Pluvius said:

'Edward will show you everything after tea. Won't you, Edward? While Miss Druid and I have a nice talk together.'

So Sarah was shown everything. The classrooms, the dining hall, the school library, all had to be looked at and admired. There was also a scattering of boys here and there, who stood up at sight of her, like soldiers on parade, or with conscious looks melted away from the alarming presence.

'Is it you they're afraid of, or me?' she said.

'Not at all,' he answered vaguely. 'I mean . . .' He looked away, stiff and unsmiling.

She glanced timidly at his profile, wishing he would look at her and fearing lest he should.

'This is the library,' he said, after an awkward silence. 'They come here when they want to be quiet, and read.'

'I see.'

'They can do their prep here if they like. At least the seniors can. Because of the no-talking rule.'

'Are you very strict with them, Mr Linton?   Do you beat them a lot?'

'Not often.'   He looked startled.   Then smiled shyly at distance.   'And then only the smaller ones, who can't hit back.'   But before she could answer he was serious again.   'My uncle doesn't believe in that kind of thing. It's not quite like other schools, you know.'

'I'm sure it's very nice,' she said politely.

'It must be a great bore for you, being shown round like this.'

'Not at all.   But I see it is for you.   Please don't waste any more of your time on me.   I'm sure it's very precious.'

And now, at last, he did look at her, in sheer astonishment, a blush mounting to his cheek.   'Have I offended you, Miss Peacock?'

'Of course not.   How could you?'   She spoke with affected lightness, but her voice trembled.

'I would rather do anything than that,' he said harshly. 'Anything in the world.'

Above the noise of her hurrying heart she heard herself say: 'Please don't exaggerate.   Tell me more about the school.'   A sort of panic seized her.   'Could we go outside, do you think?   I should like to see the garden and the cricket-field and everything.'

In the open air she would be safe, she thought, from the folly that was possessing her.   He was, after all, a quite ordinary young man.   Hold fast to that.   Tall, fair, good-looking in a queer way, but not, oh definitely not, handsome.   At the tea-table, with his uncle and aunt to support him, he had seemed alert, self-possessed, even gay; but now, his high spirits were quenched, his movements

were abrupt and selfconscious, and his severe black
garments hung awkwardly, seeming not to belong to him.
The elegant young gentleman had been displaced by a
big, loose-limbed, awkward boy. Why then did his
glance disturb her, and the deep music of his voice make
her nerves tingle? Why this ridiculous, half-maternal
impulse to do something, anything, that would restore to
him his former self-assurance?

That part of the garden which was visible from the
drawing-room window was out-of-bounds to the boys, but
elsewhere in the grounds they might roam as they pleased.
There were trees for climbing; there was a paddock where
a pony grazed; and from the cricket-field beyond came
the sound of boys' voices, softened by distance. The hour
was serene, the earth contained in a glowing stillness, as
Sarah and her escort walked slowly across a series of three
terraced lawns and entered a sun-spangled copse.

'The playing-field is over there,' said Edward Linton,
with a vague gesture. 'They're practising at the nets.
You can hear them.'

'Yes. How peaceful it is here. I sometimes wish I
had been a boy.'

'I am glad you're not.'

'Are you? Why? Do you like being a schoolmaster,
Mr Linton?'

'I suppose so. It passes the time. My father's idea is
to set me up on my own, when I've got more experience.'

'It must be wonderful to be so learned. But then men
are, aren't they?'

'I don't know the answer to that,' said Edward Linton.
'Let's not talk about me.'

'What shall we talk about, then?'

'About you, if you don't mind. There's something you ought to know.'

She stared at the ground, dazzled by his nearness and afraid of what must come. It's too soon. It can't be true. Things don't happen like that.

'I expect it won't interest you. I expect I shall offend you again.'

'In that case you'd better not tell me,' said Sarah, with heroic firmness.

'I must,' he said, almost angrily. 'Forgive me, but I must. You're the most beautiful girl I've ever seen.' There was a moment's silence between them, and as if conscious of anti-climax he added in a desperate, defeated tone: 'That's all.'

She raised her eyes to his, shyly, with a tremulous half-smile. 'But that's quite a lot, isn't it, Mr Linton?' He took a quick step towards her. 'No. Don't say any more. Not now. It's too soon.'

Turning, she saw Patience Druid emerging from the house, in search of her.

§ 5

DEAREST Sarah (wrote Catherine), I am glad you are having a nice time. There is no news, nothing ever happens here, and we all miss you very much, especially me. Robert was half-expected on Sunday but didn't come, it's over three weeks since you and I saw him, and no letter or anything. Of course there is no reason why he should write to me but it seems rather funny all the same considering everything, I mean Mrs S's strange behaviour, but perhaps he is afraid of Mama's seeing the letter, if not I do not know what to think, it is rather worrying because I cannot believe she is the sort of person that could make him happy but men are so strange. You will perhaps say it is no business of mine and you are quite right in a way but one cannot help taking an interest seeing he is a friend of the family and Papa's partner. Papa has a slight cough, I think he knows more than he says but never opens his lips and I dare not ask, apart from everything else it is quite time he came to Sunday luncheon again I should have thought but perhaps she will not let him. I wish you were home again there is lots to talk about, I *might* tell you a secret and you could give me some good donkeyfied advice dear elder sister, I being *only a child* as Mama is always telling me though nearly 21. Mama had quite a little scene with Cook yesterday but it has blown over thank goodness and all smiles.' Now I must bring this letter to a close with much love from your affec sister, Catherine.

Sarah had this letter in her bosom and in her mind when on Saturday afternoon, taking one of her solitary walks, she visited Meonthorpe parish church. She was not a particularly imaginative girl, but church interiors, more especially when no service was in progress, had a curious attraction for her. St Gabriel's stood apart and alone, all but its spire hidden from the road by trees and high hedges. Entering it she had the sensation of stepping out of time into a region of quick, luminous silence, in which the essence of bygone centuries and of centuries still to come was distilled. The afternoon sunlight, stained by the tall, coloured windows, slanted across the flagstone floor. The inexorable, deliberate tick of the tower-clock was like the beating of an immortal heart. Forgetting her intention of strolling round to examine the memorial tablets, the tombs, the recumbent stone figures, she sank into a pew and let the quietness flow into her. . . .

She was roused, recalled from a long journey, by the sound of footsteps approaching down the aisle. They came to a halt. A voice spoke. A well-remembered voice. Edward Linton's.

'Are you all right? Is anything the matter?'

She looked up at him, dazed. 'I think I was dreaming. What's the time?'

'I've been waiting for you outside,' said Edward Linton. 'I saw you come in. Do you mind?'

'There was a young man here,' said Sarah, clutching at a vanishing memory. 'Not you. His name was David. He thought I was his mother.' She shivered slightly, and got up.

'You *have* been dreaming,' said Edward gently. 'Shall we go outside, into the sunshine?'

Meekly, still half-bemused, she followed him out of the church.

When they reached the porch he turned to her, lightly touching her hand. 'You're going home on Monday. This may be my last chance.'

'Yes,' she said.

'I think you know what I want to say.'

'Do I? Yes, perhaps I do.'

'Well, then . . .'

'But you must give me a little time.'

'Oh, no!' He seized her by the arms and turned her

towards him. 'I daren't do that. It's now or never. You've taken possession of me. I can't think of anything else.'

'I'm sorry,' said Sarah, smiling uncertainly.

'Sorry!'

'Sorry to be such a nuisance. You sounded quite angry.'

'Did I? No wonder.' He gazed at her ardently, half-smiling, but still with a hint of sternness, or desperation. 'Do you, by any chance, like me at all, Sarah?'

'I like you very much, Edward.'

'Thank you,' he said quaintly. 'Will you marry me then?'

'Isn't it rather early to talk of that?'

'Will you?'

She sighed, relaxing into his arms. 'It looks as though I shall have to, if you've made up your mind to it.'

CHAPTER SIX

Catherine and Robert

§ 1

BACK at Lutterfield, Sarah, as always on such occasions, had the blissful excitement of rediscovering her home, of finding everything unchanged. Because she had seen new places and new faces, and because above all she had found in Edward Linton the answer to a long-maturing doubt, the ten days of her sojourn at Meonthorpe seemed in retrospect like an age; yet here, in her absence, time had apparently stood still. House, garden, countryside, mother and sisters, all were blessedly the same. In view of all that had happened to *her*, it was difficult to believe that Mama, Catherine, and Julia, Alice and Jenny and Cook, Harry Dawkins and Old Piggott, were any of them a minute older than when she had left them a lifetime ago. One thing only was different, and disconcerting: Mr Peacock was away in London, on a business visit. For more reasons than one she was impatient to see him, and hardly knew how to wait till his return.

'Something's happened to you, Sarah,' said Catherine, when after a long, garrulous, family evening they reached the private haven of their bedroom.

Sarah smiled evasively. 'It's lovely to be back.'

'Yes, but something's happened,' Catherine insisted. 'Hasn't it?'

'I hope Papa comes home soon,' said Sarah, getting into her nightdress.

Catherine was already in bed, sitting up, expectant. Sarah joined her. She blew out the candle, whose wick, the flame departed, gave forth an acrid, hovering stench; and presently, in the intimacy of darkness and warmth, she told her story.

'Oh Sally! How wonderful for you!' Catherine said. 'I'm terribly excited. Aren't you?'

'I'm not altogether displeased,' Sarah admitted. 'But he may have changed his mind by now.'

'Humbug said the hedgehog. You know he hasn't. I expect there'll be a letter tomorrow. Will he come to stay, do you think?'

'That depends, doesn't it.'

'On Mama, you mean. Yes, there's sure to be a commotion. When will you tell her?'

'Not till Papa comes home. It's a secret, mind, till then. Now tell me about Robert.'

'I think, I'm not sure, he'll be coming next Sunday. Papa said something. Isn't it funny of him not to write, though?'

'I expect he thought it unwise. Do you like him very much, Kitty?'

'I might,' said Catherine, 'if he liked me. But I don't suppose he does. Not much. Besides, there's that woman. It must be wonderful to be in love. To let yourself, I mean. I do think you're lucky, having Edward. I'm dying to see him. Is he nice, Sally?'

'He is not entirely lacking in attractive qualities.'

Catherine gurgled. 'Is that what you said when he asked you to marry him? How gratifying for him, as Papa would say.'

'I don't know about gratifying, but there were no complaints.'

'It's such a comfort, Sally, having you back. Don't get married too soon, *please*!'

'No chance of that,' said Sarah, rather sombrely. 'He's not in a position to marry yet. Besides . . .'

'Besides what?'

'We might have a double wedding. That would be fun.'

'You and Julia, do you mean?' said Catherine slyly.

'Of course. What else?'

'As for me,' said Catherine, 'I shall be an old maid. I may even go into a decline and fade away, like Mary Godolphin in *Rosemary and Rue*.' Now that she had Sarah again, to confide in and laugh with, her heart was lighter, her lovesickness eased. 'Shall you tell Papa first, about Edward? He's sure to be on your side.'

'Will he be? I wonder.' Sarah was not so confident.

Mr Peacock returned two days later, but not until Thursday was she able to put her question to the proof. A visit to London on his part was a rare event: for his womenfolk it had all the wonder and excitement of an odyssey. They crowded about him, plying him with questions and greeting with delighted indignation his teasingly brief replies. Had he stayed with Uncle Richard? Yes. Had he been to a theatre? No. Then what *had* he done and seen? What adventures had he had? He had got up in the morning, he assured them, and gone to bed at night, and in the interval had encountered a number of people all of whom, though Londoners, had eyes in their heads and noses above their chins. As to whether he was glad to be home again, he

M

must have time to consider the question; but at least he could promise to endure the circumstance with fortitude. Sarah alone, playing his own game, held somewhat aloof from the inquisition, knowing that much as he enjoyed frustrating their curiosity he would sooner or later, in his own time, when the din had subsided, tell them all there was to be told. Meanwhile the salient fact that emerged was that the purpose of his visit had been achieved: all arrangements had been made for the opening of a London office of Messrs Peacock and Crabbe, in Lincoln's Inn Fields.

Upstairs, on the first floor, was a small room known as Papa's study, to which Mr Peacock resorted when he wished to enjoy the pleasures of solitude. Catherine in early childhood had once described it to a visitor as 'the place where Papa sleeps', and it was true that sometimes, with a calf-bound volume nestling in his lap, he would close his eyes for a few moments, reasonably confident of being neither disturbed nor detected.

'May I come in, Papa?' said Sarah, peering round the edge of the door.

'Eh? Certainly, child.' He put down his pen.

She advanced into the room. 'Am I interrupting your letter?'

'The fact is incontestable,' said Mr Peacock. 'It would be idle to deny it.' He smiled amiably. 'But the letter can wait. It will come to no harm.'

'I want to talk to you,' said Sarah, perching herself on the arm of the nearest chair.

'Yes?' He glanced at her sharply, over his spectacles.

'I met someone while I was at Meonthorpe. Rather a nice person.'

'Excellent, so far,' said Mr Peacock judicially.

'I wondered whether it would be a good idea to ask him to come and stay with us for a few days, during the school holidays.'

'Am I to understand that the young gentleman is still at school?'

'Don't be difficult, Papa. He's an assistant master. Actually, he's older than I am.'

'Poor fellow. How does he support the burden of his years?'

'The point is,' said Sarah firmly, ignoring the heavy banter, 'we . . . like each other. And . . . the fact is, he has asked me to marry him.'

'Has he indeed? Wasn't that a little rash of him, on such a short acquaintance?'

'I think you'll like him, Papa.'

'I'm already disposed to like him, my dear. Impetuous he may be, but he shows excellent taste.'

'Thank you, Papa.'

'But that's not to say that I can do with him as a son-in-law.'

'Would you care to know his name?' said Sarah. 'Or would that seem to you an irrelevance?'

'The answer is Yes, my dear Sarah, to both questions. To know his name may turn out, eventually, to be a convenience. On the other hand, it can have no bearing on his eligibility.'

On the strength of this meagre encouragement Sarah proceeded to tell all she knew of Edward Linton. She became aware, as the recital dwindled to its conclusion, that it amounted to painfully little.

'You have known each other,' said Mr Peacock, 'for little more than a week. You have spoken with him twice, I gather, or is it three times? You have spent an aggregate of perhaps half an hour in his company. Are you, on the strength of that, proposing to spend the rest of your life with him? Really, my love, you surprise me. I thought you were a sensible young woman. Do I need to remind you that marriage is a long business, and a difficult one? At the moment, I've no doubt, you imagine you are in love. That's very important and very agreeable, but it's not, I assure you, enough. Have you, may I ask, ever felt like this before?'

'Never,' said Sarah, blushing deeply.

'So much the worse. The experience is new to you, and therefore overwhelming. It may be that the young man is all, or nearly all, that you think him. But you are not, not yet, in a position to judge. You must give yourself time, my dear. And,' he added significantly, 'you must give *him* time, poor fellow. Has it occurred to you that he may already be half-repenting his impulsiveness? That's a thing that has been known to happen.'

Sarah had indeed been tormented at intervals by just that doubt; but this very morning it had been resolved.

'Yes, Papa. But I had a letter this morning, if you remember? The one that Mama was so curious about.'

'I see. And you haven't spoken to your mother?' Guiltily, staring at the ground, Sarah shook her head. 'You realize, don't you, that she'd be very hurt if she knew of this conversation? This will need careful handling, child. Whatever you may have privately resolved, an official engagement, at this stage, is clearly out of the question. My advice is this. Let the young man find a pretext for visiting Newtonbury, and from there call and pay his respects to Miss Sarah in due form. He will then, if all goes well, be invited to stay with us for a day or two. I'll propose it myself if necessary. But as for what you've told me, my dear, I've already forgotten it. Let that be understood. His arrival will be a complete surprise to me.'

'Oh thank you, Papa,' said Sarah. 'That's a wonderful idea.'

§ 2

ON Sunday morning Catherine woke at first light, and could not sleep again. This was the day, so long looked-for, when Robert Crabbe was coming to luncheon. Recently, and especially since Sarah's homecoming, she had contrived to keep the thought at bay; but now it was unavoidable and must be examined in all its aspects. She was angry with him, and still more so with herself for having exposed her heart to no purpose. His five-weeks silence had not failed of its effect. At first she had been prolific in excuses for him, but now could no longer see his behaviour as anything but a snub, gentle and well-deserved, but bitterly unwelcome. Since he evidently had no use for her devotion, what better could he have done than ignore it? So she argued within herself, trying to be inflexibly just. Yet still her heart rebelled, clinging to its foolish dream. To meet him again would be painfully embarrassing for them both, she believed; yet the possibility that he might not come today after all was a torment. Even to see him would be something, would be almost everything.

'Are you awake, Sarah?'

Getting no answer she slipped out of bed, padded across the room, and flung back the curtains, letting sunlight flood in. Then lifting the ewer from its basin she poured out some water and began her ablutions, wishing that the process were a noisier one. The house was quiet, no one was yet stirring, and a direct assault on Sarah's slumbers at this hour was against the code; but there was always a chance that with a little surreptitious encouragement she might wake of her own accord and put an end to this anxious intolerable solitude, this alternation of hope and dread. Sarah asleep had the trustful look of a young child: as well she might, having Edward for her own. Catherine rejoiced in her sister's happiness but could not quite subdue a pang of envy that to Sarah, who had always been inclined to make fun of such things, not to herself who so much desired it, had come this lightning visitation, love at first sight. She'll be married before long. And then, perhaps, Julia—who knows? And I shall be left alone, to be with Mama, and grow old.

A drowsy voice from the bed murmured: 'Is it time to get up?'

'Not really,' said Catherine, gliding quickly to the bedside, towel in hand. ''But don't go to sleep again, *please*, donkey, unless you most dreadfully want to. It's Sunday. I was tired of lying awake, so I got up.'

'Very commendable in a young girl,' said Sarah, 'this eagerness for church. Is it the thought of Mr Pardew's preaching that excites you, dear child?'

'Yes, Papa,' retorted Catherine. 'What else could it be? But perhaps Mr Garnish will take the service today.

He's a good deal better, Julia says, in spite of the Budge.'
She seated herself on the bed and fixed expectant eyes on
Sarah. 'It's Sunday,' she said again. 'I can hardly
bear it, Sally.' Her looked belied the words. The small
alert face, enhaloed by the flame of her hair, glowed with
a vital, irrational happiness. 'Do you think he'll come?'
she said breathlessly.

Sarah smiled. 'Of course he will.'

'I'm not sure that I want him to, now,' said Catherine,
her eyes clouding. 'It's all rather frightening.'

'I think you do, Kitty.'

'Yes, I suppose I do, really. And yet . . .'

'I know,' said Sarah. 'Don't worry. Everything is
going to be all right.'

'You remember what we were talking about last night?'

'It begins to come back,' Sarah conceded, 'as the mists
of sleep disperse. We were talking about your lonely old
age. Or at least you were.'

'I rather think it was nonsense, don't you?' said
Catherine judicially. 'I mean, even if he doesn't like
me much, it's not the end of the world.'

'It certainly isn't.'

'Of course, I should never marry anyone else.'

'Of course not,' agreed Sarah, with scarcely perceptible
irony.

'But it'll be fun being an aunt,' said Catherine wistfully.

'We shall both be aunts in time,' said Sarah. 'And
Julia too. Poor Julia!'

'Why do you say that?'

'Mama will never let us all go. Not if she can help it.

And Julia, you know, suffers from an enlarged sense of duty.'

'That won't make any difference,' said Catherine, 'if she falls in love. Perhaps Mr Pardew will be the one. She sees a lot of him, because of the Sunday School. And Mama thinks he's wonderful.'

Of Mr Pardew's wonderfulness they had a chance to judge for themselves a few hours later. The Vicar's boasted recovery did not amount to much : he left his bed for an hour or two each day, but neither Julia nor Dr Witherby, though they pretended otherwise, could suppose that he would ever be able to resume his duties. They tactfully refrained from telling Mr Garnish that his 'smart young curate' was acquitting himself well in the pulpit. Responsibility had endowed Hugh Pardew with a new dignity and self-assurance. He would never be an inspired preacher, but this morning his manifest sincerity won respect even from Catherine, who, not daring to think of what lunchtime would bring, yet unable to forget it even for a moment, tried hard to concentrate on the sermon.

In the churchyard, on the way out along the narrow gravel path flanked with tombstones standing in rough grass, mute memorials of names long forgotten, of men and women beyond reach of this quivering late-September sunlight, there were neighbours to be greeted and to exchange a moment's gossip with. Then came the walk home, parents leading, daughters following in a row, each with a prayer book nestling in her muff. Catherine was now in a complicated state. She moved in an emotional vacuum between dream and reality, hardly knowing which was which. Her tormented psyche, confronted by a choice between hysteria and partial anaesthesia, chose the wiser, safer alternative; but the resulting numbness left no outward mark on her behaviour; aware, though she did not belong to it, of the immediate world about her, the wide-arching sky, the running hedgerows, the chalky lane, she joined without effort, and indeed without thought, in her sisters' talk, while within her was an entranced silence, and within that silence, beating against its high walls, the voice of her anxiety, to which she dared not listen, incessantly chattered.

Robert was waiting for them at the gate of the house, having arrived in their absence and stabled his horse in the yard. He was there. He was actual. He was a dream made manifest. Something, something of glamour, was lost to her in the process. Eagerness, having unbelievably attained its object, died within her. She experienced a moment of sick reaction. The moment passing, everything was normal again: ordinary, matter-of-fact. Robert was here. There was nothing more to wish for. Her heart resumed its long-suspended motion.

He was exchanging greetings with the parents. He was lifting a hand in casual salute to the girls, still some twenty yards distant. Talking with Mrs Peacock he disappeared into the house.

Catherine's next sight of him left her new problem still unresolved. Was he what she had thought him, or was he, after all, a man like other men, no thing of wonder? He said 'Hullo, Catherine!' and she responded in like manner, cool and friendly. That was the policy she had resolved on, for her pride's sake; and here, with her family about her, it was easy, as well as necessary, to pursue it. But gradually the shock of finding him actual, and therefore subtly different from her feverish imagining, wore off, giving place to a sense of miracle. Her frozen feelings thawed: the dream resumed its sway. He is here, she said again, but with a new meaning. He is here, and I am seeing him, and he is Robert.

Covertly, during the long, leisurely luncheon, she watched him, being careful, unlike her former ingenuous self, that no one should observe her doing so. She saw, or thought she saw, that he was preoccupied, unhappy. His face in repose had always had a certain sombre gravity: that, and the quality of the smile that would suddenly and unexpectedly irradiate it, were the chief part of his personal attraction for her. But today there was an absentness as well. Conversation flowed with no apparent effort, and Catherine played her small necessary part in it, but Robert's contribution was meagre until, halfway through the meal, as if uneasily conscious of his long silences, he became suddenly loquacious and launched into a long account of a great new work he had been reading, by his favourite modern poet. It was the story, told again and again, in a series of dramatic monologues, of a murder and its sequel, in seventeenth-century Rome. Catherine, had she been less intent on the speaker, would have been fascinated by his discourse; but the subject had features that did not commend themselves to Mrs Peacock's sense of what was suitable for discussion at table, and on Sunday of all days, and in the hearing of young women; and Robert, becoming belatedly aware of her disapproval, stopped in mid-flow, flushed, frowned briefly, and lapsed into silence.

Catherine said defiantly: 'I should like to read it. Will you lend it to me, Robert?'

'Mr Crabbe, my dear,' said Mrs Peacock, 'is not a lending library.'

'So much the better,' said her husband. 'He won't demand a subscription.'

Robert, glancing from one to the other, decided to say nothing.

In the afternoon, as usual, the two men made a tour of the home fields; and by Sarah's contriving she and Catherine were permitted to go with them. A still larger party was proposed, but neither Mrs Peacock nor Julia felt inclined for the excursion. Before it had proceeded very far, Sarah attached herself to her father and by imperceptible degrees drew him away from the others. In his tweed jacket, knee breeches, and gaiters, he was today, as always on Sunday afternoons, the country gentleman, the gentleman farmer, consciously savouring the pride and pleasure of owning these acres of good English earth, precious moiety of an estate that had belonged to his family for something over a hundred years. He stared about him in a knowing, satisfied fashion; admired the ruminating cattle; discoursed upon the quality of the grazing; tut-tutted at sight here of a gate that needed mending, there of a newly-made gap in a hedge; and in fine enjoyed himself hugely. Sarah, for her part, enjoyed him. In a minor degree she shared his interest in the farm; she was flattered to find that she was an adequate substitute for Robert in his capacity of intelligent listener, always ready with the sage comment, the encouraging question; and, seeing the distance between themselves and the others steadily increase, rejoiced in the success of her stratagem.

Catherine, however, was not happy. She was in a state of dizzy, tongue-tied suspense. She had watched her sister's unplanned, unexpected manœuvre with a mixture of eagerness and nervous dread; and now, alone with Robert at last, she could find nothing to say. With no clue to his mind, and afraid not only of anticlimax, of having this crucial moment circumvented by trivial talk, but also of the very joy she so much desired, almost she wished herself home again, surrounded by dull everyday things, safe from the agony and splendour of this intolerable crisis.

Robert too, for five interminable minutes, was silent. They walked side by side, not speaking, not looking at each other, their eyes fixed on the ground. The day was warm and mellow, but the chill at her heart made her shiver, and her breath came tremblingly. When at last he did speak his voice seemed to reach her from a great distance.

'Well, Catherine?'

He was looking at her. She met his glance with a look of polite inquiry, utterly resolved never again to betray herself. He smiled painfully.

'Well, Robert?'

'There's something I must say to you. I've no right to speak yet, but there may never be another chance, and I can't wait any longer.' He had come to a halt. She stood before him, waiting, trembling, stubbornly silent. 'I'm in love with you,' he said. 'That's how it is. I ought not to be. It's all wrong. But I am.'

It was said, but she could not yet believe it.

'Are you sure, Robert? Are you quite sure?'

His answer, his burning look, disposed of all doubt. But the joy, so long hoped for, was too sudden. She could not yet bear it.

'Thank you for telling me,' she said, in a small, cold voice.

'Is that your answer, Catherine? Is that *all* your answer?'

'Should I say more? Must I say that I love *you*? But you know that already. I made it too dreadfully plain.' Interrupting his protest she said: 'Are you sure it isn't mere chivalry that you feel for me? Or, worse still, pity? You needn't, you know. I shall get over it in time. And even if I don't——'

He seized her hands. 'I love you. I'm drowned in love.' His touch revived her, making the blood flow again. But both were conscious that the world, in the persons of Mr Peacock and Sarah, was still with them: out of earshot but not out of sight.

'I'm too old for you,' said Robert. 'I realize that.'

'No. You're exactly right,' she answered, gently disengaging herself.

'Besides,' he went on, as though she had not spoken, 'I'm not a good man.'

She would not argue that point, lest he should be provoked into enlarging on it.

'Aren't you, Robert? Never mind. You will be, now.'

'Yes, of course, but——'

'No,' she said quickly. 'Don't tell me anything. I'd rather not know. Hadn't we better move on?'

He assented. They began walking again.

'There are difficulties,' he said, 'grave difficulties. That's why I ought not to have spoken.'

'I'm glad you did. I think I should have died if you hadn't.' She smiled up at him. Tears stood in her eyes. 'Am I being very silly, Robert?'

'Not silly,' he answered. 'Heavenly. But ill-advised. I'm warning you against me, Kitty.'

'Too late for that,' said Catherine happily. 'The damage is done.' They stopped again, to look at each other. The trouble in his eyes troubled her. He bent over her, forgetting caution. Their lips met in a brief, butterfly kiss.

'We shall have to be very patient, my dear, and secret. Your parents will be against me, and quite rightly, because I don't deserve you.'

'When shall we tell them? Today?'

'No.' He shook his head sadly. 'We must go very carefully. I'm not out of the wood yet.' He hesitated before adding: 'There's someone ready to make trouble. I needn't say who. It's possible I may become a public disgrace. If that happens, my dearest, I shall go away and you must try to forget me.'

She smiled, tenderly scornful. 'If you go away I shall go with you, Robert. Don't imagine you can get rid of me, because you can't. Not unless you stop loving me.'

'I shall never do that.'

'Very well then. That's settled,' said Catherine comfortably. In her present mood of exultation she was ready to defy all the world. Answering the thought she discerned in his mind, 'I'm not,' she assured him, 'so very young, after all. I shall be twenty-one, you know, in December.'

§ 3

CATHERINE was no longer the ingenuous girl she had been three months ago: the situation in which she then found herself had discovered in her an unexpected talent for self-concealment. When she and Robert caught up with the others and returned with them to the house, when all the family and their guest were assembled at the tea-table, and when half an hour later she watched her lover mount and ride away, she behaved with exemplary calm and propriety. A close observer during the meal might have noticed that she had moments of starry-eyed abstraction and that her glance, if it strayed towards Robert, did not linger there but was quickly averted; but by contributing to the conversation just enough and no more, as became the youngest member of the party, she succeeded in being inconspicuous. No one knew, not even Sarah, that she was hugging a precious secret to her bosom. No one guessed, when the farewells were being said, what it cost her—nor with what sombre romantic pride she paid the price of discretion—to stand a little aloof, to refrain from darting forward to help Robert saddle his horse, to refrain from possessively touching him, to let him go without one eloquent look or intimate word. Since Robert for reasons she could only painfully surmise had ordained secrecy, it pleased her to please him by playing her part well. Moreover, the need for conceal-ment granted, she could enjoy it for its own sake. It appealed to her sense of drama. It made her what she had so long dreamed of being, the heroine of a wonderful, hazardous, perhaps even tragic, love-story. Not that she doubted, in her heart of hearts, that the story must have a happy ending: the alternative possibility was no more than a fiery condiment in the dish of her delight.   And even if the future were uncertain, to know that Robert loved her was for the moment all-sufficient, a world-transforming ecstasy.   They were in love with each other; no one knew but themselves; and no one, except Sarah, was to be told, until the way should be made clear.   Dear, faithful Sarah!   The bliss could hardly have been borne but for the near prospect of confiding in Sarah.

The evening that followed was much like other Sunday evenings: a second visit to church, then the ritual for-gathering in the drawing-room where the girls must sit, hands in lap, mindful of what day it was, dedicating their enforced idleness to heaven.   All looked confidently to Papa, who presently, having sufficiently teased their impatience with a number of evasive pleasantries, an-nounced that he would read aloud to them for half an hour from a suitable, non-Sabbath-breaking, book.

'That will be a great treat,' said Mrs Peacock, as though it were a delightful surprise, not an almost weekly event.

'And then,' said her husband, blandly humouring the pretence, 'we'll have a little music, eh?'

His choice this evening was the gentle Cowper, whose poetry in his happier moods, remarked Mr Peacock, might be aptly described in a famous misquotation as 'the cup that cheers but not inebriates'.   But if any of the girls should feel inebriation coming on, he warned them, they must stop him at once, seeing it was Sunday.   He glanced slyly at his wife, cleared his throat, nestled deeper into his chair, leaning slightly towards the small glowing lamp at his elbow, and began reading an invocation to evening. Behind him, through the unshrouded window, the fast-waning day was still visible, a ghostly presence.

> 'Come, Evening, once again, season of peace;
> Return, sweet Evening, and continue long.
> Methinks I see thee in the streaky west,
> With matron step slow moving, while the Night
> Treads on thy sweeping train; one hand employ'd
> In letting fall the curtain of repose
> On bird and beast, the other charged for man
> With sweet oblivion of the cares of day:
> Not sumptuously adorn'd, nor needing aid,
> Like homely-featured Night, of clustering gems;
> A star or two, just twinkling on thy brow,
> Suffices thee; save that the Moon is thine
> No less than hers, not worn, indeed, on high
> With ostentatious pageantry, but set
> With modest grandeur in thy purple zone,
> Resplendent less, but of an ampler round.
> Come then, and thou shalt find thy votary calm,
> Or make me so. Composure is thy gift.'

He broke off, to direct a searching glance at Catherine and to say gently:

'Mark that, my dear child. Composure is her gift.'

'Yes, Papa,' said Catherine. How much did he suspect? Had her studious self-control been wasted labour?

He resumed the reading, and though she tried to listen, and was soothed despite herself by the gentle rhythms, its meaning went past her unheeded. When it came to an end Mrs Peacock, by general request, went to the piano and sang in her deep surprising contralto, *I know*

N

that my Redeemer liveth; Julia and Sarah played a duet; Catherine, for all must have a turn, obediently followed with a favourite piece by Sterndale Bennett; and finally Mr Peacock, without much persuasion, was prevailed upon to give them a sea song to which they were all much addicted. This was in the main a rollicking affair, with much noisy bass-work in the accompaniment to illustrate the anger of the waves; but it was redeemed from unsabbatarian impropriety by a middle section in which, the music changing to slow tempo and a minor key, a young mother drifting with her child on a raft invokes the mercy of heaven. The prayer over, the rescue achieved, all was triplets and jollity again, just Mr Peacock's style; for he too, like his wife, was an astonishingly different person when singing. By force of long habit he put tremendous gusto into the song's joyous conclusion: in earlier years it had always been a moot point whether he could reach it before one or another of his little girls was reduced to tears. Sarah on one occasion had been found hiding under the table, stifling her sobs, uncomforted by the knowledge that help for the poor castaways was close at hand, the prayer promptly answered. Now, recalling that ancient grief, she smiled maternally at her former self.

'That was glorious, Papa. What shall you sing for us next?'

Yes, it was a Sunday evening like many another. The same familiar pattern, the same comfortable cosy feeling. But for Catherine, newly translated into heaven, how different!

§ 4

NEXT morning, when she woke, that same heaven was waiting to receive her. Sunlight was a miracle and the solid world a wonder. Everything her hands touched or her eyes looked on had a new, virgin quality. The water in which she washed herself was more lithe and smooth and sparkling than water had ever been before, the cake of soap more deliciously hard, more exquisitely scented, the touch of the towel luxurious, and Sarah, in the first flush of waking, visibly an angel. It was hardly credible that only twenty-four hours had passed since yesterday morning when here in this very bedroom, with Sarah, as now, drowsily regarding her from the bed, she had stood, towel in hand, trembling at the dizzy prospect of Robert's coming. Reverting to a childlike fashion, being unable to contain her happiness, she darted across the room to Sarah and kissed her exuberantly.

'Thank you kindly, I'm sure,' said Sarah. 'But hadn't you better save them?'

'Oh, Sally! Isn't everything lovely!'

For the moment, yes. But as day after day went by, with no word of reassurance that should seal the compact and consolidate her joy, doubts and misgivings began stealing in. She had nothing but a memory to live on, a few spoken words, a single feather-soft kiss. It was precious indeed, but not enough : infinitely precious, but not enough to sustain her faith unimpaired. Aeons of time, time that changes all things, had passed since that Sunday afternoon. He had said he loved her, but did he love her still, after five, six, seven whole days? Another

Sunday came and went. Another Monday dawned. The weeks stretched before her, a monotonously repeating pattern of empty days. She applauded, and detested, the wise caution that prevented—as she supposed—his writing to her. He was wonderful. He was perfect. But she wished he were not quite so sensible. She herself wrote letter after letter, but refrained, heroically, from posting them. He, not she, must break the silence, if he would. And if he would not, it could only mean that his love had been a moment's idle fancy, already repented of and soon to be forgotten in the arms of that Other Woman.

Every day she watched and listened for the postman, and at every delivery either she or Sarah was first at the door to answer his knock. One morning there arrived a letter addressed in a strange handwriting to Mrs Peacock. The two girls, swallowing their disappointment, examined it inquisitively, asking each other whom it could be from, an unidentifiable letter being a rare event in their household. The postmark was Newtonbury, the calligraphy bold and sprawling. They carried it into the breakfast-room and placed it beside Mrs Peacock's plate.

This morning she was the last to come downstairs. Her husband, having a train to catch, had started his breakfast. The three girls waited for their mother. Jenny hovered at the sideboard, watching over the teapot, ready when her mistress should arrive to carry it, in tribute, to the table.

'Good morning, my dears,' said Mrs Peacock. Her greeting never varied. 'I'm a little late this morning. I hope you've been looking after your father?'

'Yes, Mama,' said Julia. 'Have you had a bad night?'

'Not as good as I could wish, but that's no excuse for unpunctuality.' She sat down and unfolded her napkin. 'How is the porridge this morning, Edmund?'

'In its customary state of rude health, my dear.'

'Not lumpy again, I hope?' She began pouring out the tea. 'I really must speak to Cook.'

'That,' said Mr Peacock, 'is a course I do not advise. Speaking to Cook is a danger best avoided. Besides, the porridge is excellent. She is to be congratulated on her mastery, belated though it is, of a difficult art.'

The cups circulated. The girls, Catherine in particular, waited for a sign before beginning the meal.

'Shall I ask a blessing, Mama?'

'Dear me, yes, child. Of course. How forgetful I am!'

'For what we are about to receive . . .' said Catherine.

'And for what Papa has already received,' murmured Sarah, not quite audibly.

Both she and Catherine had for the moment forgotten the letter, to which now, however, Mrs Peacock turned her attention.

'Now who can this be from? I don't know the handwriting.'

'Nor do we, Mama,' said Catherine.

'Newtonbury,' said Mrs Peacock. 'Now who can be writing to me from Newtonbury?'

'Forgive a bold suggestion, my dear,' said her husband. 'But there is, you know, a way of finding out. You could, for example, open it.'

She was already doing so. She extracted the letter from its envelope, and read. Her eyes widened. Her lips pouted ominously. Her dark brows rose. She looked up to find three pairs of eyes frankly staring at her. Only Mr Peacock seemed uninterested.

Without a word she folded the letter and replaced it in its envelope. Her silence was palpable, pointed. It continued unbroken throughout the meal. When Mr Peacock with a glance at his watch rose to go, she got up, the letter clutched in her hand, and followed him from the room, shutting the door firmly behind her.

So abrupt a departure, without explanation or apology, was without precedent. Mrs Peacock had the most precise ideas about good manners and of the need to set her children an example.

'Can it be bad news?' said Julia. 'I do hope not.'

All three waited anxiously for the sound of the front door shutting that should tell them Papa had left the house. Five minutes passed. No one dared leave the room. A premonition of disaster dawned gradually in Catherine's mind.

'Papa will miss his train,' said Julia. 'He'll be so vexed.'

Neither Sarah nor Catherine thought it worth while to answer her. She looked at them in pained surprise, wondering at their muteness.

At last the expected sound reached them, Catherine, going to the window, saw her father hurrying down the street. Mrs Peacock reappeared and with a face of frozen calm gave them, as usual, their instructions for the morning. No clue to her thoughts, except their sombre colour, was forthcoming.

'Will Papa miss his train, Mama?' Julia ventured to ask.

'Possibly. Possibly not. If so, he will no doubt catch the next.'

The next was an hour later. The long wait, spent pacing up and down the brief platform like a trapped animal, gave him plenty of time to think: far more than he needed. There was only one thing to be done, and because it was unpleasant he wished it done quickly and chafed at this intolerable delay. The carefully cultivated ironic detachment that was his defence against life's troubles failed him now. Decisive action, of a kind for which he had a profound distaste, was forced upon him.

Arrived at the office he went straight to Robert's room.

'Good morning,' said Robert.

He returned the greeting perfunctorily, then turned back to shut the door. Something in his aspect as he turned again and approached the dividing table provoked a sharp glance from Robert.

'Anything wrong?'

'I rather fancy there is, Robert.'

'All well at home, I hope?' said Robert quickly.

'My wife received a letter this morning. As it concerns you, it's best that you should read it.'

As if to brace himself for a crisis, Robert stood up. The two men faced each other across the table. The letter changed hands. Its anonymous author, self-styled a sincere well-wisher, begged leave to inform Mrs Peacock that her youngest daughter was believed to be innocently encouraging the attentions of a gentleman who, being already committed elsewhere, was not in a position to carry out any *honourable* proposal he might be rash enough to make. In spite of great reluctance to interfere, and profound sympathy with the ill-used young lady, the writer felt it only proper to warn Mrs Peacock that the gentleman's being her husband's professional partner did not preclude the possibility of legal action being taken against him, should the need arise.

'I see,' said Robert. 'Thank you. It's a pretty document.'

'Is that all you have to say?'

With great deliberation Robert put the letter down and placed a paperweight on it. A contemptuous smile sat in the corners of his mouth.

'Extraordinary woman! She doesn't even trouble to disguise her handwriting.'

'You will correct me if I'm wrong,' said Mr Peacock, 'but it occurs to me that you owe me an explanation. Let me remind you that I am Catherine's father.'

'I owe you more than an explanation, Peacock. I owe you an apology. This lying letter puts me in the wrong. It is precisely the kind of thing I feared might happen. That is why I kept silent about something you had a right to know. Until the way was clear it seemed to me useless, and worse than useless, to speak. Believe me, my chief anxiety was that if there was to be trouble, you and your family should not be involved in it.'

'Well?' said Mr Peacock. He waited for more.

'It's true that I love Catherine. I want nothing so much as to marry her. It's *not* true that I am committed elsewhere. It may have been true, in some sense, once. But not now. All that is past and done with.'

'On that point,' Mr Peacock suggested, 'the lady in question seems not to agree with you. She hints, you will observe, at legal action.'

'That,' said Robert, 'is merely malicious. A black-mailing point.'

'Nevertheless I feel bound to inquire, speaking as a lawyer: has she an arguable case?'

'There has been no promise. There are no incriminating letters. There was no intention, on either side, of marriage. And never will be, for the best of reasons.'

'And that is?'

'It's a queer story,' said Robert. He seemed reluctant to continue.

'I hope I'm not unduly inquisitive, my dear Robert. You'll do me the justice to admit that I've never pried into this affair of yours, obvious though it was. Better, perhaps, if I'd been a thought less scrupulous. But now it's become my business as well as yours. You'd better tell me everything while we're at it.'

'Very well. But don't you think we might sit down?'

'I agree that the sedentary posture is less melodramatic,' said Mr Peacock, sinking into the armchair reserved for clients.

'A fellow came to see me the other day,' said Robert, 'here in the office. An elderly, loudly-dressed black-guard, with a racecourse accent. You saw him, if you remember, when he was on his way out.'

'I remember. The fellow who tried to touch you for money.'

'That's what I told you. And it was true. But not the whole truth. He came, he informed me, as the accredited representative of Mrs Stapleton.'

'A solicitor?'

'No. Impossible. But he'd picked up some of the legal lingo.'

'Well? Go on.'

'He began by telling me that the poor dear lady (his own words) was brokenhearted, because of my cruel desertion of her; and then gave me to understand that if I did not take steps to comfort her, by resuming our former friendly relationship, she would feel compelled to take proceedings against me for breach of promise. I pointed out that as there had been no promise there could be no breach. I told him, in fact, what I told you just now: that she had no case. He stubbornly disputed that, and said that alternatively a solatium for hurt feelings would perhaps not be unacceptable to his client. He sympathized with me, he said; he knew what young chaps were; he was sure that a gentleman like me would see the logic of paying for his fun; and to oblige me he would gladly undertake, not only to carry my offer to the suffering lady, but to use his best endeavours—he'd got his phrases all pat—to persuade her to accept it. What did I say to five hundred pounds?'

'And what *did* you say, may I ask?'

'I told him to go to the devil. Whereupon he turned on an oily confiding smile, said he admired my spirit, and that I left him no alternative but to advise *Mr* Stapleton to bring an action for damages against me for what he was pleased to call criminal conversation. He was some thirteen years out of date in his law, I told him.'

'An absentee husband, eh?' Mr Peacock did not allow himself to appear surprised. 'Is there such a person?'

'Who knows? Needless to say, it was a new idea to me. Otherwise——'

'Precisely. There are limits, no doubt, to your folly.

The point, however, might be worth looking into. Such an action could hardly succeed, if what you tell me is true: the uncorroborated evidence of a guilty wife not living with her husband would smack too much of conspiracy. But it would make a loud noise, and it would ruin you professionally.'

'I agree,' said Robert Crabbe. 'I'm confident myself that it was nothing but an idle threat, but if you would prefer to dissolve our partnership . . .?'

He left the question unfinished, and Mr Peacock left it unanswered. 'How, may I ask, did this agreeable interview terminate?'

'I threatened to give him in charge for attempted blackmail, and he departed, breathing fire and slaughter.'

'I see,' said Mr Peacock. 'It's a pretty story, isn't it? But I shall not, I think, communicate it to my wife. Its peculiar fascination would be lost on her.'

That his anger was abated, his sympathy engaged, made it the more not the less difficult to say what had to be said. Though he did not approve of disorderly living, he was no prude, and had Catherine not been involved he could have contrived to take a tolerant, if slightly contemptuous, view of the affair. But, as Catherine's father, that detachment, that escape from responsibility, was denied him. Moreover this conversation had revealed to him a Robert Crabbe hitherto unknown to him.

'You seem, if I may say so,' he remarked presently, 'to take a pretty cool view of your ex-mistress. Yet I suppose you had some sort of affection for her?'

Robert flushed. His rigid self-composure broke down. 'I'm greatly to blame. I know that. I've been the damnedest fool. I've behaved like a cad, if you like. But not to her.'

'To whom, then?'

Robert did not answer.

'To Catherine, by any chance?' asked Mr Peacock, dangerously quiet. Still Robert did not answer. 'You love her, I think you said?'

'Yes.'

'And she . . .? Have you told her so?'

'Yes, God forgive me. That's what I blame myself for. I didn't intend to. It was a sudden impulse. I had intended to wait till all was clear.'

'A pity your good intentions did not persist.'

'Yes. It was unforgivable in me. You realize, of course, that no blame attaches to her. It is all mine.'

'And you,' said Mr Peacock, 'realize, of course, that in the circumstances there can be no question of your marrying her?'

Taking refuge in pedantry, 'I realize,' said Robert, 'that she is a minor, and that I am *persona non grata*.' With an air of dismissing an unprofitable subject he asked: 'What is your decision, Peacock? Are you and I to part company?'

'That, so far as I am concerned, does not arise, my dear Robert. I have, for your consideration, another plan.'

'What is it?' said Robert.

He felt like a prisoner in the dock, awaiting sentence. But the worst part of his sentence had already been pronounced.

§ 5

THE ensuing interview with Catherine was for her father even more painful. It took place in his study on the evening of the same day. Mrs Peacock, unsure of his firmness, insisted on being present.

'Do you want me, Papa?' said Catherine, hesitating in the doorway.

'Come in, child. Your father, my dear, has something to say to you.'

Catherine advanced into the room, leaving the door ajar. Mrs Peacock, having shut it, stood watchful, like a sentinel.

'Sit down, Kitty,' said Mr Peacock. 'There's no point in being uncomfortable. You too, my dear. This isn't a police case.'

'I prefer to stand, Edmund.'

Catherine waited, her courage slowly ebbing. She was not deceived by his brisk, speciously cheerful tone. She noticed that he avoided looking at her direct. A bad sign.

'What is it, Papa?'

'It's about our friend Robert Crabbe, my love. He is going away, and it is unlikely that you will see him again.'

'Going away? But——'

'He is going to take charge of our London office. It'll be a great convenience. A great convenience,' Mr Peacock repeated, 'and better for everyone concerned. Especially, my dear child, for you.'

'What?' said Catherine quickly. She was on her feet again, pale and trembling but with eyes aflame. '*When* is he going?'

'At once. Tomorrow morning. As soon as he has packed.'

She turned her back on him, took two steps towards the door.

'Don't be foolish, Catherine,' said her mother.

Mr Peacock, controlling his voice with difficulty, said gently: 'I'm afraid this piece of news is unwelcome to you, Kitty.' The sense of her youngness, his memory of the small child she had been not so long ago, worked havoc in him. 'I don't ask what your feelings for him are, but——'

'Why, Papa?' She wheeled round, to face him again. 'Why don't you ask? Do you think it doesn't matter what I feel? I love Robert, that's all. I'm going to marry him.'

'No,' said Mrs Peacock. 'That is out of the question.'

'Why? Tell me why, Mama.'

'You are a young girl, Catherine,' said her mother, in a tone of longsuffering patience. 'You must allow your father to know best. But if you insist on a reason, it is this. Mr Crabbe is not what you think him. He has behaved very wickedly. We have reason to believe he is . . . immoral. I'm sorry to have to tell you this. No doubt it's a great shock to you, but you leave me no alternative.'

'You've told me nothing I didn't know already, Mama,' retorted Catherine coldly. 'And whatever he's done he's not wicked . . . And even if he is,' she said passionately, bursting into flame again, 'I still love him.'

'Then I'm ashamed of you,' said Mrs Peacock. 'To think that a daughter of mine——'

Her husband cut in. 'Excuse me, Emily. Your mother and I, Kitty, don't see eye to eye on this point. I know Robert's value, as she doesn't. He and I have been friends and associates for many years. But we're fully agreed that in view of all that has happened he is not a suitable person for you to marry.'

'Very well, Papa.'

He looked at her curiously, troubled by the sudden submission. His wife had no such misgivings.

'*That's* better!' Her voice was warm and caressing. '*That's* more like my little Catherine. You know, don't you, my darling, that it's only your happiness we're thinking of, your father and I?'

'Is it, Mama? So kind of you both. Have you any further plans for my happiness? Or is it happiness enough that I'm never to see Robert again?'

In the shocked incredulous silence that followed she escaped, dry-eyed, to her bedroom, and there the gathering grief, no longer to be contained, found vent. For an uncounted time she lay face downwards sobbing into the pillow. But presently, exhausted, she became aware of Sarah bending over her.

'Papa has told me everything, my poor donkey.'

The embrace was loving but brief. 'Don't start me off again, Sally. I've cried quite enough. Now I must think. Now I must think what to do.'

'If you want him so much,' said Sarah fiercely, 'you shall have him. You *shan't* be made to give him up!'

'Give him up?' She stared, dry-eyed. 'I've not the least notion of giving him up. Unless he wants me to.'

CHAPTER SEVEN

A Game of Chess

§ 1

THERE followed, it is to be supposed, an anxious time for everyone. Mrs Peacock, though incapable of doubting her own judgment, was not uncompassionate. Secure of having her own way, which was all she ever demanded of life, she was quite ready to forgive and forget. Forgetting, however, was not so easy. Catherine's dutiful surrender had taken her by surprise: she had been prepared for a more protracted resistance: and the girl's quiet submissiveness in the weeks that followed, no sulks, no tears, no outbursts of rebellion, not only disarmed her but gave her some moments of uneasiness. She relied on time and absence to do their remedial work, but remembering her own young womanhood she could not disguise from herself that meanwhile the dear child was unhappy. Several times she found it necessary to assure her husband that they had acted for the best, and that henceforward, until the process of healing should be completed, they must treat Catherine very gently.

'I agree with you, my dear Emily,' said he. 'I am resolved to beat her not more than three times a week.'

Catherine, then, was forgiven; but her mother's anger against Robert Crabbe was increased rather than diminished. No punishment, she insisted, could be too bad for him, and the sooner Edmund could contrive to dissolve the partnership the better she would be pleased. After the third repetition of this remark Mr Peacock, hitherto silent on the point, answered with a bland smile that he had no such intention.

'Business, my love, is *my* domain. Yours, in which I do not interfere, is domestic felicity, of which we enjoy so great an abundance.'

Instantly recognizing defeat, she said no more. She was annoyed indeed, but mingled with her annoyance was a perverse satisfaction in having a husband she could not always control. Opposition from anyone else was insufferable, a cardinal crime; but in Edmund, though tiresome, it could sometimes be almost a merit.

Every week now, with unfailing punctuality, a letter arrived for Sarah bearing the Meonthorpe postmark, to be snatched, hidden away, and gloated over in private. No one knew, except the four immediately concerned, that sometimes, not so often as could have been wished, the envelope contained not only Edward Linton's letter to Sarah but a sealed enclosure for her young sister. Sarah herself, not Catherine, had devised this simple, audacious plan, and had written to Lincoln's Inn Fields suggesting it. Robert's answer had been awaited in a twitter of trepidation. Both girls felt guilty, on Papa's account, and surmised that Robert, being a man and therefore afflicted with precise unpractical notions of what was and was not honourable, might have scruples about deceiving their parents. It was even possible that a definite promise had been extracted from him. His answer set their minds at rest, at least on this latter point. Conscience consists in part of a fear of being found out,

o

and every time a letter arrived undetected that fear lost
something of its power. Before long they were within
sight of enjoying their strategy for its own sake and no
longer needed to argue its grim necessity, a point on which
Sarah had been emphatic from the first. Not to have let
poor Kitty see Robert even once, even to say goodbye,
was to Sarah's mind an unkindness that justified any
deception, though she did wish that Papa were not
involved, Papa who had been so understanding about
Edward.

'He's useful, my Edward, isn't he?' said Sarah. 'I
hardly know how we should have managed without him.'

'Useful!' echoed Catherine indignantly. 'I shall love
him for ever! When do you think he will come to us?'

He would come, as it turned out, sooner than they had
dared to hope, and by a route less circuitous than the one
artfully proposed by Mr Peacock. Sarah, like Catherine,
had discovered in herself a talent, born of necessity, for
intrigue. His letters so far had been a miraculously kept
secret, but she had made a point of mentioning him and
confessing to a friendly interest in him, both with a view
to preparing the way for his eventual arrival and because
her woman's wisdom told her that half the truth, having
an appearance of candour, would be more effective for
her purpose, and more disarming of suspicion, than a
secrecy that could not be indefinitely maintained; and
there came a day when with an air of pleased surprise she
boldly announced at the breakfast-table that—would you
believe it?—he had written to her.

'Edward Linton, Mama. You remember my telling
you about him?'

His letter, composed with great care, gave Sarah a new sense of Edward's cleverness: he had improved on his instructions. She passed it to Mrs Peacock without a tremor. Beginning *Dear Miss Sarah*, he modestly introduced himself, reminded her of the occasion when he had had the pleasure of meeting her and showing her round the school, and hoped that she would forgive his presumption in writing to her. He thought she would wish to know that old Mr Pluvius had been ill with bronchitis but was now happily out of danger. Mrs and Miss Druid had been *most* kind and attentive. So indeed had all the neighbours, but none so much as Mrs and Miss Druid, who continued, he was glad to say, to enjoy excellent health, as no doubt she knew. There was, however, a serious outbreak of measles among the boys, and the school was breaking up on November the 14th, several weeks in advance of the normal end of term, so that he was likely to have more idle time on his hands than he quite cared for. The passage from Virgil that she had been good enough to inquire about was to be found in the *Georgics*, which she, being so much interested in farming, would perhaps like to read? It began *Alternis idem tonsas* . . . and he ventured to append a rough translation. In conclusion he expressed the hope that they might some day meet again, and subscribed himself, most faithfully hers, Edward Linton.

'Very nice,' said Mrs Peacock. 'He seems to be a well-bred young man.' She handed the letter to her husband.

'H'm,' said he. 'I like the sound of him. Does he play chess, Sarah?'

'Yes, Papa, I'm sure he does,' said Sarah, freely

inventing. 'No one could live in the same house with Mr Pluvius without playing chess.'

'Then I wonder if he could be persuaded to visit us, having, as he puts it, idle time on his hands?'

'I think he might, Papa. That would be nice.'

'Do let's ask him,' said Catherine. 'Don't you think so, Julia?'

Julia, smiling uncertainly, looked to Mama for her cue.

'What do you say, Emily?' said Mr Peacock. 'Shall we risk it? It would liven us up to have a visitor, don't you think?'

Meeting his glance Mrs Peacock read her husband's mind, or part of it. He was thinking, she supposed, of Catherine. It was she who needed enlivening, and what more calculated to do that, and more, than the company of an eligible young man?

'Very well, Edmund. Sarah shall write to him, if you think it proper.'

'But shall you be able to manage, Mama?' said Julia. '*I* shan't be much help to you, I fear, now that poor Mr Garnish is taken worse again.'

'Never mind,' said Catherine. 'Sarah and I will entertain him, won't we, Sally? That is, when he's not playing chess with Papa.'

'That's my sensible chick!' said Mrs Peacock, smiling fondly. This flash of the old Catherine, hidden too long in a cloud of listlessness, comforted her. Her thoughts raced ahead, foreseeing romantic possibilities. A *young* man, with a neat handwriting and a civil way of expressing himself. So much more suitable than a dubiously respectable widower of thirty-six. A month ago her habitual possessiveness would have resisted the idea automatically; but now, in view of all that had happened, she was more than ready to see her chick safely married to some really nice man.

§ 2

NO ONE at home, least of all her mother, disputed Julia's right to devote some hours of each day to the aged Mr Garnish, whose end, it could hardly be doubted, was now so near. Although she had visited him in the first place timidly and tentatively, moved by nothing but compassion and a sense of duty, by now, finding he depended on her and looked eagerly for her coming, she had become fiercely maternal, seeing him—in his dotage, stripped of all dignity—as a forlorn frightened child confronting the unknown. He was weary of living, yet afraid to die: the doctrine he had preached for half a century had apparently lost all meaning for him. Shocked, but only dimly conscious of the irony of the situation, she a young woman, he the accredited man of God, she talked to him of heaven and its glories, life everlasting, the reunion with loved ones who were waiting to welcome him; for it was no longer possible, in the face of his despair, to pretend that he would get better. At intervals he had spasms of pain, angina pectoris, during which he ceased to be human, became a groaning, grunting animal, and she, watching, prayed that he might die and be at rest; but the stubborn life in him would not yield. The spasm over, even the fear of its recurrence, than which nothing was more dreadfully probable, did not reconcile him to death. She was deeply puzzled by his attitude, as well as distressed. It conflicted not only with all she had been taught to believe but also with her firm persuasion that the prospect of being reunited with his wife must be a comfort to him.

'But think, dear Mr Garnish. If it should please God to take you to himself you'll see your dear Essie again. How lovely that will be!'

'I don't want to see her. She's being very unkind to me.'

'But surely . . . !' For a moment astonishment bereft her of speech. 'You were always happy together, weren't you?'

'That was a long time ago. She doesn't like me any more. She torments me.'

'Oh no! You mustn't say that.'

'She does, I tell you. She's here in this house. Here in this room. She's listening to us, laughing at us. I can't see her, but that's her artfulness. She keeps out of my sight. But she's here. Oh yes! Mocking me. Trying to frighten me.'

Julia shivered. But her voice when she answered him held no hint of dismay.

'Tell me, do. What makes you think that?'

He resisted her questions. He was cunning in evasion, like a child with a shameful, frightening secret. But at last, after a long duel, she got it out of him. Mrs Budge, it appeared, had seen the late Mrs Garnish peering in at the window just as dusk was falling. That was the first apparition. The very next day she appeared on the stairs when Mrs Budge was on the point of descending them. She was dressed, asserted Mrs Budge, in an oldfashioned style, with a large feathered hat, as in her picture. When challenged she paid no heed but came gliding, floating on. Mrs Budge, so the story went, stood at the stairhead bravely barring the way; and the next thing she knew was a blast of cold air, chilling her to the bone, as the apparition passed through her. Turning she saw it vanish through the shut door of the bedroom. So back she went, zealous to protect her dear master by telling him all about it: at first indirectly, in a series of dark hints, but finally, with every appearance of anguish, in plain speech. 'She's here now. Look, over there! Can't you see her? She's coming nearer. She's looking at you. She's hovering above the bed, like the demon she is.' Everything was as in the picture except that the face was distorted by a cruel, hungry, derisive smile. 'Ah, poor dear, now you're taken bad again,' said Mrs Budge. 'She's gone now. She's got her wish. Budge is with you, never fear.' Mr Garnish's response, inevitably, was yet another heart-attack, a grinding mounting agony that lasted four minutes—or was it four hours?—and left him whimpering and exhausted. The ordeal was protracted beyond its usual term because something, she didn't know what, jogged her elbow as she was pouring out the medicine, the pain-subduing medicine on which he so anxiously relied. Three times, since then, the portrait—'touched by no mortal hand,' said Mrs Budge —had been found lying face downwards on the floor.

'It's not true,' said Julia. 'Don't you see, it *can't* be true! Your Essie would never do that. She was always so good and kind. And now she's in heaven, with gentle Jesus.'

'Lost and damned,' he retorted angrily, shutting tight his eyes. 'A tormented spirit. But why do they let her torment *me*?'

Mrs Budge had done her work too well. Nothing Julia said could avail against his stubborn, despairing conviction.

'Dr Witherby,' said Julia, 'shall hear of this.'

She went downstairs, to await the doctor's arrival.

He was late this morning: once again there was an epidemic in the village. Never had she looked so eagerly for his coming. The room where she waited, standing by the window that commanded a view of the approach, was hardly less far gone in decay than its master upstairs. The carpet, dull red, and once luxurious, was faded and worn; feathers oozed from holes in the cushions; the chimneypiece with its array of ornaments, the uncovered mahogany table, and indeed every horizontal surface, were visibly coated with dust. The ornate ormulu clock had stopped, perhaps years ago. The walls were stained with patches of creeping damp. It was a dead room, dead and deserted, its dreariness enhanced by mute witnesses to a happier, confident time, now long past. There were two pleasant landscapes in heavy gilt frames. There was a pencil sketch, embellished in water colour, of eleven young gentlemen in cricketing attire, one of them, stalwart and broadly smiling, Tom Garnish. Near the empty, dusty grate stood a pole-screen whose Jacobean design, of birds and flowers, had been worked, Julia believed, by his young wife during the first year of their marriage.

The house, to Julia's sense, was strangely silent, with

a silence that made her shudder to remember the stricken
man upstairs and the embodied malice lurking unseen
in the kitchen quarters. Neither Mrs Budge nor her
daughter had shown themselves this morning. Julia, as
always now, had effected her entry by the use of a
duplicate key which Dr Witherby, without asking anyone's permission, had had cut for her. The ghost-story,
she surmised, was part of Mrs Budge's retort to that bold
strategem.

At last she saw him, picking his way through the
wilderness that had once been a garden. An odd-
looking creature, not unlike an exuberant gargoyle. Yet
he seemed to her at this moment an angel from heaven.
She ran quickly to open the door.

'Good morning, Miss Julia. Think I was never coming?'

At sound of his voice, at sight of his robust masculinity,
the tumult was stilled in her.

She answered composedly: 'Good morning, doctor.
Before you go upstairs I want to talk to you.'

He followed her into the room she had just vacated.

'Well? How's my patient this morning?'

'Not well. He'll never be well again.'

The ambiguity, and the manner in which it was
uttered, made him say briskly, impatient of euphemism:
'Do you mean he's dead?'

'No, more's the pity.'

'Ah yes. I daresay.' His eyebrows soared. 'I'm
inclined to agree with you. But unprofessionally, mind.
As a medical man it's my business to keep him alive.'

'It's horrible,' said Julia, 'he's frightened. Frightened
out of his wits. Mrs Budge . . .'

Dr Witherby's facial contortions as he listened to her story, glaring eyes, switchback brows, wide angry grin, aggressively jutting jaw, would in any other circumstances have made her want to laugh. Today they did not seem very funny.

When she had finished speaking his features slipped back into their normal shapes and situations, thus restoring his customary look of sardonic, unsurprised melancholy.

'So that's it, eh? I hardly thought the woman had it in her.'

'What shall we do, doctor?' Not waiting for an answer Julia said with quiet urgency: 'Will you fetch her for me, please? I want to talk to her—in your presence.' The last words had a comfortable sound. Dr Witherby's presence would make all the difference.

In a few minutes he returned, with Mrs Budge, tight-lipped and formidable, in tow.

'Good morning, Mrs Budge,' said Julia. 'Mr Garnish has been telling me a strange story, about a ghost.'

'A ghost, miss? The poor old gentleman's not himself.'

'Yes, Mrs Budge. A ghost. The ghost of his late wife, which you, I understand, have been seeing lately. Dr Witherby and I would like to hear your version, if you please.'

'If the Vicar's told you,' said Mrs Budge, boldly staring, 'what's more to say? He knows as much about it as me.'

'Not quite, I think. It's you, isn't it, that see this curious manifestation? The Vicar knows only what you have told him. The first time was on the stairs, wasn't it?'

'Yes, miss. No, miss. The first time was looking in at the window.'

'Ah yes, the window. And then the stairs, I think?'

'That's right. But no good 'll come of talking about it. Them as are dead don't like it. They turn nasty.'

'And after that,' said Julia smoothly, in quite her mother's manner, 'there was that alarming incident in the bedroom. Something made you spill the medicine, didn't it?'

'What if it did? I'm not to blame.'

'Quite so. But it was a pity, wasn't it? Without the medicine he might have died.'

'Night and day I'm on the go,' said Mrs Budge. Her voice was shrill. 'Watch over him like a mother I do. Bed-pans and all, but I don't complain. Not that it's what I'm used to, not by any manner of means.'

'Mrs Budge,' said Julia, gently inquiring, 'would you like to be hanged?' By now she had all but forgotten Dr Witherby. In the small cunning eyes that glared at her she saw astonishment and a momentary terror, quickly veiled by a parade of indignation. 'Because if you would, you're going the right way to work.'

The eyes fell. The hands twisted. 'I dunno what you're talking of.'

'Don't you, Mrs Budge?' said the lawyer's daughter. 'Then I'll explain. Frightening someone to death, dear Mrs Budge, is murder. And *trying* to frighten someone to death is *attempted* murder. We don't believe your story, Dr Witherby and I. Nor do you, Mrs Budge.' The incessant repetition of the name was like a satirical caress. 'Have you, may I ask, any relations living?'

'What's that to you, pray? I didn't come here to be called out of my name. Call yourself a lady! I know better. You needn't think you can scare me. Oh dear no! And I'll tell you something, Miss Clever Peacock. This'll be *my* house before I'm much older, and I'll thank you to get out of it, double quick.'

'Yes,' said Julia, unaware of Witherby's amazed admiration, 'you've a married sister at Mercester, I think you once told me. That will do very nicely. You will now go and pack your belongings, Mrs Budge, you and your daughter. There's a train to Newtonbury at twelve o'clock. See that you catch it.'

'What——' began Mrs Budge.

'In plain terms you're dismissed,' said Witherby, speaking for the first time.

'Indeed? Fancy that now! I'm taking no orders from you, doctor, nor her neither. Here I am and here I stay, till the master says otherwise. And he won't, don't you worry. He'd be lost without me, after all I done for him. Fingers to the bone, and always the pleasant word. It's a plot between the two of you, and no better than you should be I daresay. *I'm* in charge here, and for a very good reason. It's *my* house, I tell you straight, or soon will be, and every stick in it. I've got it in writing, see? All signed and everything.'

'Signed by whom, I wonder?' said Julia. 'By the Ecclesiastical Commissioners? The vicarage, you know, is their property.'

'Ah,' said Dr Witherby, 'but this rather alters the

situation, Miss Peacock. If the good Mrs Budge is sole legatee . . .' He directed a grave look at Julia, one eyelid significantly drooping. 'Perhaps, Mrs Budge, you will be kind enough to show me the document.'

'Not me. I'm too old a bird to be caught with chaff.'

'As you please,' said Julia pleasantly. 'But you won't refuse to satisfy our curiosity on one point. Whose is the signature on this piece of writing you have?'

Scornful in triumph, Mrs Budge answered: 'His upstairs, of course. Who else's?'

'Yes indeed. *Who* else's?'

'No one else's, my fine madam. So there!'

'No witnesses?' asked Julia. The woman looked blank. 'Isn't that interesting, Dr Witherby? No witnesses. Poor ignorant creature, she's had all her wicked trouble for nothing. You may go now, Mrs Budge, and get on with your packing. We shan't need you again.'

'We'll see what the master's got to say about that,' retorted Mrs Budge. She turned her back on them, making for the door.

'Stop!' bellowed Dr Witherby. She turned again, to face him with an ugly uneasy smile. 'If you go near my patient, woman, I'll break every bone in your body. Do you understand? And if you're not out of this house within half an hour I shall send Miss Peacock for the police and have you locked up.'

She faced him with grinning, gaping fury, laying bare her yellow teeth; but under the bright beam of his anger her defiance suddenly dissolved.

He stared her out of the room.

'Come, Miss Julia, we'll go to him, lest she does him a mischief.'

Trembling now, shaken by the discovery of a Julia so ruthless in anger, so unlike her normal self, she followed him upstairs and stood limply in the background while he approached the bed. The old man lay very still, his eyes closed. Witherby bent over him. 'It's all right,' he assured her. 'He's asleep.'

Finger on lip, he approached Julia. 'What now?'

'I shall stay with him,' said Julia, 'till the end. Will you tell Mama, please, and fetch me my night things? She'll know what's necessary.'

He nodded, and came nearer.

'Julia, you're a wonderful woman. By gad you are!'

His two hands lightly touched her shoulders. She made no movement, either in response or evasion. He hovered for a moment, hesitating; then, gently, briefly, kissed her brow.

'Thank you, doctor,' she murmured, colouring slightly. 'Please go now. He'll be safe with me till you return.'

§ 3

IN addition to his pleasant looks and good manners, Edward Linton had everything to recommend him to Mrs Peacock except a large fortune. As her husband remarked, it was a sign of grace in him that he had had the foresight to be born the only child of eminently respectable parents. His father, it appeared, was vicar of a parish in Sussex, and his mother second cousin to a baronet. The latter fact, of which he seemed slightly ashamed, emerged accidentally and did him no irreparable harm in the eyes of his prospective mother-in-law. As such she already privately regarded herself, noting with great satisfaction Catherine's pleasure in his company. That he had come to them on the strength of his acquaintance with Sarah did not prevent her from seeing that he had eyes only for Catherine, who now, in the light of her newly restored happiness, grew prettier every day. For Sarah she had other plans, not yet precisely formulated, in which sometimes Jack Claybrook figured, sometimes his brother Will: either would be suitable. But that could wait: at the moment she had Catherine on her conscience. And it gratified her to perceive that young Linton was finding favour with dear Edmund, was indeed in some danger of being monopolized by him to the exclusion of the girls. They played chess assiduously, and they talked the same ridiculous language.

'So you hail from Sussex, eh Linton?'

'Yes, sir. I'm afraid so.'

'Never mind, my boy. We won't hold it against you. One of the southern counties, I believe?'

'Rather a large one, sir. And it has, if you remember, a coastline.'

'Ah yes. I think I've seen it on the map.'

'Really, sir? That's most encouraging.'

'And now, having seen Lutterfield, the centre of civilization, you're proposing, Sarah tells me, to start a new school in these parts.'

'My father has some such idea for me, either here in the Midlands or elsewhere. Not necessarily a *new* school.

An old one would do, a going concern, provided the headmastership fell vacant.'

'Quite so. Have you considered Eton or Harrow?'

'No,' confessed Edward. 'Do you recommend them, sir? Would they be worthy of me?'

'Have you never thought of taking holy orders, Mr Linton?' said Mrs Peacock. 'But no. I think I shall call you Edward.'

'Please do, Mrs Peacock.'

'We all will,' said Catherine eagerly, who in fact had never called him anything else.

'I feel sure,' said Mrs Peacock, 'that you would make a good clergyman.'

'Very kind of you, Mrs Peacock. But mistaken, I fear.'

'Such a nice, dignified life. And so useful.'

'It *has* been suggested,' admitted Edward. 'My parents at one time were quite set on it. But I felt I had no vocation. And there are other reasons.'

'Other reasons?'

'I suppose you might call them intellectual scruples.' He caught a warning glance from Sarah. 'My usefulness, if any, must lie in another sphere,' he added hastily.

'Ah,' said Mr Peacock. 'That masterpiece of Eliza-bethan compromise, the Thirty-nine Articles, sticks in your throat perhaps? I don't wonder. You prefer to teach facts, and to the young.'

'I'm sure Edward meant nothing of the kind,' said Mrs Peacock. 'Did you, Edward?'

'The truth is, Mrs Peacock, I do not feel worthy of so high a calling.' He could almost hear Sarah's sigh of relief. 'It demands very special qualities, don't you

think? Qualities that I am very conscious of not possessing. My father has them in abundance. Infinite
patience and understanding. He, if I may say so, is
father to the whole parish. He spends half his time
listening to their troubles. Listening, he says, is the chief
of his duties. He's like Chaucer's Poor Parson of a
Town, you know. Except that he's not, luckily, so very
poor. *But Cristes loore, and his apostles twelve, / He taught,
but first he followed it himselve.* And my mother, too. She
does her part, and it's no small one, I assure you.'

'It seems to me,' said Mr Peacock, 'that your true
métier is diplomacy, my dear fellow. But we mustn't
try to deflect you from your chosen course. And school-
mastering, after all, has one great advantage in common
with parsoning. They can't answer you back.'

'You'd be surprised, sir. Some of the brighter lads
will argue the hind legs off a donkey when they're in the
mood. However, I don't mind that. Anything is better
than a drowsy acquiescence. Why, they say, didn't the
Romans speak English, sir, like sensible chaps? Because
it wasn't their native language for one thing, I tell them.
And because, for another, it hadn't yet come into existence. Please, sir, why hadn't it, sir? . . . And then
we're off. It's a dodge to get me talking history instead
of bothering them with declensions and conjugations.
They're cunning little brutes.'

'But you rather like them, all the same?' suggested
Sarah.

'In a way,' admitted Edward, grinning. 'You see, I
was one myself once.'

'And not,' said Mr Peacock, 'so very long ago. I can
still discern traces in you, Edward, of that original sin.'

P

'Oh dear!' cried Edward. 'I do hope not!'

Even Mrs Peacock, though the point of the joke luckily eluded her, joined in the general laugh. There was no doubt about it: the house had become a livelier place, and the girls visibly happier, since Edward's arrival. She would try to persuade him to stay over for Catherine's birthday—or at any rate to come back for it after visiting, as was proper, his parents. By then, she felt sure, something decisive would have happened.

But the presence of Edward, already it seemed one of the family, did not persuade them to forget Julia, who for the past few days had been living and sleeping at the vicarage with only a village girl for companion. The Budges, their boxes duly searched, had departed that same morning, leaving behind them an odour of unsanctity which it was Julia's chosen task to dispel. Her sisters, escorted by Edward, went to see her every day.

Her dark eyes were larger nowadays. Her tea-rose complexion had lost its warm bloom.

'*Dear* Julia,' said Sarah, 'you need a rest from it. Go back with Kitty and let me stay.'

'Oh no. Thank you, darling, but no.'

'Mama says I may,' said Sarah. Much as she would hate to leave home while Edward was there, she felt obliged, and the more so because of that reluctance, to persist. 'It really would be best. We shall have *you* getting ill next.'

'No,' said Julia again. 'He's used to me. He needs me. It won't be for long now.'

'Well, then,' put in Catherine, 'wouldn't you like one of us to stay *with* you? Me, for instance. I should like to. Not Sally. They need her at home to cope with Edward. Don't they, Edward?'

Edward blushed, glancing shyly at Sarah. 'Oh no. You mustn't consider me, *please*! If Miss Julia would like to be relieved——'

'But she wouldn't,' said Julia firmly. 'I won't hear of it, girls. I'm quite determined.'

'Do you know, Julia,' said Catherine, 'you get more like Mama every day.'

'I wish I could believe that, Kitty dear. And now you must excuse me, all of you. Good-bye, Mr Linton.' She gave him her hand. 'I do hope they're looking after you properly, these sisters of mine.'

'No complaints so far,' Catherine assured her.

Rather timidly Sarah said: 'How *is* he this morning? I've been afraid to ask.'

'No better, dear. He'll never be any better, the doctor says. But he's not frightened any more, thank God. Now I must go to him. Good-bye.'

The first part of the walk home was accomplished in thoughtful silence. Breaking it at last Sarah said:

'I ought to have stayed. Poor Julia! She looks worn out.'

'How could you?' said Catherine. 'You did your best. There's no moving Julia once she's made up her mind. And I know how she feels.'

'She's very beautiful, your sister, isn't she?' said Edward.

'But of course!' said Catherine.

'So different from both of you.'

'Really, Edward! Is that quite polite, do you think?'

He laughed. 'Oh, you're beautiful too, my dear Kitty, in your sweet, childish way.'

'Thank you for nothing, Mr Linton. And what about Sarah?'

'That,' said Edward, 'is a subject for more private discussion.'

Two days later Julia's ordeal came to an end. The death of the old man on whom she had lavished a mother's care left her feeling lost, exhausted, but in some deep sense fulfilled. She had charmed him from his fears. She had reconciled him to what must come. He died at peace, soothed by the touch of her hand.

§ 4

'WELL, Emily, my love,' said Mr Peacock, having lured his wife into the study, 'it seems that we are to lose a daughter.'

'What do you mean, Edmund?' she demanded in a joyous flutter. 'Are you trying to frighten me?'

'Not at all. There is no occasion for alarm, I think. Unless you dislike the young gentleman.'

'Which young gentleman? Come to the point, do!'

'Can you not guess? You surprise me. It's Edward Linton. He has asked my permission to pay his addresses.'

'Ah! So that's how it is! I thought so. And you've given him your permission?'

'My dear Emily, you flatter me. As if I should dare, without first consulting you!'

'Nonsense, Edmund! Don't pretend to be henpecked. And don't pretend you didn't say yes, because I'm quite sure you did.'

'Am I to understand, then, that you approve?'

'You know I do. I've made no secret of liking him. It will be a most suitable match in every way.'

'If the young lady consents, yes, I agree with you.'

'She'll consent fast enough. You need have no doubts on that score. I've seen it in her eyes a hundred times. So would you have done, Edmund, had you been her mother.'

'That privilege, alas, has been denied me. Paternity was all I could rise to.'

'It shows how right I was,' declared Mrs Peacock, 'to take the stand I did. I knew she would come to her senses, given time.'

'There, I'm afraid, I do not quite follow you, Emily.'

'Oh yes, you do. I know you were half-hearted about it, but you know very well we did the right thing when we sent your precious Robert about his business. And this proves it, if proof were needed.'

Mr Peacock, perceiving her drift, settled down to enjoy himself.

'It would have been a mistake, you think, to let him marry our Catherine?' he inquired courteously.

'A mistake? No. An outrage. A disaster.'

'Possibly. Possibly not. But forgive me. It's not quite clear to me what bearing that affair can have in this present situation.'

'What bearing! Every bearing! If she'd been allowed to engage herself to your Mr Crabbe she could never have had Edward, that's obvious.'

'Nor can she now, my love.' Mr Peacock smiled beatifically. 'Unless she and Sarah should decide to share him. An improbable contingency, you will agree.'

'Sarah! What's Sarah to do with it? You don't mean . . . you can't mean . . .'

But he did.   His nod, his delighted smile, proclaimed it.

'But it's absurd!' cried Mrs Peacock.   'It's impossible. I don't believe it.   You're teasing me, Edmund.   It's Catherine he's in love with.   You've only to look at them to know that.'

'In that case, my dear, we must lose no time in acquainting him with the state of his affections.   He himself, at the moment, is firmly under the impression that he wants to marry Sarah.   What a singular mistake! I really must speak to him about it.'

Before Mrs Peacock could collect herself for speech, the door behind her softly opened.

'May we come in, Mama?'

On the threshold stood Edward and Sarah, hand in hand.

CHAPTER EIGHT

Twenty-first Birthday

§ 1

'THANK you, Mama, it's very kind,' said Catherine. 'But honestly, I don't *want* a dance.'

'How odd of you, Catherine, to talk like that. I can't believe you quite sincere. Not want a dance on your twenty-first birthday! I never heard of such a thing. In *my* young days I should have been only too delighted. Let me see now, who can we have? The Claybrooks, that's two. Your Cousin Barnabas, that's three. Edward, of course, and perhaps he could bring a friend: we can trust his judgment. Then how about Captain Beckoning? He's back at the Manor again, I hear. It would be a nice neighbourly gesture to invite him; and he looks so splendid, doesn't he, in his regimentals? And your Uncle Richard, and your Uncle Thomas, if they can spare the time. How many does that come to? Eight, I think.'

'Two and a half men for each of our girls,' said Mr Peacock. 'They can fight for the other half. I shall look forward to a most amusing evening.'

'Nonsense, Edmund. Our brothers will hardly want to dance.'

'Will they not, poor old gentlemen? But *I* shall, my dear. May I have the first dance, Kitty?'

'Not Captain Beckoning, Mama, I do hope,' said Julia. 'He's a tiresome person.'

'How *can* you say that, Julia dear?' exclaimed Mrs Peacock, with an *Et tu Brute* look. 'Such a respectable family! His father the Colonel is one of the very *nicest* men. It's quite time he found himself a wife.'

'I was under the impression,' remarked Mr Peacock, 'that he already had a wife. Is it your idea that he should start a harem?'

'I'm speaking of young *Arthur* Beckoning,' said Mrs Peacock severely, 'as well you know, Edmund.'

'If he does come,' said Sarah, 'he can dance with Cousin Barnabas. They can talk crops together.'

'God forbid that I should discourage your enthusiasm, my dear Emily, but have you thought how all these people are to be accommodated? We have only, I think, two suitably furnished spare bedrooms.'

'Julia can share with her sisters for once. I'm sure she won't mind.'

'Of course not, Mama.'

'And my brother and brother-in-law,' said Mr Peacock, 'will no doubt be happy to make themselves comfortable with Jenny and Alice. We will give them their choice. That leaves Edward and his hypothetical friend in one spare room, and our military gentleman in the other, unless he takes a fancy to Cook. It will be a famous arrangement.'

'Really, Edmund!' Mrs Peacock was not amused. 'In front of the girls too!'

'They'll come to no harm, my love. They're growing up, we must remember. And they make allowances for their poor frivolous father. Don't you, girls?'

'Of course, if you're bent on making difficulties——

'We're not, Mama,' said Sarah, cutting in. 'But won't eight gentlemen be rather more than we can manage? Indeed it will be nine with Papa, and not nearly enough females to go round. There are only four of us.'

'I'm aware of that, Sarah. Your father and the uncles do not count. Dancing is for young people.'

'That still leaves us outnumbered, Mama.'

'So it does. Thank you, my dear, for being so helpful. We must find another young lady. Your friend Ellen Skimmer, Catherine. That will be very nice and suitable.'

'And with whom is *she* to sleep?' inquired Mr Peacock.

'If necessary, we can engage rooms at the Waggon and Horses. As for Captain Beckoning, he'll go back to the Manor, of course. There's no problem there.'

'Let's hope the weather keeps fine for him. Not much fun turning out on a cold December night. But a soldier should be accustomed to rough living, so I daresay he'll make nothing of it.'

'We must do everything we can,' said Mrs Peacock, 'to make the day a great success, for dear Catherine's sake. Our one thought—isn't it, Edmund?—is to give her a happy birthday. You know that, don't you, Catherine?'

All eyes turned to Catherine.

'In that case, Mama, may I speak? I'd really sooner we didn't give a dance. What I'd like best is a little dinner party. Quite small. Just family and a few friends.'

Mrs Peacock made a gesture of despair. Her patience was being sorely tried.

'Very well, Catherine. If that's your wish. So I've had all my trouble and thought for nothing.'

'Not for nothing, my love,' said Mr Peacock, 'if by trouble you mean this conversation. For my part I've greatly enjoyed it.'

'I must say it seems unnatural in a young girl. But never mind. There shall be no dancing. I must think again, it seems.'

'Come, Emily, let us swallow our disappointment, you and I. Let us even concede, since it is Kitty's choice, that a dinner party would be rather more manageable.'

'Very well, Edmund, Let us take that view.'

Catherine looked at Sarah, as if to gather courage from her. Then with an effect of reciting a prepared speech she said:

'And, as it will be *my* birthday party, Mama, I would like, if you please, to invite Mr Crabbe.'

Silence and consternation. Catherine had gone deathly pale. Julia and Sarah held their breath. Mr Peacock, with a covert look at his wife, cleared his throat noisily.

'That, my dear,' said Mrs Peacock with exaggerated gentleness, 'is quite out of the question. What is more, I don't wish to hear that name again. How can you be so foolish, so wilful, Catherine?' she continued after a pregnant pause. 'We quite thought, your father and I, that you'd got over that nonsense.'

Catherine looked to her father, but he would not meet the look.

'It isn't nonsense, Mama. And I shall *never* get over it.' She rose and moved to the door. 'Thank you for planning a happy birthday for me. It was very kind.' Her voice trembled, on the verge of breakdown. 'But you needn't have troubled. I don't want a birthday.

I don't want any presents either. I don't want *anything* if I can't have Robert.'

She was gone. The door slammed behind her.

'A good exit-line,' said Mr Peacock. 'She has quite a sense of theatre, our Catherine.'

'She gets it from you, Papa,' said Sarah, returning the ball.

She was not misled by his airy manner into supposing him undisturbed by Catherine's outburst, and was willing to help him evade its discussion. Nevertheless, and not for the first time in this context, she was disappointed in him. Was it possible that he agreed with Mama? Remembering Olive Stapleton she had to admit that it was more than possible. Or was he merely, as usual, pursuing his lazy man's policy, anything for a quiet life?

She herself had her own private reasons for preserving an appearance of neutrality. Mrs Peacock, to everyone's surprise, maintained a severe silence. When at last she opened her tight-shut mouth it was to speak of other things.

'Very well, Mama,' answered Julia. 'I'll see about it at once.'

Sarah, making her escape, went in search of Catherine.

§ 2

PREPARATIONS for the birthday continued, and with Catherine's co-operation, as if nothing untoward had happened. Within an hour of the storm's breaking the skies had cleared and sweet reason resumed its sway. A talk with Sarah persuaded the sinful girl to change her tactics, make a formal apology to dear Mama, and be reinstated yet again in the maternal bosom. Convinced that her defiance had been premature, she became once again the contrite, dutiful daughter, whose mother knew best.

Even had she persisted in her naughtiness it would have availed nothing. With or without her consent the birthday would have been celebrated: the alternative was too preposterous to be considered. Family decency required that the child should be made to enjoy herself, whether she would or no. And now, mercifully, she gave every sign of accepting her destiny with a good grace: in return for which Mrs Peacock generously agreed that there should be only a simple dinner party instead of the threatened dance. On that point Catherine was immovable. After a series of conferences a list was at last drawn up and the invitations dispatched.

Uncle Tom was the first to arrive, and characteristically, having made a muddle about the date, he arrived ten days too soon, wearing a deerstalker cap and an Inverness cape. Everyone rejoiced in the mistake, both because it was so like him and because he was a general favourite. Tom Peacock, fifteen months younger than his brother Edmund, looked several years older by reason of his baldness and spareness and his untidy grey moustache which was apparently his chief source of nourishment since he was for ever chewing it. He and Edmund had been Cambridge undergraduates together for two of their three academic years; but Tom, unlike his easygoing brother, had taken ferociously to scholarship, won high honours, secured a Fellowship, and ever since had been the delight and despair of the young gentlemen who

sat at his feet—slippered feet as often as not, though
sometimes, on high ceremonial occasions or in wet
weather, he would wear a pair of ancient down-at-heel
boots, laced with the nearest piece of string or whatever came handiest. He was preternaturally tall, lean,
angular, with a long stringy neck, jutting ears, small
blunt nose, innocent blue eyes, a high narrow dome of
forehead not unlike a human knee, and a small prominent
chin with which he pointed his more emphatic remarks.
He lived most of his time in the Middle Ages, could tell
you with confident particularity how many people
succumbed to the Black Death in the parish of Little
Puddlington, yet had surprising flashes of modernity.
The bicycle upon which during two laborious days he
had transported himself and his bulging haversack from
Cambridge was the very latest model, as he never wearied
of declaring. He had violent political opinions and
combined with his habitual absentmindedness a passionate
belief in the strenuous life. Every morning, summer and
winter alike, he took a cold bath and rejoiced in his
suffering, convinced that it did him a world of good : the
daily ritual cost Jenny and Alice much labour, pumping
and carrying water and mopping up the residual flood
from his bedroom floor. In fine he was stubborn,
learned, goodnatured, and affectionate, and so far as
could be discerned utterly without humour. In a somewhat puzzled fashion he enjoyed being laughed at,
especially by Edmund, but whether he ever saw the joke
was a point much debated in the family.

Being unmarried and celibate (that he should be anything else was unimaginable), he was free to devote

himself to a series of inanimate loves, the latest being his new bicycle—'my machine' as he proudly called it. This super-glorious object, a marvel of applied science, was accommodated in a convenient outhouse; and there he could often be found, by one or another of his nieces, perched in the saddle, fondling the handle-bars, happily dreaming of rides accomplished and others still to come. He did indeed take it out for a 'spin' every day, as though it had been a favourite dog, until an untimely fall of snow made the going too hazardous even for him.

'My machine, Sarah,' he would say reverently. 'Isn't she a beauty?'

'I'm Catherine, Uncle Tom. But never mind.'

'Ah! Catherine is it? Of course. So it is.'

'What are you doing, Uncle, out here in the cold by yourself?'

'Just sitting, my dear. Just sitting. She's a Phantom, that's what they call her. A Reynolds and Mays model. She made her first appearance last year, at the Crystal Palace. Rubber tyres, you see. Not like your old bone-shakers. And suspension wheels, with wire spokes in tension.'

'I'm afraid I don't know what that means, Uncle. But I'm sure it's something very nice.'

Three days after his arrival he burst into the breakfast-room clad in cap and cape and carrying his bundle which he dumped in a corner before taking his seat.

Mrs Peacock stared in wonder. Her daughters smiled happily.

'Feeling cold, Tom?' said Edmund.

'Just a cup of tea,' said Uncle Tom, 'before I take the

road. No time for more. And thank you, Julia my dear,' he continued warmly, beaming upon his sister-in-law, 'for my delightful visit.'

'But, Thomas,' Emily protested, 'you're not thinking of leaving us so soon!'

'Must make an early start, don't you know. Long way to go before nightfall.'

'But the birthday, Uncle Tom!' cried Julia. 'It's not for a week yet, and that's what you came for.'

'Catherine's birthday,' said Sarah. 'Her twenty-first.'

'The Catherine they allude to, Tom,' explained Edmund, 'is a niece of yours, and our youngest daughter.'

'This one, Uncle,' said Catherine, pointing at herself. 'Me. The redhead.'

Mrs Peacock corrected her. 'Auburn, my dear.'

'Ah yes,' said Uncle Tom. 'Sweet Auburn, loveliest village of the plain. That reminds me. I've something for you, Catherine. With my best love. Now where did I put it? He jumped up, pushing back the chair, and after a surprisingly brief search in his pockets produced a cheque. 'There you are, my dear. Buy yourself a trinket.'

'Oh, Uncle! How kind of you!' All joined in the chorus of thanks. 'But you *will* stay for my birthday, won't you?'

'Of course. Of course. Wouldn't miss it for the world.' Divesting himself of his outdoor coverings, and dropping them on the floor, he resumed his seat and settled down to enjoy his breakfast.

That was Uncle Tom. Everyone rejoiced in him: even the servants to whom his untidiness gave so much trouble, and even Emily, shocked though she sometimes was by his unconventional manners. To the girls and their father his elderly innocence was a continual feast.

And what of Mrs Peacock? Was not *her* side of the family to be represented at the dinner party? Indeed it was. There was her brother, Uncle Richard Bartlow, and there were the Druids. Uncle Richard was a dried-up but genial little man who, having no taste or talent for farming, had gravitated to London. He now occupied a commanding position, monarch of all he surveyed, in Threadneedle Street: according to his brother-in-law Edmund, no one dared approach him without murmurings of apology and ritual genuflexions. Having no nearer kin, for he was married only to his career, he duly arrived on the morning of the great day. So, a little later, did Uncle Druid, garrulously explaining, with the support of many a sagacious proverb, why Aunt Bertha, his son Barnabas, and his daughter Patience, who sent their fondest love, were unable to accompany him. So too did Edward Linton, his perverseness in proposing to the wrong girl now fully forgiven. The Claybrook brothers, who though not family might some day become so, were expected in the evening.

Laden with gifts and good wishes, the guests arrived. Catherine by now was unbearably excited. But for one circumstance, which she hardly dared think about but could not for a moment forget, the birthday promised to be all she could wish for.

§3

THEY were eleven at table, a predominantly male party. The seven men included Edmund and three uncles, all of whom, being unmarriageable, were nothing to Mrs Peacock's purpose. Sarah's Edward being already bespoken, her only hope, and that a slender one, was the Claybrooks. She observed with satisfaction that dear Catherine, in her new evening gown, was looking prettier than ever, her cheeks delicately flushed, her eyes sparkling. As for the absence of aunts, that could not be helped and was anyhow no great matter. She was annoyed with Bertha Druid for not coming, and still more for sending Mr Druid in her place, for she had difficulty in accepting him as belonging to the family; but Jane and Clara, who were elderly and ailing, the only other survivors of a numerous brood, she had not expected; and Edmund—it had been part of his attraction for her—possessed no sisters. She gazed upon her guests with a benign complacency, only regretting that she had allowed herself to be talked out of sending an invitation to the Manor. Such a handsome fellow, Arthur Beckoning, and so well connected. The very thing for Catherine.

Seven tall candles—it had been Edmund's whim to leave the lamps unlit—created a glowing island of intimacy. Their soft lustre, reflected in silver and glass, lit up the eleven expectant faces. Elsewhere in the room firelight contended with the surrounding shadows. In the centre of the long table stood a bowl in which, bedded in moss, Christmas roses bloomed: emblem, thought Mrs Peacock, recalling something she had read, of that purity

Q

by which she set so much store. They had been Julia's
idea: Julia, the one daughter on whose loyalty she could
utterly rely. She did not know what a pang it had cost
Julia to refrain from proposing that Dr Witherby should
be invited.

'The festive board,' said Uncle Druid, rubbing his
hands together, 'maketh glad the heart of man, as the
Good Book says. And woman too, eh Emily? Woman
too,' he repeated, feeling within him the birth-pangs of a
new thought. 'Male and female,' he announced triumphantly, 'created he them. That's how it is. Am I right,
Edmund?'

'Incontestably, my dear sir. It's an eccentric arrangement, but it has its advantages. Our Catherine, for
example. Here's wishing you joy, my love.' He raised
his glass.

'Joy!' echoed a chorus of voices.

'And security,' said Uncle Richard. 'Gilt-edged.'

The felicitations over, Uncle Druid was again moved to
unburden his mind of its accumulating treasure.

'A body's birthday,' said Uncle Druid, with emphatic
deliberation, 'comes but once a year. It is meet, therefore, that we should be merry.'

'Within reason,' remarked Uncle Richard. 'Always
within reason. A very sound vintage, this, Edmund.
Full-bodied. Mellow. Delicate bouquet.'

'Glad you like it, Dick. Made from grapes, they tell
me.'

'Comes but once a year,' repeated Uncle Druid,
holding in mid-air his fork, on which was impaled a
brussels sprout. 'But the twenty-first birthday, be you

man or be you woman, comes but once in a lifetime. Here today and gone tomorrow, as the saying is. There's a thought for you there, Catherine.'

'Yes, Uncle. So there is.'

'A wine like this,' said Uncle Richard, 'is a sound investment.'

'In a year from now,' said Uncle Druid, 'you'll be twenty-two. Think of that.'

'Pays good dividends,' said Uncle Richard.

'And this time last year, Uncle Druid,' said Sarah, 'the poor little thing was only twenty.'

'True, my dear. Very true. And there's a lesson in that, too.'

'An arithmetic lesson,' murmured Edward.

'Thomas, you're not eating,' said Mrs Peacock. 'Wake up, do.'

'Eh? What's that? Dear me, I fear I was dreaming.'

'Dreaming of his bicycle, Mama,' said Catherine. 'Is it quite happy, do you think, Uncle Tom? Oughtn't we to take it something to eat?'

Uncle Tom smiled vaguely. 'I was trying to recall a saying of St Bernard's. But for the moment it eludes me. Must be getting old.'

'Time flies,' said Uncle Druid. 'We all get older, even the youngest of us. Day after day, week after week, year after year. Take your Cousin Barnabas now, Catherine. Your Cousin Barnabas, Sarah. *He's* older than he was. Close on forty, his mother tells me.'

'Fancy that!' said Julia sympathetically.

'Yes, Julia my dear. Your Cousin Barnabas. And

only yesterday, it seems, he was cutting, as they say, his first tooth.'

'Ah,' said Mr Peacock, 'there's a deal of dillwater has flowed under the bridges since then, eh Druid?'

'*I* don't get older,' said Will Claybrook, 'and don't intend to. Never better in me life. How about you, Jack?'

'Same here,' said Jack, busily munching. 'Good fodder. Healthy life. Plenty of hard work. Sleep like a baby.'

'Tip of my tongue,' said Uncle Tom. 'It's in the *De baptismo*. Very apt to the occasion. Perhaps you can help me, Linton? St Bernard of Clairvaux, you know.'

'Not I, sir,' said Edward. 'The only St Bernard I ever knew had four legs.'

'A good dog,' said Uncle Druid, 'is a man's best friend, I always say. Bar his mother, mark you. Bar his mother. Dead and gone now these many years, poor dear soul. Take my old sheepdog now. Jack we call him. No offence to you, Mr Claybrook, and none taken I hope. I've had him for years and his dam before him, and that's not swearing, Emily, dear lady, it's a manner of speaking, as you might say his mother. Violent speech was never my way. I'll tell you what that dog's got,' said Uncle Druid generously, 'and I daresay it will surprise you. He's got wisdom, he's got understanding, he's got loyalty. Bring 'em along, Jack, I say. And what does he do?'

'He brings them along?' suggested Edward diffidently.

'Sure enough,' declared Uncle Druid, 'he brings them along. Bring 'em along, Jack, I say, but don't hustle them. They're mortal creatures, I say, like you and me, Jack, like all of us. And what does he do?' He paused for dramatic effect, then said, making eyes of wonder: 'He brings them along. A bark here. A snap there. But all as mild as a nodding nursemaid.'

'A most sagacious animal,' said Mr Peacock. 'It would be a privilege to meet him. Come, Tom. Drink up, man. Or I shall think Cambridge has corrupted you.'

'I believe you, Edmund,' said Uncle Druid. 'We understand each other, him and me.'

'Very gratifying,' said Edmund, hovering at hand with the decanter. 'Let me give you some more wine, my dear fellow. It may loosen your tongue.'

'Faithful and true, that dog is, and never a flea worth speaking of. There's many a lesson we could learn from the likes of him.'

He emptied his refilled glass, nodded at the company, and lapsed into silence with a sense of duty well done.

Catherine, as the feast moved to its conclusion, became conscious of an inward trembling. Now was the moment. She braced herself for a great effort.

'Is anything the matter, Catherine dear?'

'Nothing at all, Mama.'

'You look pale. Are you feeling quite well?'

'Perfectly, thank you. Papa, may I ask you a question?'

'Eh? Certainly, my love. I am all attention.'

'It's on a point of law,' said Catherine. The trembling had subsided. Her voice was steady and clear. 'Am I right in believing that now I'm twenty-one you are no longer legally responsible for me?'

'That, in a strict sense, is true. What a singular question!'

'And that from now on I can do what I like?'

'You are still your father's daughter, my dear,' said Mrs Peacock.

'Yes, Mama. I'm not questioning that. What I mean is that if I were to disobey him he couldn't, legally I mean, lock me up in my room, as oldfashioned fathers used to do. That is so, isn't it, Papa?'

'Near enough, Kitty. Near enough. And by the same token it might be argued that I'm relieved, by your great age, of the obligation to feed and clothe and house you. If you're interested I'll take counsel's opinion on the point. But I'll tell you here and now, for your re-assurance, that I have no immediate intention of standing on my legal rights, whatever they may be. Your sisters, you will have noticed, are still with us, though both are of age. So pray compose yourself, my dear. You need have no fear I shall starve you

'Nor lock me up either?' said Catherine.

'Nor lock you up either, dear child. I think I can safely promise that.'

'Would it amount to assault and battery, do you think, Papa? Or would they call it false imprisonment?'

'That again is a point I shall have to look up. At the moment I can recall no precedent.'

'When you've quite finished talking nonsense...' said Mrs Peacock, rising.

All the men, except Uncle Tom, scrambled to their feet.

'Just a minute, Mama.' Catherine, too, stood up. 'There's something you ought to know, you and Papa. And Uncle Tom. And . . . everybody.'

'Well, Catherine?'

Everyone was looking at her.

'Please don't make a fuss, because it's quite decided,' said Catherine. 'I'm going to marry Robert Crabbe.'

'Tut!' exclaimed Uncle Tom. 'What a duffer I am! It's not in the *De baptismo* at all. It's in the *De gradibus humilitatis*. Let me see now, how does it run? Just give me a moment.'

They gave him more than a moment. The silence painfully lengthened while Mrs Peacock, frozen with anger, recovered her power of speech.

'Fortunately, Catherine, I did not hear what you said. And I forbid you to repeat it.'

'Just as you like, Mama.'

'Edmund!'

'Yes, Emily?'

'Have you nothing to say to Catherine?'

'Nothing at the moment, my dear. Unless you wish me to felicitate her?'

'You heard what she said?'

'Very distinctly. And as you, I understand, did not, I will rehearse it for you. She has decided, she says, to marry Robert Crabbe.'

'In the spring, Mama,' said Catherine, 'if you'll have me till then. If not, we can make it next week.'

'Be quiet, Catherine. The subject is closed. You know perfectly well your father will never consent.'

'My consent, Emily, as Kitty has been careful to

establish, is no longer required.   It's checkmate, my dear.
And as neat a one as I've seen.'

'Very well, Edmund.   Then you must disinherit her.
There's no law against that.'

'True.   But the gesture would lack humour, I feel.
Believe me, my dear Emily, our best plan by far is to try
to look pleasant about it, since the young lady has made
up her mind.'   He met Emily's basilisk look with his
most charming smile.   'Edward, my dear fellow, may I
trouble you to fetch the port decanter?   You'll find it
on the sideboard.'

'With pleasure, sir.   This port, I conjecture,' remarked
Edward, returning to the table, 'is older even than
Catherine.'

Mrs Peacock, magnificent in defeat, said smoothly, all
trace of anger gone:

'Come along, girls.   Let us leave the gentlemen to
their wine.'

CHAPTER NINE

Epilogue

ON an afternoon in 1919, and out of uniform at last, Nicholas Crabbe, sole surviving member of the firm of Peacock and Crabbe, formerly of Newtonbury but now and for many years functioning solely from Lincoln's Inn Fields, lifted the shining brass knocker of his grandmother's house and performed with it a delicate tattoo. While he stood, waiting, a great load of time seemed to drop from his middle-aged shoulders. Hardly more than five years had passed since his last visit, but the scene was saturated in the quality of a much earlier time, when his mother, who was now seventy, had been young and gay. Gay she still was at moments, in spite of what the war had done to her; her courage was a constant marvel to him; and but for Aunt Julia's dissuasion—'Such an ordeal for you, Kitty, with your poor sciatica!'—she would have been with him today. Nicholas was the youngest of three, and the only survivor, his brothers Edmund and Thomas having by understating their ages contrived to get themselves killed in Flanders. His mother and Aunt Julia, Uncle Witherby's widow, now shared a house with Aunt Julia's Emily, not too far from where Aunt Sarah and Uncle Edward lived, with their children and grandchildren at no insuperable distance. Dutifully, having a strong sense of family, he had visited them all within a week or two of his demobilization; and now it was Granny Peacock's turn. Granny Peacock, full of years, by whose stubbornness even Death himself was daunted.

The door opened.   A pair of startled, incredulous eyes stared at him.

'Hullo, Miff-Miff!   How are you?   I'm Nicholas Crabbe, in case you don't remember.'

'Mr Nicholas!   How nice!   As if I could forget!'

If anyone could make Nicholas Crabbe feel like a boy again it was Miss Smith.   Here she was, in her eighties, the same as ever: still straight as a rod, still neat and prim, her mid-parted Quakerish hair still the colour of bleached straw, her long face—empty of all but kindliness —making her look, as to him she had always looked, like a sentimental goat.

'Come along in now and rest yourself,' she said anxiously.   'I'm sure you must be tired after your long journey.   Mrs Peacock *will* be pleased.'

'Will she?   I wonder.   How is she, Miffy?'

'Pretty well on the whole,' said Mary Smith.   'She has, you know, her ups and downs.'

'Of course,' said Nicholas.

While the talk ran on he was aware, as never before, of Mary Smith and her story, too placid for pathos.   It had been her destiny, cheerfully embraced, to live always at second hand, ministering to others: first as nursery governess, and then, and for something like thirty years, as companion to a tatchety old woman.   She had lived from day to day, from week to week, never looking far ahead, and the years had gone by unnoticed, bringing quarrels and discontents, he surmised, but no decisive reason for making a change, even had that been possible.

At intervals, so he had heard, there had been angry talk, on both sides, of her going; but nothing came of it, nor ever would. She had in fact nowhere to go; and since no one but Mrs Peacock now had need of her, what could she do but stay?

'So the old lady's pretty well, is she?'

'She's wonderful for her age, is dear Mrs Peacock. She has her cough of course. The tubes aren't what they were, doctor says. And she gets a little mixed in her thoughts. You mustn't mind that, Mr Nicholas. It's only to be expected at ninety-five.'

'Yes indeed,' said Nicholas.

A long silence paid tribute to the miracle of Mrs Peacock's longevity.

'You shall see her presently, when she's had her rest. She'll be ever so delighted. And now you'll be ready for a cup of tea, I'm sure. I'll go and tell Violet. She's getting your room ready. Such a treat for her.'

Left to himself, he turned back into the small square entrance hall which he knew so well and had remembered so often. The rose-coloured fanlight over the front door shed a warm illumination into the red-carpeted room, to mingle with the plain daylight filtering in through the glass doors opposite, which gave on to the garden. Standing in this quiet neutral interior with the street door at his back and a vision of lawn and trees and October sky confronting him, he felt himself to be at the very centre and heart of his grandmother's habitual being. The house was rather smaller than he had remembered it, but otherwise still the same: the same taste and smell; the same colour; the same tall gravely-ticking clock, whose face was that of an old friend; the same enclosed pocket of unchanging time.

Some twenty minutes later, after he had drunk a ceremonial cup of tea with Miff-Miff, she ushered him into his grandmother's presence. Mrs Peacock now spent her days in that small annexe to the drawing-room which, because it had two wide windows and a double glass-panelled door opening on a level stretch of lawn, they had been used to call the 'garden room'. Here, on an April afternoon half a century ago, an earnest young curate, Mr Pardew, had been politely, if reluctantly, received by Sarah and Catherine, and with Sarah had played a memorable game of croquet on the sunk lawn that was only just not visible from these windows. That, however, was a corner of past time to which Nicholas Crabbe had no access: his memories of this house and garden, scene of many a joyous holiday, with a young mother and two brothers to keep him in order, a grandfather to engage him in amusing adult conversation, and Granny herself resolute to spoil him, began seven or eight years later.

'Here's Mr Crabbe to see you, Mrs Peacock. Isn't that nice?'

'Eh?'

'Mr Crabbe, dear.   Master Nicholas that was.'

'I heard,' said Mrs Peacock.

She sat, very straight, in a tall-backed chair by the fire-place, in which a slow coal fire was burning.   Her primly-shod feet rested on a low stool, and her arms on the arms of the chair, her splayed hands enclosing the rounded mahogany ends.   She had grown stouter in old age, and the flesh of her face hung loosely like leather bags on the prominent bone-structure. Draped in black taffeta, her head surmounted by a gleaming white cap, she stared fixedly, morosely, at the garden.

Nicholas stood before her like a suppliant, awaiting her pleasure.

'Well, Granny, how are you?'

At the sound of his voice she turned a dim grey gaze upon him.

'Good morning, Robert Crabbe.'

'Good afternoon, you mean, don't you, Mrs Peacock,' said Miff-Miff obtusely. 'And it's not Mr Robert, you know. It's Nicholas.'

'Hold your tongue,' said the old woman. 'I don't need a girl to teach me what's what.'

'Very well, Mrs Peacock dear. If you don't need me at the moment, I'll slip away.'

'Robert,' said Nicholas, as the door closed on Miff-Miff, 'was my father, you know.'

Mrs Peacock was seized with a paroxysm of coughing. When it was over she glared with dull anger at Nicholas, seeming to accuse him.

'I'm Nicholas,' he said. 'Your grandson, Granny. You remember Nicholas.'

'Eh?' She seemed not to have heard him. 'I see how it is, Robert Crabbe. You've killed one wife and now you want another to kill.'

He could find no answer to that. He let it go.

'He shan't have her,' declared the aged voice, 'no matter what Edmund says. Partner? No such thing. He's a trickster. Always was.'

'Let's get things clear,' said Nicholas gently. 'You're dreaming, Granny. I'm me, not my father. He died three years ago. I'm Catherine's son, Nicholas. Her youngest.'

'Catherine? What's Catherine to you?'

'My mother,' said Nicholas firmly.

'Your mother? Catherine's youngest? Then you must be young Nicholas. Yes, and you're the very spit and image of your father, I do declare! Well, Nicholas, aren't you going to kiss your old granny? ... That's right. Best let bygones be bygones, since what's done can't be mended.'

'Nice to see you looking so well, Granny.'

'I daresay.'

'My mother sends her best love,' said Nicholas, in a loud cheerful voice. 'So do they all, Granny. Aunt Sarah, Aunt Julia, Cousin Emily, everybody. Who do you think I saw the other day? Cousin David. David Linton. Had lunch with him. He was asking after you.'

'What?'

'David Linton. Your grandson. Sarah's boy. Grown-up children of his own now, you know. When you see Granny Peacock, he said, don't forget to give her my love, Nicholas.'

She was not listening.

'There's something for you on the chimneypiece, boy.'

'Thank you, Granny.' He made a parade of looking on the chimneypiece and pocketing a half-crown. 'Thanks awfully,' he said, reverting to schoolboy idiom.

In the old days this ritual had been a sign that the

audience was over, but today, as he neared the door, her querulous voice stayed him.

'Look in that drawer, Nicholas my dear. The big bottom one. There's a bundle there, unless Mary Smith has been poking and prying. Letters and rubbish. Peacock and Crabbe. Crabbe indeed! No wonder they had to shut up the office when Edmund went.'

The only piece of furniture in the room, apart from chairs and a table, was a Jacobean oak chest of three drawers, the lowest and deepest of which had been designed to accommodate the plumed Cavalier hat of its first owner. To humour her whim, though he would have been glad to escape, Nicholas opened this drawer. It ran smoothly to meet him, with scarcely a sound. Inside it was a heap of miscellaneous papers: letters to the firm, all sorts and sizes, with spidery copperplate copies of some of the answers. Gathering up a handful he spread them on the table, drew up a chair, and sat down.

His eye travelled idly over the faded calligraphy, picking out a few sentences here and there. Dear Sirs, I have compromised with my Uncle in the matter referred to in your note of this morning. He is to sign the Transfer: I am to return the Interest. Will you be kind enough therefore . . . Newtonbury July 1st 1877: Dear Sirs, We have seen our Client, who has a great reluctance to litigate with a Brother and has in consequence given us authority to arrange the accounts with you and settle the sum to be accepted; and if your Client will give you the same authority, and a little latitude, we shall have no difficulty in finally adjusting the business when we next meet. . . . Dear Sirs, In the matter of Brown and Jarvis and Another, we have signed and registered Judgment on the Warrant of Attorney, and it will not be necessary to revive the Judgment at the expiration of the year as the Warrant of Attorney contains a clause dispensing with a *scire facias*. Annexed are our charges herein. Yours faithfully.

'Very interesting, Granny,' said Nicholas. 'I'm glad you kept them.'

Something else had been kept, which he could not bring himself to mention. It did not belong among these letters: it must have slipped in by mistake. A silhouette of a little girl, cut out in black paper and pasted on a piece of cardboard. It was a miracle of delicately suggestive art: the young ingenuous profile, the slightly parted lips, the eyelashes, the rhythm of neatly dressed hair tied with a ribbon at the coltish nape. Turning it over he made out a faded pencil inscription: *Emily Ann Bartlow, 1834, aged 10 years.*

He glanced covertly at his grandmother, her eyes now closed, her hands folded in sleep; then looked again at what she had once been. He sighed, listening to the enormous silence; glanced towards the wide garden window; and stared at the shadow of evening that moved, like time itself, no pace perceived, over the sunlit grass.